MURPHY'S RANGERS
MASSACRE

HEROES OF WORLD WAR II: BOOK 2

ERIC MEYER

Copyright © 2022 Eric Meyer

All rights reserved.

ISBN: 979-8361132669

PROLOGUE

The Second World War began in September 1939, when the Third Reich invaded Poland, claiming territory that belonged to the Fatherland. Many said the new Germany had risen from the ashes of the First World War that ended in November 1918. For one man, Major Gottlieb Kreis, the war began a year earlier, in 1917, in the mud and horror of the trenches on the Western front. He was aged five when his mother informed him his father Herman Kreis was badly wounded. He was too young to understand what it meant, but he explained when he returned home, paralyzed from the neck down by an American bullet.

The casualties suffered on both sides were huge, and after the ceasefire the German nation became accustomed to trains, trucks, and carts returning from France and Belgium laden with dead and wounded. His father was one such casualty, and like many such men, he was embittered. With good reason, he'd been wounded in the leg and stumbled in the mud of no man's land during a furious attack. Bleeding badly and unable to move, the Americans counterattacked, and Kreis looked up to see an American soldier pointing his rifle at him, snarling in the unfamiliar language he didn't understand.

The hatred was all too understandable. He was spitting curses, his face savage, his lips twisted in rage. A moment later he kicked Kreis hard, so he rolled over in the mud. The American fired two shots, and those two bullets did the real damage. Both impacted his spine, one below the neck and one and lodged between the lower vertebrae. He felt a fleeting agony, and then nothing. He assumed the bullets had grazed his back, but when he tried to use his arms to pull himself forward, they didn't respond to the commands sent to them by his brain. He thought he was suffering from shock, and there was nothing else he could do but wait patiently for the medics to arrive. If it was the Americans, he'd end up a POW, but with luck, his people would emerge victorious and get him to an aid station. The medics could patch him up and he'd rejoin the battle.

It didn't happen. The Americans found him and took him to a forward hospital, where they treated his wounds. They gave him the bad news, paralysis from the neck down. At first, he didn't believe it, but as the days and weeks passed and he couldn't move, he began to accept his life was over. He worried about how his wife and family would deal with having a quadriplegic to care for, and he dictated a letter to another badly wounded man, also a German, who was due for repatriation to Germany and promised to deliver it to his wife. The letter arrived, and she took the bad news as befitted an efficient German housewife, preparing the house to receive him when they brought him home.

As he grew up, Gottlieb Kreis listened to the story, again and again, pressing his father to repeat every single detail. He regretted he couldn't describe the American soldier who'd shot him in the back so he could find a way to take revenge. He persuaded the son to leave it alone and said there was no point in pursuing it. Despite this, Gottlieb could see the rage that burned in his eyes, and it was the beginning of his hatred for all things American.

He grew up at a time when Adolf Hitler was bringing his Nazis to power, and he became a fanatical supporter of the Party. When he was old enough, he joined the Army as a cadet, and helped by his Nazi credentials he worked his way up to his current rank of Major in the Wehrmacht. As the SS blossomed into a new and more formidable military force, he applied for a transfer, only for the Army to refuse permission, and he stayed in post. Champing at the bit, desperate for a chance to avenge the events of the previous war, he got his chance in 1939, joining the attack on Poland in command of a unit of artillery.

Events conspired against him when the half-track he was traveling in struck a mine and overturned, causing him to suffer a concussion, and he was unconscious for almost twenty-four hours. When he recovered, the medic marked him as unfit to continue as a frontline soldier, and they gave him command of a logistics unit, comprising several trucks, most of them the German-built Opel Blitz. Although a few were French, flimsy Renaults seized by his transport team and included horse-drawn wagons. It made the business of carrying supplies to the front slow and dependent on finding forage for the horses. He hated it, almost as much as he hated the Americans, but he carried out his duties scrupulously, always hoping for a chance to get back into the action. His supply vehicles took part in the invasion of France and then came Barbarossa, the invasion of Russia.

He proved himself more than capable, getting supplies to the frontline troops, despite the formidable obstacles of alternating mud and freezing weather. Again and again, he begged his superiors to transfer him to a front-line unit, or the SS who were grabbing much of the glory. Each time they refused. His reputation for getting the supplies through to soldiers desperate for food and ammunition was his undoing, and he continued to command the supply train. The war was going badly in Russia when the Allies invaded Normandy, and they rushed reinforcements, troops, and armor to counter the new threat. Gottlieb Kreis was part of those reinforcements, and his bitterness at them forcing him to take a secondary role resurfaced.

He'd arrived back in France, back where a cowardly American soldier had shot his father in the back all those years ago. Yet unable to take revenge.

What am I? A fucking truck driver, fetching and carrying, a glorified delivery boy! If an opportunity arrives for me to get into the action, I'm determined to take it.

His trucks had halted fifteen miles west of Rouen close to a railway siding, and he was awaiting the arrival of a train with ammunition and supplies for the front. The war was close. Although too far to hear the noise of bullets and shells, Allied aircraft roamed the skies, shooting and bombing enemy targets. He'd made certain to keep his vehicles under the cover of a clump of trees several hundred yards from the railway line, and an hour ago rocket-firing Typhoons fighters had attacked a train.

Fortunately, their aim was wide, and the train continued on its way, with just minor damage to a single rail that engineers rushed out to repair to keep the line open.

He checked his watch again, impatient for the arrival of his supplies. There was still no sign of it when a Kubelwagen braked to a halt nearby, and an infantry Colonel climbed out. A real fighting soldier with a Knight's Cross, Germany's highest decoration at his throat, and waited for Kreis to approach.

Kreis saluted, and the other man nodded. "Major Kreis, I have new orders for you. A scratch force of ten artillery pieces and two hundred soldiers is traveling on the train, and they need transport. You will hitch up the artillery, and the soldiers will ride on your trucks, along with the supplies. Major, things are not looking good. The Allies have stormed ashore in large numbers, and although we've brought up our heavy panzers to push them back, the battle is still very uncertain. They desperately need these guns to form a defensive line west of St. Lo in case the enemy manages to break through. Can I rely on you, Kreis? If the worst comes to the worst, this will be our last line of defense to hold them back."

"Jawohl, Colonel. I will not let you down. We will drive these invaders back into the sea." He threw up his right arm in the prescribed Nazi salute, "Heil Hitler!"

The Colonel nodded slowly. "Yes, Heil Hitler. Good luck, Major."

As he turned away, Kreis thought the man muttered, "You'll need it." But he could've misheard.

The Kubelwagen drove away, and a half-hour later the train arrived, a line of flat cars loaded with artillery pieces and troops. The guns were the 7.5cm Infanteriegeschütz PAK-40s, effective against both armor and infantry, and he was impressed. He was unimpressed with the crews, who were sloppy. Under the command of a captain, who looked too old to be in command of a fighting unit, they moved slowly, as if they had all the time in the world; as if the Allies weren't pouring hundreds of thousands of men and mountains of equipment ashore. He marched over to the captain, who saw him coming and saluted.

Kreis noted his Iron Cross First Class, and once again felt a twinge of envy, but he also noticed the scars on the man's face, and his right hand encased in a black leather glove, a sign he'd probably lost that hand in action. Even so, he was an officer, and he ought to do better.

"Captain, tell your men to snap to it. My orders are to get them into position as fast as possible in case the Allies manage to break through our lines."

The officer shrugged. "If you wish, but they won't be happy. They're tired after a long journey from the Eastern Front, and they haven't eaten all day."

Kreis bridled. Food was of little importance when the future security of the Reich was at stake. "I don't care, Captain. Just get them moving. By the way, I'm sorry to see you were wounded. You've seen some action, where did it happen?"

"Stalingrad."

He didn't say any more. Any man who'd survived that charnel house deserved respect. He watched, fuming in impatience as they continued to move the guns from the flat cars to the waiting trucks. They were still moving too slowly, stumbling along like automatons, tired and hungry, which was through no fault of their own. But their uniforms were scruffy, stained, and ripped, and he made a note to take it up with the officer when they'd finished the loading.

They got the guns hitched up to the trucks and formed chains to pass the wooden crates of ammunition and supplies across. When they'd finished, they climbed aboard and found space to make themselves as comfortable as possible. There wasn't enough room for all of them, and several men climbed on the gun carriages, but eventually, they were ready. He gave the order for the convoy to move out.

It was almost dark, which was a relief, giving them some protection from the marauding aircraft that seemed to command the skies. As he'd done so many times, he wondered about the whereabouts of the Luftwaffe.

Why aren't they overhead, shooting down the potent English and American fighters?

He cursed the man in command, the obese drug addict Hermann Goering. The man who'd promised to keep the skies over the German Empire clear of enemy aircraft, and who'd manifestly failed.

They rolled through the French countryside and almost died. A man traveling in the open on the gun carriage towed behind Kreis' truck saw them in the moonlight and shouted a warning.

"Enemy aircraft! Take cover!"

Kreis' unit was no stranger to these emergencies, and they reacted fast. They were traveling parallel to a branch line of the railroad, and alongside it, he spotted the dark outline of the mouth of the tunnel.

"Get off the road, and into the tunnel!"

His driver flung the wheel over, drove onto the tracks, and

into the mouth of the tunnel. It was very long, maybe one hundred yards, but long enough for the rest of the trucks. Except one, the rearmost truck, and the first fighter swooped, an American Republic P-47 Thunderbolt. The cannons blazed as it closed on the unfortunate truck with its towed artillery piece. The Pratt & Whitney 18-cylinder air-cooled radial piston engine roared defiantly as the pilot gunned the throttle to maximum, and eight Browning .50 caliber machine guns blazed. As the aircraft went past, it dropped two 250-pound bombs that exploded yards away from the truck. Destroying the artillery piece and damaging the vehicle, but it kept moving forward. The driver made a valiant attempt to reach the safety of the tunnel, but the Thunderbolt wasn't alone, and three more fighters lurked, ready to pounce. They pounced, and the truck disappeared beneath sheets of heavy machine gun fire and high-explosive, a flaming pyre that lit up the area and turned night into day.

They circled for what seemed like hours, perhaps waiting for the Germans to emerge, but Kreis knew what waited for them, and nobody objected when he told them to stay in the tunnel until they were certain they'd gone away. Eventually, they left, but he gave it another hour in case they'd set a trap and called in more aircraft to circle overhead. When he was sure the sky was clear, he gave the order, and they cautiously drove out the other end of the tunnel and found their way back onto the road.

After their brush with the Allied fighters, they encountered little traffic on the route west, until they reached an intersection, with a detachment of military cops, Feldgendarmerie. He climbed out to get directions from the

NCO who appeared to be in charge.

"We're heading toward St. Lo, which road do we take?"

The man shook his head. "Forget it, Major. The enemy has reached Evrecy, and our troops are fighting to hold them off. There's no way through."

"Sergeant, we have to get through. It's vital we establish a new defensive position."

He shrugged. "Major, it's too late. I doubt anything can save Evrecy, and even Panzer Lehr, our elite tank battalion, is looking for a way out. We'll be lucky if we can get all our tanks out and pull them further east."

"I don't understand, what's gone wrong?"

"What's gone wrong is there're too many of them, and not enough troops to hold them back. Evrecy is the key, and when it falls, the enemy will use it as a springboard to push more troops and armor this way. We may as well face it, we're finished."

Kreis felt a growing excitement deep down.

If I can't carry out my orders, why not do something even more important? It's time to strike a blow for the Fatherland. Time to fulfill the vows I made when I joined the Party, and when I took up my commission in the Wehrmacht.

He felt a surge of adrenaline pouring through his body.

It's time to become a fighting soldier.

"Which road do I take for Evrecy? Quickly, man, I need the route!"

He pointed along the road leading off to the north-west. "That way, but you'll run into a shitload of fighting."

That was exactly what he'd been waiting for, the chance to hit back at the hated Americans. He nodded to the sergeant and climbed back into the truck. He gave the order, the engines started, and they took the road the NCO had indicated. Gottlieb Kreis was going into battle in honor of his father, and the Fatherland.

The Captain, who was also riding in the cab of the leading truck, squeezed between Kreis and the driver, glanced at him. "You got directions?"

"I did."

"How far to our new position?"

"Evrecy is around fifty miles."

"Evrecy? That's the wrong direction? St. Lo is further south."

"Change of plan, Captain. We're going where we're most needed."

"What's at Evrecy?"

"Glory."

They reached the town just after dawn and took cover inside the town. The German defenders had left, and just like the NCO had said, a gap had opened through which the enemy would come pouring through once they became aware of it.

He ordered the troops to dismount, hitch the artillery, and prepare for action, but not everybody was happy. The Captain, whose name was Fritz Neumann, interrupted him while he was giving orders.

"Major, I'm not sure this is a good idea. I doubt this position is defensible. My men have orders to establish a position thirty miles east of St. Lo, and it makes more sense than sitting here waiting for the enemy to arrive in strength and wipe us all out. They outnumber us. They have more men, more guns, and more armor, as well as air superiority. If we get out now, we can still carry out our orders."

"Captain Neumann, those orders have changed. I am your superior officer, and in my judgment, it is more important we defend the town and prevent further enemy breakthroughs. We're here, and this is where we stay."

Neumann raised an eyebrow. "And this is where we die?"

Kreis gave him a cold stare. "No, Captain. This is where the Americans die, should they be foolish enough to come here. My orders are to kill them all. When they come, show no mercy."

He nodded slowly. "I understand, but what about prisoners?"

"Captain," he murmured icily, "I said my orders are to kill them all. What don't you understand?"

"Sir, we cannot kill prisoners. Such an act is inhuman, illegal under the Geneva Convention. This isn't the Russian Front."

"I don't care. My order stands, and you can tell the men if any of them fail to carry out the order, I will shoot them myself. Clear?"

Neumann nodded. "Yessir. Heil Hitler."

* * *

They were a reconnaissance company, part of the 9th Infantry Division. They'd sent them ahead of the bulk of the Army to check out reports the town of Evrecy was undefended. Led by newly promoted Captain Frank Lesser, he was uneasy about his orders. They'd landed on Utah Beach, and although they'd lost a few men, it hadn't been as bad as they'd expected. As opposed to Omaha Beach, where he'd heard they had a much tougher time. Armor had come ashore with the Battalion, and with flocks of fighter aircraft overhead, he felt confident about the way things were going, until they gave him his current assignment. Aircraft had reported the town of Evrecy empty of defenders, and his assignment was to go check it out.

"Frank, it's a walk in the park," the Battalion Commander told him, "Reach the town, make sure it's clear, and stay there until our troops arrive. It's a chance for your men to strike out and put into practice everything you've learned in training. If you do run into the Jerries, it'll just be isolated pockets, and you should be able to roll them up without any trouble. The worst you'll encounter is the occasional machine gun, and you've been well trained to take care of them. You have the flamethrowers?"

"Yessir, two flamethrowers."

"That's good. If you run into a Kraut machine gun nest, use them, and you won't have any trouble. Any questions? No? Okay, get your men to Evrecy, dig in, and wait for us."

He'd got his men moving, all ninety-six of them. Less than normal for a company of infantry, but the brass had decided in their wisdom to shuffle men around, reinforcing those units expected to bear the brunt of the action, by taking men away from those they anticipated having an easier time. If everything went to plan, he didn't expect to run into difficulties. They said the town was empty of German defenders, so they could stroll in, check it out, and send the motorcycle messenger they'd assigned to him to take the good news back to HQ.

A simple assignment, and they climbed into the four Company trucks and drove through the French countryside. The journey was pleasant, with no sign of German soldiers, and just as important, the only aircraft in the sky were Allied. The sun was shining, and Captain Lesser began to relax as they reached the town, and nobody was shooting at them. They dismounted in the town square and prowled around to make sure the place was indeed empty. Apart from a few civilians who'd refused to leave, but they made themselves scarce, the only sign of them the occasional fleeting glimpse of a beret or headscarfed head peering through a grimy window before it abruptly disappeared.

The place was empty, and they drove to the east side, took shovels and entrenching tools, and began to form a defensive position. Men filled sandbags with earth, while others had begun the process of digging slit trenches. The flamethrower crews found a good position behind a hut tumbled stone wall, and they started to stack up the blocks of stone to repair the damage. When they'd finished, they could pop up and engulf the enemy in flames should they appear. Lesser was more than happy with the way things were going, until he wasn't happy. The first indication something was wrong was the noise of trucks approaching from the east. It had to mean Germans, and he shouted at his men to get behind cover.

There was little cover. The slit trenches were still too shallow, the emplacements for the flamethrower crews partly built, and he had no choice but to order them to retreat to the first houses on the easternmost side of the town. He was in the upstairs window of a house, with the rest of his men deployed in two adjoining houses. At first, he was nervous, but he reminded himself there was almost a hundred of them, equipped with two machine guns, two flamethrowers, and four infantry mortars; enough to defend themselves from a few Germans who'd probably taken a wrong turn. A moment later the hood of the first truck appeared, laden with supplies and men. He counted around fifteen men.

"Stand by. Wait until I fire. Don't worry men, this'll be a breeze."

"Captain…" Joe Merrick, a veteran NCO, clutched an M1 Thompson, and he didn't look happy, "I'm not too sure about this. This could be a good time to pull out."

"Pull out? You can't be serious. This is our first real action, and I intend to make sure we give a good account of ourselves."

A second truck rolled into view, but he saw no reason for alarm.

What are another fifteen men? There are almost a hundred of us, and when we open fire, they won't stand a chance.

"Captain, I really think we should pull out."

He waved the suggestion away. "Not in a million years, Sergeant. We came here to fight, and we're gonna show these Krauts how it goes." He raised his voice. "All of you, lock and load. Let 'em make another few yards and hit them."

He gripped his M3 Grease Gun and took aim. His finger curled around the trigger, he took up first pressure, and almost before he knew what he was doing, he'd started shooting. A line of bullets arced toward the lead truck that swerved away, and he grinned as the rest of his men opened fire. He felt exhilarated. This was the way to fight a war, surprise an enemy, and show them what American soldiers could do.

"Give 'em hell, men. Don't give them a chance to run away."

"Captain, they're not running away."

He glanced at the NCO. "What do you mean, they're not running away? They turned their trucks around, which means they must be…" He looked again, and for the first time, he saw them, "Oh, my God, sweet Jesus. Artillery."

"Yeah, artillery. Maybe we can pull out before it's too late."

"I…uh… I…"

He watched in horror as more trucks arrived, each laden with troops and pulling a vicious-looking artillery piece. The men on the trucks were clearly no strangers to action. One moment they'd been lolling amidst the crates and sacks, and they were a sorry-looking bunch, disheveled, their uniforms almost in rags. Too late, he understood the reason for the lack of spit and polish. They'd seen some hard fighting, and unlike his men, these were no rookies. They were hardened veterans, probably of the brutal, vicious fighting on the Eastern Front, and they went into action with a speed and precision that left him awestruck.

In less than one minute the first artillery piece was unloaded, and the crew was loading the first shell. The rest were seconds behind, and when they started throwing shells, his company had no way to defend themselves.

"Sergeant, give the order to pull back, now! Run!"

He shouted the order, and men scrambled to get out of the houses, but they didn't get far. The guns bellowed, sending a rain of high-explosive shells that demolished houses. Shrapnel tore into running men, killing and wounding half of them before they had a chance to get far. Captain Lesser stumbled and fell when a slice of shrapnel sliced into his leg, but Joe Merrick was next to him. He scooped him up onto his shoulders and carried him the rest of the way. The others made it back to the town square where their trucks were waiting for them, and they boarded two trucks in which to drive away. Straight into the enemy who'd anticipated the move and had driven around the town to intercept them on the other side. Two trucks were waiting for them, blocking the road, crammed with infantry, and they'd mounted an MG-42 machine gun on the cab of each truck.

Merrick gave the order to stop. "We can't get past them, and if we try to turn around, they'll hit us with those machine guns. Don't forget they have those artillery pieces, so whichever way we go we're fucked."

The driver stomped on the brake pedal and ground to a halt, with the other truck pulling up close behind. In the cab, Lesser was losing a lot of blood, but he protested they ought to do something. "We came here to do a job, Sergeant. We can't just go back with half the company dead."

"Sir, you'll lose the other half of the company if we don't stop. Our best chance is to disappear into the houses and use them for cover, work our way out of here, and try to get back to our lines."

Lesser didn't reply. He'd fainted from loss of blood. The Sergeant carried him into the nearest house and walked through to the rear yard. He was staring into the muzzle of three MP-40 machine pistols, alongside a dozen enemy troopers who looked like they were just burning for an excuse to squeeze the trigger. They were screwed. The Germans had moved faster than he'd have believed possible, showing tactical understanding learned from a score of fierce battles, and he grudgingly admitted they'd got the drop on them.

He laid down his weapon, shouted for the rest of them to do the same, and stepped out with his hands in the air. The only man to have escaped was the motorcycle messenger, who'd stopped on a hill outside the town to look back and see what happened. He couldn't believe it. He saw Sergeant Merrick lay down his weapon and surrender, the rest of the men did the same, and then the shooting started. German soldiers hosing down men who'd put down their weapons, expecting honorable treatment, but they treated them like rabid dogs. Tearing them apart with sheets of gunfire, and although some attempted to retrieve their weapons to shoot back, it was too late.

He watched, unable to tear himself away until the ground was littered with bodies, stained with their blood. He saw an officer walking among the corpses and badly wounded men with his sidearm clutched in his hand. He paused by each body, took deliberate aim, and fired a single bullet into the head, moving to the next and doing the same. The dispatch rider, Corporal Ernest Mellor waited until it was over. Waited until the officer strutted away and called his men. They disappeared back into the town, and he assumed they were leaving. It had just been bad luck the Germans had arrived before they had a chance to set up defensive positions. Even more bad luck they were towing artillery pieces, and as if things couldn't be worse, it was obvious they knew their business.

There was nothing more for him here. All he could do was get back to Battalion Headquarters as fast as possible and report what he'd seen. It was nothing less than a war crime, an act of mass murder. What mattered was to find out where those Germans went and find out the identity of the officer who'd given the order for such brutal slaughter.

CHAPTER ONE

13 June 1944

Army Ranger PFC Jack Murphy had found a comfortable spot to relax for a couple of hours until it was time to move off. Since they came ashore on Omaha Beach, the fighting had been hard, and they'd taken heavy casualties, wiping out almost a half of First Platoon. A few replacements had appeared, but they were still below strength. Among the replacements were the new platoon commander, Second Lieutenant Carter Adams, and a new sergeant to replace the previous man who'd died heroically. The new NCO was a grizzled veteran, Master Sergeant Tom Rooker. He's spent his life in the Army, and early indications were promising. Of average height, with dark hair and dark, brooding eyes, he looked tough, and he was tough. A weather-beaten face with a broken nose and a patchwork of scars, he looked tough and determined; the kind of guy who'd take on all comers and beat them down with sheer strength of will and brute force. Maybe he was a bit long in the tooth, but he'd demonstrated his ability to keep the platoon out of trouble. The kind of trouble a rookie officer could get them into, if the brass saddled a platoon with a rookie officer. They'd saddled First Platoon, Bravo Company, Army Rangers, with a rookie officer.

Murphy glanced at PFC Dan Kelly, his best buddy, who'd dropped down beside him. He'd started to snooze. "I wouldn't get too comfortable. We're sure to be moving out before for long."

He yawned. "They told us we could take a rest, and that's exactly what I intend to do."

Kelly was no outdoorsman. He hated the outdoors, resented every second since they hit the beaches. Not that he had anything against France. At least, not Paris, France. He was counting the days until they arrived in the 'City of Light.' Anticipating the women, the fine wines, everything a city had to offer. And the countryside lacked.

He didn't resemble a sophisticated city boy, built more like a wrestler, or a boxer, which was closer to the truth. After he left school, he made his money touring the carnival circuit, taking on all comers to earn a few bucks. Descended from Irish immigrants, he had pale, blue eyes and pasty skin. His hair was odd, not quite blonde, not quite ginger, but somewhere in between. On occasion, another soldier thought to josh him about strange color, until they saw his muscled bulk and the eyes that regarded the world with a fierce intensity. Probably derived from his warlike ancestors, who'd fought an unending fight to stay alive in the violence that was a feature of Ireland during its formative centuries.

Murphy grinned at the buddy who'd been beside him every step of the way since they came ashore. "Knock yourself out, but the Sarge is coming toward us, and that looks like Lieutenant Adams trying to catch up."

"Shit."

They both got to their feet, nodded to Rooker, a no-nonsense, no-shit kind of guy, and sketched a casual salute to Lieutenant Adams. He looked uncertain, worried, and that told them a lot. Told them the shit was about to hit the fan.

"We need to be ready to move out at a moment's notice. The Germans don't look like they're about to give up. The Brit armor ran into an ambush and lost a heap of vehicles at Villers-Bocage. Now those same heavy panzers are loose. We don't know where they are. The Airborne are heavily engaged outside Carentan, and they're taking heavy fire from enemy mortars and machine guns. We need a breakthrough, and we needed it fast. Aerial reconnaissance has shown a gap in the German lines. It's a town named Evrecy, and it looks like they've pulled out and left it undefended. As soon as the orders come through, we'll be going forward to check it out. If it's true, our troops and armor can drive through the town and get in the enemy's rear to hit them from behind, but we need to be sure. Things have got confused, and it was thought some men were sent in from the 9th Infantry Division to check it out. But there has been no response, which is why they're sending us in."

"What the Lieutenant is saying," Rooker grunted, "Is get your sorry asses off the ground, draw ammunition and rations for one day, and make sure you're ready to leave when he gives the order."

Adams nodded. "We'll move fast, so anything you don't

need stow it somewhere. Light weapons only, nothing else."

"Grenades?"

He shot Murphy a sour glance, which was no surprise. They were direct opposites. Murphy was an outdoorsman, five feet eight inches, with pale, watery blue eyes, a freckled face, and a shock of sandy-colored hair. Of medium build, he looked ordinary, at first glance. Until he stripped to the waist, displaying a body packed with muscle, the result of the hobby that filled most of his spare time. He was a climber and liked nothing better than pitting his skills against the treacherous slopes of the neighboring mountains.

Carter Adams looked like he'd be more at home in a library, leafing through musty old books. He wasn't a good fit for the Rangers, but the Army had sent him, and they had to make the best of it. He'd disliked Murphy on sight and made sure to always give him the shit assignments.

"No grenades, you won't need them."

"Lt, is that wise?"

"I said no. Clear?"

"Yessir."

Carter and Rooker went on to brief the rest of First Platoon. Reluctantly, Murphy emptied his pack to remove the gear he wouldn't be taking with him. Most of it was climbing gear. Stuff he'd brought along into Normandy, and it had proved useful, although not for climbing mountains. There were other places to climb, like the deep shaft he'd descended when they attacked an enemy artillery emplacement tucked deep into a hillside. He checked his weapons, the Springfield M1903 he'd managed to swap out instead of the M1 Garand they'd issued to him. The bolt-action Springfield was a joy to use, packing five

.30 caliber cartridges in the stripper clip, and back in Montana, he'd become something of an expert shooter.

It wasn't his only weapon. Like most Army Rangers, including enlisted men, he carried a sidearm, and like most, his was a .45 caliber Colt M1911 automatic. Accurate at short-range, it was rugged and reliable, a handy backup in a tight situation. Although frowned upon, he carried a third weapon, and it was unconventional. A German MP-40, taken from an enemy soldier he'd killed. It was kind of like the M3 Grease Gun. Short, compact, and the magazine carried thirty-two 9mm rounds, which made it useful for close-quarters fighting when a man who knew how to use it could clear an enemy squad in a single shattering burst. Murphy knew how to use it. With the stock folded, the weapon was a mere twenty-four inches long, and he carried it slung on his back, with several spare magazines in his pack.

He glanced at Dan Kelly, who also carried an MP-40 taken from a dead German, as well as an M1911. He didn't see any point in swapping out his M1 Garand. He'd told him with a grin, "Jack, it'd be a waste of time. I may as well face it, I'm a lousy shot."

They drew rations and ammunition, stuffed them in their packs, and went to check on another platoon member, PFC Arnold Morgan. He'd suffered a neck wound the previous day when they'd run into a German machine gun nest set up to delay the Allied advance. They'd taken care of it and wiped out the crew, but Arnold took a bullet. At the time it had seemed a lot worse, with blood pouring from his neck. When the medic cleaned him up, he discovered a deep gouge that'd missed the serious arteries or veins.

"You're gonna be okay, Private Morgan. I've put a dressing on it and some antiseptic ointment to take care of any infection. Rest up to twenty-four hours, and you'll be back in action, fit as a flea."

"How about forty-eight hours?"

He'd grinned. "No chance."

Arnold was busy with his M1 Garand, and he didn't notice them as they walked up behind him. The dressing made the wound look bad, but it didn't look like it would cause him problems.

"Hey, buddy, what's the deal? How is it?"

He glanced around, saw Murphy, and grinned. "If the bullet had gone a tad deeper, they'd have sent me home."

"If it had gone a tad deeper, they could've sent you home in a box."

The grin faded. "I guess there is that. Hey, I never thanked you for what you did."

"I didn't do anything special. I saw a German and I popped him, is all."

"Murphy, he had me bang to rights. I thought that bullet had done for me, but he thought otherwise, and he was getting ready to take another shot. That's when you jumped up and blasted him with that Kraut machine gun you carry. If you hadn't been there, I'd have been dead."

"One of those things, Arnold. You'd have done the same for me."

"All the same, I owe you."

"You owe me nothing. Forget it, and next time, don't get in the way of an enemy bullet."

The smile returned. "You can bet on it."

He moved away with Kelly, walking back to join the rest of the platoon. Before they got there, James Curtis, the Brit war photographer embedded with the battalion tried to grab them. He was a pain in the ass, always asking questions, always trying to persuade them to adopt heroic poses so he could snap pictures and send them back to his newspaper. Some of the men were prepared to go along with it, but neither Murphy nor Kelly were inclined to be a part of obviously faked pictures.

Before they could get away, Curtis blocked their path. "Say guys, I'm still trying to line up some good action shots I can use for the readers back home. You men are heroes, and all I'm asking is a few minutes of your time to set something up, snap a couple of pictures, and you'll be famous." He brandished his camera, a German-made Leica 35mm.

Murphy faked an apologetic smile. "Sorry, pal, we have things to do, places to go."

"It'll only take a minute."

He grabbed hold of his arm to stop him from walking away, but he snatched his arm away. He spun the photographer around. "Mister, if you wanna take action shots, you can come with us when we go into battle. That's where you'll see the real heroes."

"Uh, another time. How about I take a quick couple of snaps before you go."

The arrival of a jeep saved them. Driven by Ron Lucas, a new man who'd already acquired the nickname 'Lucky Lucas,' due to the way he fell into every easy detail. Like acquiring better rations reserved for higher ranks. Like driving the jeep, which meant a more comfortable ride when the rest of them hiked to the front or rode in the back of a boneshaker of a truck. Within twenty-four hours of his arrival, he'd shown himself an ass crawler, becoming the company commander's blue-eyed boy. What caused the real resentment was his magical ability to disappear when the shooting started. Nobody liked him. Except for Bravo Company Commander Captain Robert Washington.

Murphy ignored Lucas and was more interested in the person seated in the passenger seat, a French girl. Soon after arriving in Normandy, he'd met Clemence Delon, terrified after being stalked by a Nazi officer. She stayed with the platoon for protection, even after Murphy put a bullet in her pursuer, and they'd become close, despite attempts by HQ to remove her and send her home. She'd proved herself useful, and they agreed to keep her on as an interpreter. As well as speaking English, she was also a fluent German speaker, and because linguists were in short supply, they allowed her to stay as an unpaid adviser.

She'd proved her worth in other ways. Clemence Delon had run a farm when Murphy ran into her, and when he saw her, he felt as if the ghost of Rachel Gold, the girl who'd been murdered by a rogue cop back in Whitefish, Montana had returned from the dead. She had dark hair always tucked beneath a peasant scarf, and she was short, a little taller than a child. Yet the look from her dark, flashing eyes told him everything he needed to know about her, a steely, inner determination and toughness. This was France, the country that'd given birth to Joan of Arc, and she was one helluva a fighter. There was a further benefit that no man could deny. She was pretty. In the mud and grime of warfare, she reminded a man of the things he was fighting for.

He helped her out of the jeep, and she gave him a smile. "Jack, it's good to see you again. How're things?"

Just hearing her voice was a tonic, English spoken with that unmistakable French lilt, enough to melt the heart of any red-blooded man. "It's good to see you, Clemence. What're you doing here?"

"I…"

Before he could reply, a rifle bullet came out of nowhere, a sudden loud crack, and somebody cried out. Men scattered, racing for cover, and Murphy scooped up his Springfield and began searching for the sniper. He couldn't find him first, not until a second bullet whined through the air, narrowly missing the French girl.

"Clemence, get behind cover!"

She jumped behind the jeep and threw herself on the ground. Some of the men had started firing, but the shots were wild, and not likely to score any hits. Dan Kelly lay next to him, searching a clump of trees about eight hundred yards away. "I could swear that last shot came from in that small wood. What do you think?"

He nodded. "I reckon so, too. It'll be difficult flushing him out. It's open ground between us and him. How about you give him a burst from the MP-40? If he moves, I'll see him, and I can nail the bastard."

Dan looked doubtful. "That's some distance, do you think you can get him?"

"He shot one of our guys, so, yeah, if he can do it, I can do it. Why don't we give it a try?"

"You got it."

More men were firing, some in the direction of the wood, and others aiming every which way. They'd no idea of the location of the sniper, but Murphy had watched when the second shot was fired, and he was pretty sure his estimate was correct, and the guy was tucked inside the wood, probably high in a tree to give him a good field of view. He threw the Springfield to his shoulder and peered through the telescopic sight. The previous owner of the rifle, killed on Omaha Beach, was an enthusiast, and he'd fitted the weapon with a Winchester A5 Telescopic Sight. It was an antique, two feet long, yet the optics were of high quality, and despite other men shaking their heads in disbelief when they saw it, he swore by its precision build and unfailing accuracy.

The trees swung into focus, and he moved the rifle barrel side to side and up and down in tiny movements, searching for the target, but there was nothing. The guy had camouflaged himself well, and he'd get one chance. A split second when Dan emptied his MP-40 in the general direction, hoping something would move. Probably a small branch, or even a leaf, but it would give him what he needed, a target, something to shoot at.

"Ready?" Dan murmured.

"Hit it."

The German machine pistol chattered, spraying bullets into the distant trees. The effective range maxed out at two hundred yards, and at eight hundred yards, the bullets would be no more lethal than throwing small pebbles. But with luck, the shock of his position coming under fire would be enough to make him move. Dan fired, keeping the trigger depressed until the magazine was empty. Murphy waited, and at last, he saw him. Or at least, he saw a part of him. Several leaves parted, and in the gap, he saw a reflection. Something metallic, or even glass, like a telescopic sight, but whatever it was, he had him.

There was no time for fancy technique. As Dan's burst

tailed off, he exhaled and took up first pressure on the trigger. Put the crosshairs on the target and gently squeezed the trigger. One bullet cracked out of the muzzle, and at the velocity of almost three thousand feet per second, it traveled the distance in one second flat. The branches around the target moved, the leaves rustled, and a dark figure tumbled out, falling to the ground.

Someone shouted, "You got him!"

Sergeant Rooker was already shouting at Lucas to grab another man and drive over to check the body and make sure he was dead. Dan grinned. "Now that's what I call shooting. I guess you haven't lost your touch."

"I was lucky, is all. I heard someone cry out after the first shot, who got hit?" He looked around, and the French girl had crawled out from behind the jeep. She was attending to a man lying on the ground in a pool of blood, "Christ, it's Arnold. Clemence, how is he?"

She looked up and shook her head. "I'm sorry, he never stood a chance."

"Those Krauts should know when to pack up and go home."

Sergeant Rooker walked up to them and glanced down Arnold Morgan. "The problem is, Murphy, they don't know when to pack up and go home. Not until we hit them so hard, they wish they'd never been born. A pity about Morgan, I guess he was just unlucky, in the wrong place at the wrong time."

Clemence glanced at him. "He was unlucky, and Lucas was lucky. He was standing in front of Morgan, but a second before the sniper fired, he dropped something and bent down to pick it up. If he hadn't moved, the sniper would've got him.

He got Arnold instead."

"Lucky Lucas," Kelly grunted, "It's always the good ones die, and the bad ones live."

"Luck of the draw," Rooker snapped, "Don't make anything of it."

The jeep returned, and instead of carrying a corpse, they had a casualty lying on the back seat. Murphy's bullet had hit him square in the chest, but it'd missed his heart and other vital organs, leaving him bleeding badly and in need of urgent attention, but he was still alive. The Lieutenant glanced at him and told Lucas to get him to the medics at Battalion Headquarters. "Miss Delon, you'd better go along. You can travel in the rear of the jeep with the wounded man. When you get there, stay there. I don't want you here."

She sketched him a mock salute. "Yessir, Lieutenant."

He gave her a sour look. "And don't come back."

Murphy didn't what her to leave, and he had mixed feelings. The battlefront was no place for a girl, especially when she was the girl he'd planned to spend the future with. Back home in Montana, he'd fallen for another girl, Rachel Gold, when he rescued her from the mountains above his hometown of Whitefish. He belonged to the local Mountain Rescue team, and they called him out when she got into trouble with some friends. After a daring operation when he plucked her to safety off the mountain in the face of overwhelming odds, he loved and lost her almost in the blink of an eye. He dated her just once. Soon after she was found dead, her body hidden in the woods. Murdered, and he'd found the man responsible, a local cop, Sergeant Jeff Abbott.

By coincidence, Abbott had joined the Army Rangers, his

outfit, and when he realized Murphy knew he was responsible, he tried to kill him on several occasions. He failed. Abbott and his friend Pérez were dead, their bodies now rotting in the rich Normandy soil. As far as he knew, nobody knew who killed them, except his best buddy, Dan Kelly and Clemence, so he felt safe, as safe as any man could feel in the middle of the battle for Europe, fighting a cunning well-equipped and skillful enemy. An enemy that could call on legions of heavy tanks and hard-bitten, veteran soldiers who'd proved their mettle in the slaughter of the Eastern Front. It was going to be tough, but he was a Ranger, and Rangers were tough, enough to kick the Krauts where it hurt. Show them they couldn't arrogantly assume they were the Masters of Europe. That America and the Allies were better.

When it was all over, he wanted nothing more than to get his life back. Working in Ernie's Gunshop in Whitefish, Montana. Indulging his love of climbing, and hunting. And hopefully, Clemence Delon would agree to come with him. To start a new life in the States and the crisp, clean air of Montana. He knew she'd be happy, if it were within his power, he'd make damn sure of it. And make sure he didn't lose her.

Not again. Not like Rachel. A guy can only stand so much, and I'd go out of my mind.

He heard the noise of an engine, another Willys Jeep. At first, he thought they were coming back, but this one carried the insignia of the Military Police. It pulled up close to him, and a large-bellied cop with a face like a rusty bucket and wearing the stripes of a sergeant approached a Ranger and spoke for a few seconds. The man shrugged and pointed to Murphy. "That's him."

He hitched up his pants and walked, or rather strutted

toward him. "You're PFC Jack Murphy? The guy they call 'Angel' Murphy?"

He hated the nickname. It went back to his volunteer work in Whitefish when his mountaineering skills had enabled him to rescue trapped climbers in situations most regarded as impossible. People said he must have sprouted wings to get to climbers perched at high altitude on tiny ledges, impossible to reach, but somehow, he always made it, and he'd never lost a single one. But he let it go. "What's up? What do you want?"

The man's eyes narrowed. "You're supposed to say what's up, Sergeant?"

He shrugged. "If there's something you want, spit it out."

The eyes narrowed slits. "Have it your way. My name is Sergeant Duane Bishop, Military Police."

"Uh-huh. You still haven't told me what you want."

He hitched his pants up again around his protruding belly. "Does the name Jeff Abbott mean anything to you?"

"Sure it does, I knew him back in Whitefish, and I was with him in Normandy. If you're looking for him, he's dead."

"I know he's dead, and that's why I'm here. Me and Jeff joined the cops at the same time, went through training together, and we had our first posting together in Billings. We were pretty close, so I want to find out how he died. Somehow it doesn't seem right. Jeff was more than able to look after himself, and I can't imagine some Kraut getting the drop on him."

It wasn't a Kraut, Bishop, but he got what he deserved.

He shrugged. "I wouldn't know about that. I didn't see it happen."

"I heard different. Some guy said he'd seen you and Abbott in the same sector, and you had to have seen what happened."

"Whatever he said, he's wrong. I don't know where Abbott was when he got hit, I didn't see him."

"They found his body and brought it back, what's left of him. I'm not happy with the official explanation, so I've put in a request for an autopsy. When they carry it out, I'll be able to follow it up some more."

"Whatever. Like I said, I didn't see it happen, but my guess is when they do the autopsy all they'll find is a chunk of German lead."

"Or a chunk of American lead, maybe. I'll know soon enough, and if it pans out the way I think it will, I'll be back to talk with you some more."

"Knock yourself out, Bishop."

"It's Sergeant Bishop."

"Yeah. Listen, pal, I can't waste all morning chatting with you, I have work to do. Real work, like killing the enemy. Maybe you'd like to join us, see some real action?" Bishop didn't reply, but he saw his skin go a couple of shades paler, "I thought not. So long."

Lieutenant Adams was waiting for them, and he rejoined the platoon. When he looked back, Bishop was still watching him, and he knew he could have trouble with that guy. Did he believe he'd killed his pal Abbott? Maybe he did, maybe he didn't. He was the kind of guy who wanted someone to blame, would hold a grudge, and would keep looking until he'd found someone to pin that grudge to. Murphy had been close, and so he assumed he'd killed him. As it happened, he was almost right. Abbott and his pal Pérez had been trying to kill him after he found out the cop had killed Rachel. They almost succeeded, but

Clemence had intervened and killed them both. Only him and Dan knew the truth, and it would stay that way. Not that he wouldn't have put a bullet in him, but it hadn't worked out that way.

Now they were jumping off on a new mission to the town they'd called Evrecy. According to headquarters, the town had emptied of Germans, so it would be simple. Check out the town, make sure the enemy wasn't in evidence, and send a message back so the tanks and infantry could drive through the gap; piercing the enemy lines and wheeling around to take them by surprise. That was the plan, and as every soldier knew, plans were the first casualty of war. Besides, the Lieutenant mentioned one or two factors they ought to consider.

"We've lost sight of the panzers. The 101st Heavy Panzers, they're the ones who gave the Brit armor a heavy kicking at Villers-Bocage. The other outfit is the Panzer Lehr, also equipped with heavy tanks, Tigers, and Panthers. In theory, the Panzer Lehr Division is somewhere to the north, and the 101st to the south, but they may have moved to a new position."

A man groaned, and Rooker gave him a hard look. "Pipe down and listen. Lt, what about infantry and artillery? Do they have anything close to the town?"

He shook his head. "I can answer that with an emphatic no. No guns, and no infantry." A couple more of the men jeered, but he held up his hand quiet, "I get it, we're not equipped to tangle with heavy armor, but we have trucks, and if we run into trouble we can get out of it fast. USAF has also promised to fly frequent reconnaissance flights, and if they see the enemy, they'll warn us in good time."

"How?"

He stared at the Sarge, mystified. "How? I don't understand?"

"Lt, our radio got busted, and they don't have a spare, so they're sending a motorcycle messenger with us to report back to headquarters. That's a slow means of communication. If they see enemy tanks, how will they warn us?"

"Uh, I have no doubt they'll think of a way. Maybe send the messenger back."

"If we're surrounded, it'll mean getting past enemy armor? You're saying our lives depend on a messenger getting past the panzers?"

"Sergeant, Battalion put this plan together, and they'll have thought through every last detail."

"Yeah, right."

"That's enough, Sergeant. We leave at dawn."

"I thought we were getting ready to pull out right away."

"I've decided to wait until dawn. That way we can see what we're getting into." He put an ingratiating smile on his face as if trying to persuade Rooker his way was the best way, "Better than running into a squadron of German tanks during the night."

"It'd be better if we arrived while it's still dark, Sir. We still don't know what we're gonna find when we get to Evrecy."

"Sergeant," he said in a voice that suggested his patience was wearing thin, "The Germans are not there. This is a simple reconnaissance, nothing more."

"Simple, right."

They unhitched their packs, put down their weapons, and settled down to wait, searching for places to bivouac for the night. At dawn, they boarded the truck, and the Lieutenant led the way in the jeep. The drive to Evrecy was uneventful, and their worst fears were unrealized. There was no sign of enemy armor, and the only aircraft in the sky were friendlies, who swooped down, recognized the white Allied star painted on the hood of each vehicle, and left them alone, apart from a British Spitfire that gave them a friendly waggle of the wings.

With a sense of relief, they reached the outskirts of the town. Adams surveyed the buildings and streets through his binoculars and passed them to Rooker. "See what you think, but it looks clear to me."

The Sarge took his time, moving the lenses from side to side, examining everything in minute detail, and he passed the glasses back to the Lieutenant. "It looks quiet, Lt. Too quiet. We should take a look first; make sure they're not waiting for us. If it's clear, we can drive in, spread out, and check out the rest of the town. Let me take a couple of men in and have a look around."

He nodded. "If you think so but make it quick. This is a simple mission. I don't want to turn it into a major operation."

"Me, either, but that's kind of up to the Jerries, don't you think? Murphy, Kelly, come with me."

The three Rangers ran forward, doubled over in case the enemy had left snipers inside the town, but they reached the first of the buildings without running into trouble. Rooker led the way into the town, and he paused when he saw movement.

"Cover me, I saw something inside a window. There's somebody over there. Could be something, could be nothing, but I'll check it out."

They dropped to the ground and watched as the Sarge raced forward, kicked open the door of the house, and dashed inside. Several minutes later, he appeared in the doorway.

"It's okay. It's one of our guys. He's hurt bad, and we need to attend to his wounds before we move on, or he'll die."

They jogged over to the house and went inside. It was gloomy, and the soldier lay on the floor in the center of the room. Even in the poor light, they could make out the dark liquid seeping out around his body. Rooker was already pulling out dressings from his pack, and he wrapped them over the wounds to stop further blood loss. The man's lips were moving, and he told Murphy to try to make out what he was saying. He nodded, knelt next to him, and put his ear close to the man's mouth.

"What is it, pal? What're you trying to tell us?"

"It… was… murder."

"Uh-huh. What happened?"

"Ambush. We weren't expecting it. All dead. Except me, and I don't think I'm gonna make it."

"Sure you'll make it. How many died in the ambush? Did you say all of them?"

He coughed, and a spray of blood spewed out from his mouth. Rooker wiped the blood from his mouth and gave him sips of water from his canteen. After another minute, his lips moved and with a huge effort, he spoke again. "Prisoners."

"Okay, I get it. They killed some and captured the rest, so they're prisoners."

"Killed them." The voice had dropped to a hoarse whisper.

"They murdered them?"

They had to wait almost another minute for the answer. "Yes."

Seconds later, he was dead, and Rooker gently leaned over

and closed his eyes. They glanced at each other. "Jesus Christ, what's going on? Did I hear right, this guy just said the Krauts murdered American prisoners?"

Kelly nodded. "That's what he said. Is it possible? I mean, I know they can play hardball, but that's on the Eastern Front, where they say warfare has descended into primitive butchery."

Murphy went to the window and glanced out into the street. He saw it was empty, and he looked back at Rooker. "If they ambushed this poor guy's unit and killed them, they have to be close. Did he mean it happened inside the town, or somewhere else and he was heading back to our lines when he was too weak to carry on?"

"No idea, but we need to get further into the town and make sure. We have to leave him here, and we'll notify Graves Registration when we get back. Let's go."

They left the house and continued walking toward the center of Evrecy. But this time they were more careful. Rooker hugged one side of the street, Murphy the other, and Kelly brought up the rear, constantly looking back to make sure there wasn't a squad of Nazi storm troopers crawling up their backsides. They reached the end of the street, and the square at the center of the town lay in front of them, about three hundred yards ahead. There was still no sign of life, and they turned into the street to reach the center, stopping after the first ten yards.

Something was wrong, badly wrong. A narrow, dark lane at the side of the street, and something was moving, flies, clouds of flies. As their eyes grew accustomed to the gloom, they saw them. Bodies, piles of bodies. All of them were in American uniform, and now they got it. The Germans had executed American prisoners inside the town, and the unexpected butchery appalled them. As did the sudden realization the enemy was there.

They looked up and down the street and saw movement. They weren't flies feasting on the bodies of dead soldiers. It was the men who'd killed them. They were here, in the town, despite the confident assertions of Battalion. Rooker hit the cobbles, and they joined him, lying flat, keeping out of sight. But it was too late, the enemy had seen them, and they came under fire from a score of rifles. A machine gun opened up, then another, and they scampered inside the nearest house. It was empty of civilians, and Murphy ran to the rear to look for a way out. Rooker looked out the window to see if they were coming along the street, and it was a fatal mistake.

They didn't just have rifles and machine guns. An artillery piece bellowed, and a shell hit the next house. It fired again, and then another opened up, and two shells smashed into the house they were standing inside. They demolished most of the front wall, causing the upper floor and roof to collapse. They'd made it to the rear of the house, but the Sarge hadn't. An avalanche of masonry and timbers had trapped him in the rubble.

Kelly stared in disbelief. "He's dead! They got the Sarge!"

42

CHAPTER TWO

14 June 1944

They stared at the heap of rubble covering the spot where they'd seen Rooker a few moments before. The guns were still firing, and the interior was a thick cloud of dust, making it impossible to see more than a couple of feet, but they ran back to get him out. Frantically pulling at chunks of masonry, tossing them aside, ripping up heavy roofing timbers mixed with slates, and they saw him. At least a part of him, his boot, sticking out from beneath a concrete slab, and Murphy grabbed the end and tried to lift it. It wouldn't budge.

"Dan, lend a hand. We need to shift this so we can free him."

They gripped the slab between them and heaved, using every ounce of their strength. Slowly, it moved enough for him to wedge a length of timber under the slab to hold it up, and

Rooker was there, almost invisible in the dust, and he wasn't moving. They dragged him out and between them carried him to the rear of the house. There was nothing in the rear yard, and they pulled him out into the open, laid him down, and to their relief, his eyes opened, and he looked at Murphy.

"What happened? There was a big bang, and then nothing."

"The Germans happened. They're in the town, all over the place, and they have artillery. A couple of shells hit the house and partly destroyed it. Sarge, have you broken anything?"

He moved his limbs. "I don't think so. Help me up."

He got his feet, swayed for a few seconds, and got his balance. Master Sargent Tom Rooker was nothing if not as tough as boiled leather. "I'm okay. Before we get out of here, we need to find out what we're up against. Then we need to get back to the platoon and warn them. I guess they will want to call in an airstrike to take care of those Nazis, if they're still here when they arrive. I'd sure like to get my hands on the guy in charge for ordering his men to kill prisoners. He shrugged, "I doubt it'll ever happen. We need to get out of here, let's go."

They slipped from backyard to backyard, careful to stay out of sight, until they were back at the edge of the town, and that's when they heard the sound of engines. Lieutenant Carter Adams had lost patience, decided he didn't need to wait, and they were within fifty yards of the town, driving in the Willys with the truck following. He decided to stop on the edge and proceed on foot, for they switched off the engines, but it didn't go silent. Their engines had covered the noise of the German Opel Blitz driving toward them. The truck, laden with troops was towing an artillery piece, followed by another truck, and they moved with the slick precision of veteran troops.

Guttural German voices shouted orders, and men rushed into position. Some unhitched the gun and turned it to point toward the platoon. The rest threw themselves behind cover, and the bullets began to fly. Caught out in the open, First Platoon lost half-dozen men almost before they came aware they were under fire. The Rangers scattered, disappearing into ditches and behind stone walls, but they weren't out of trouble. The artillery fired a high-explosive shell, demolishing the truck, and another shell made mincemeat of the jeep.

Rooker looked every which way, searching for a way to help them, and it looked impossible. They were three men against twenty Germans, armed with everything from rifles and machine pistols, to a light machine gun. A moment later the second truck arrived, and more soldiers leaped into action.

"We have to do something," he growled at Murphy, "But I'm out of ideas. Grenades, how're you fixed?"

"He told us to travel light, Sarge. No grenades," He didn't remind him they'd said the town would be empty of Germans. A pause, "But I have the Springfield. I can take out the gunners if you can handle the rest of them."

He measured distances. "We'd have to get much closer before we hit them. Follow the wall where it loops outside of the town and loop back. If we keep out of sight, we could get close enough, but it'll be tough."

He handed him his MP-40. "Dan has one of these, and you have the Thompson. You can use mine, Sarge. That'll give you a lot of firepower, I just hope it's enough."

"It'll have to be enough," he snarled. His jaw jutting out in a posture they'd seen before, his warlike posture. The way he looked when he was about to wade into the enemy and give them hell, "Let's do it."

They snaked across twenty yards of open ground and reached the safety of a stone wall. Continued on their hands and knees, keeping their heads out of sight, and it was a long crawl. In the meantime, the Germans weren't idle. They'd spotted Adams' platoon, and first one and then the other gun crashed out, blasting them with high-explosive shells. They fired again, and twice more, then stopped shooting. Murphy could see the Lieutenant had pulled them back behind the wrecked and burnt-out Panther, and the heavy armor shielded them from the blasts. Shell after shell impacted the armor, but it wasn't until the Germans switched tactics and started using armor-piercing shells that everything changed.

Rooker grimaced. "The bastards are chewing holes into the hull of the tank. Sooner or later they're gonna go all the way through and out the other side, and our guys are toast. We have to move faster."

Murphy had been thinking the same thing, and they had seconds left to act. He glanced through the long telescope mounted on his Springfield. "I can nail the gunners from here if you can take care of the troops. How about it?"

Both men looked toward the enemy position, and it was going to be a tough nut to crack. Rooker measured the angles and finally nodded. "Okay, I think we can do it, but we're gonna have to break the record for the hundred-yard dash. Kelly, are you up to it?"

"Do we have a choice?"

"Nope. Murphy, get ready."

He rested the barrel of the Springfield on the top of the

wall. "Ready."

"Go!"

He squeezed the trigger, and the disciplined German troops collapsed into chaos as his steady, precision shots targeted the gun crews. One by one they went down. There were three men for each gun, six men in all, and five bullets in the stripper clip. Each of his first five bullets scored a hit, and in a swift movement, he checked out the empty clip and slammed in a replacement. Just in time, the sixth and last surviving member of the gun crews was scuttling into safety, heading for a house at the edge of the town. If he hadn't panicked and had dived for cover, he'd probably have been out of sight, but Murphy aimed ahead of the running man, leading off his shot to allow for his speed, and fired. The guy stumbled, got up, and resumed running, and he thought he'd missed. But he hadn't missed. He'd winged him. When he fired again, he put a bullet high into his back, probably into the heart, for he flung up his hands and fell flat on the ground where he lay. Unmoving.

The other two Rangers were running toward the rest of the Germans, and Rooker was an incredible sight, with the Thompson clutched under one arm and the MP-40 under the other. Dan ran alongside him, emptying his machine pistol, reloading, and firing again. The hurricane of bullets they put out took the enemy by so much surprise they were slow to return fire. They'd been preparing for the final assault on the platoon sheltering behind the tank, leaving them exposed. Several men went down beneath the storm of bullets, but the rest hurriedly took cover. Protected from the two Rangers charging at them, but not from Murphy.

He judged the man in command would be the best target,

and he put the crosshairs on an officer who stood out in the open. Squeezed the trigger, watched his body jerk backward, worked the bolt, and put another round in the chamber. Kept up a methodical rate of fire, bullet after bullet, empty the clip, insert a fresh clip, work the bolt, aim and fire again. It shouldn't have happened. They were veteran troops, hardened in the cauldron of the most vicious fighting in Europe, seasoned by the horrors of the war in Soviet Russia, yet it did happen. The survivors panicked and ran. Men were leaping to their feet, fleeing back to the shelter of the town, and the three Rangers took down four more before they reached safety.

Suddenly, everything was quiet. The shooting had stopped, no rifles, no automatic fire, no artillery, nothing. A light aircraft flew over, the drone of the engine breaking the silence, and they saw a Cessna Bird Dog fly overhead. The wing tilted as the pilot banked over to get a better view of what was going on in the town, and he came in low enough to make out the Rangers on the ground. He may have seen the abandoned artillery pieces and the Opel Blitz trucks they'd used to tow them, and maybe he saw the bodies of the soldiers they'd killed. Whatever the reason, what he spotted on the outside of Evrecy confirmed what they'd told him back at headquarters. The Germans had pulled out, and the evidence of the bodies and the abandoned vehicles and guns was enough to convince him not to waste gas spending any more time overflying the town.

He flew lower and waved to the men emerging from behind the Panther, and a couple waved back. He'd seen what he'd expected to see, what they told him he'd find, and he banked again and flew away to the west. They stared at the departing aircraft in astonishment.

"The stupid fucker!" Kelly snarled, "Is he blind?"

There was no need to reply, and they jumped back to rejoin Adams and the rest of the men. They were out in the open, with Adams grinning, unaware of what awaited them inside the town, assuming they'd got the job done. Until Rooker disabused him of that notion, his voice would've carried all the way to Omaha Beach. "Lt, get them into cover. Now!"

He blinked. "What…"

"There're more of them, plenty more. They're all over the town!"

"Uh, right. Men, get back behind the tank."

"Not behind the tank. They have plenty more artillery pieces, and when they come out, they'll fill it full of holes."

"Then what? We've lost our transport, so we'll have to get out of here on foot."

"Negative!" he shouted, "Our priority is to warn them the Germans are still in the town before they send the entire company into a trap. Get the motorcycle messenger moving with a message we need more men, and when he's on the way, we'll have to go in and do what we can to hold them back until reinforcements arrive."

He looked embarrassed. "The motorcycle messenger was on the truck. He's dead."

"Get somebody else to ride the motorcycle."

A pause. "It went up with the truck."

Rooker sighed. "So we're on our own."

"Yes. Sergeant, we don't have any choice, we have to pull back."

He hesitated, unhappy about leaving a bunch of Germans in charge of the town they were supposed to have abandoned.

Murphy had other ideas. "Lt, we can't pull back. Our guys think the town is undefended, and the chances are they'll send in more troops to occupy it. They'll run straight into the Krauts, and we know they have plenty of artillery. It'll be a bloodbath."

Adams shuffled uneasily, coughed, and finally glared at him. "Private, I get what you're saying, but there's nothing we can do. We lost men, and we're down to around a dozen? We don't know how many guns they have in the town, but…"

"Maybe not, Lt, but there're more trucks in the square, and if each of them is towing an artillery piece, we could be looking at a lot of firepower. As well as Christ knows how many soldiers. We don't know for sure."

"That's the way I see it, there's nothing we can do."

"There's always something we can do. First, we need to finish what we came here for, find out how many Germans, how many guns, and what we're up against, so we can report back to Battalion, and they can deal with it. An airstrike, artillery, whatever it takes."

Adams didn't look happy, but he concluded he had to take back definite information about the situation in Evrecy, and despite the objections of Murphy, Kelly, and Rooker, he sent in four Rangers to carry out a recce. It was the right thing to do, but the wrong men. New men. Anderson, Smith, Snyder, and Carradine, men who had yet to fire a shot in anger; an auto mechanic, a clerk in a shoe store, a postal worker, and a bank clerk. They were good and enthusiastic men, but inexperienced, and he recalled the chilling determination of the Germans inside Evrecy.

He argued with him, said he'd do it, and Kelly volunteered to go with him, but Adams was having none of it. "These men need experience, and provided they stayed out of trouble, they'll be okay."

"At least wait until it's dark, so they'll have a better chance."

"We can't waste any more time on this. They go now."

They raced toward the town, doubled over to keep a low profile, and along with the few remaining Rangers he watched their progress from five hundred yards away, tucked behind a ruined shepherd's hut. To his relief, they reached the town without running into trouble and disappeared into the first houses. The minutes dragged on, and minutes became hours. It was almost dark when they heard the shots. Not the cluster of uneven shots that denoted a pitched battle, this was a single volley of rifle fire.

Dan glanced at him. "I don't want to say it, but that sounded to me like a firing squad. The Krauts captured them, and they've killed them."

"Murdered them more like. Shit, we need to do something about those bastards." He looked at the Lieutenant. "Lt, you heard that?"

Adams' skin had gone gray, his eyes had dilated, and he looked like a haunted man. A man haunted by the knowledge he'd just sent four soldiers to their deaths. He looked at Rooker. "What do you think, Sergeant?"

"I agree. They've murdered them."

His skin went a paler shade of gray. "I shouldn't have sent them."

Nobody replied, and they waited in silence, staring toward the town, looking at each other, and looking at the Lieutenant. Murphy said they'd have to do something, but for once the Sarge agreed with Adams, and he refused to go along with sending any more men into a town that had become a death trap.

"Not until we have more men, artillery, and maybe some tanks. In the meantime, the smart move would be to get back to Battalion and tell them what's happened here. Headquarters will need to know the gap they expected at Evrecy doesn't exist, that the town is occupied by Germans with heavy artillery, and until they've knocked them out, the route is closed."

They started back, and Murphy couldn't stop himself thinking about those rookies on their first mission, murdered by some fucking Nazi. They made it back to Battalion HQ, and things were happening fast. General de Gaulle had crossed to France aboard the destroyer 'La Combattante,' a ship of the Free French Navy, to take command of the Free French Army. A buzz was going around that he was joining the British Commander, General Montgomery, on a whirlwind visit to the headquarters of the 9th Infantry Division steamrollering through the German defenses to capture town after town.

Things were going well, at least in some areas, but not all. Murphy recalled those guns hidden inside the town of Evrecy, and maybe they'd forgotten about the German 101st Heavy Panzers, and the Panzer Lehr Division equipped with a mix of heavy tanks and assault guns. Where were they? Nobody knew. They'd lost sight of them. But he suspected they weren't far from Evrecy, and it was almost as if the Germans scented the trap and were waiting for the Allies to walk straight into it.

There was something else that nagged in his mind, and eventually, it came to him. They'd talked about the 9th Infantry Division, and those bodies of American soldiers he'd seen inside the town had worn the unit flashes of the 9th Infantry Division.

Slaughtered by some arrogant Nazi, and the four Rangers who'd gone in had undoubtedly suffered the same fate. The area bustled with activity, men running backward and forward, and he waited with the few remaining survivors of First Platoon for orders. In the meantime, a truck brought up metal containers of hot chow, and he gratefully lined up to grab something to eat.

They were spooning an unappetizing stew from their aluminum mess cans when the reason for the bustle became apparent. The arrival of a convoy of vehicles, and in the center a Dodge Command Car, the vehicle preferred by many American and British senior officers. Including a famous face, a slight, wiry-looking man wearing a woolly sweater and a rakish beret. General Montgomery, in command of British forces, was taking an hour out to visit one of the nearest American units.

He leaped nimbly out of the vehicle, and men stiffened to attention. Montgomery wasn't alone. An American two-star general accompanied him. Rooker murmured he was General Earl Shriver, in command of the 27th Infantry Division.

The way he said it made Murphy give him a sharp look. He had mixed feelings about senior officers. There were good generals and bad generals. There weren't many like Ike or Patton. And this guy didn't look like either.

"Not another asshole?"

"His reputation follows him. In triplicate."

He sighed. "If I never see another general again, I'd be more than happy. What's the big deal with Shriver?"

"They say he's a stickler for regulations. His men call him 'By the Book' Shriver. He uses for his bible the Manual of Military Operations, and he has very definite ideas. One of them is a dislike of Special Forces. He thinks we're loose cannons, and they oughtta incorporate the Rangers into the regular infantry, probably into his division. He runs a tight ship, spit and polish, lots of drilling."

"Sounds like a real bundle of fun."

"Yeah, like you wouldn't believe. A pal of mine belongs to the 27th, and he spends most of his time working out how to transfer out. Every time he applies, Shriver blocks it. He's that kind of guy."

There was another surprise for Murphy, in the shape of another Brit. Like Monty, he was an older man, but unlike Monty, he knew him well. Major Andrew Fraser of the Scots Guards. The craggy-faced Major was dressed in what appeared to be mostly civilian clothes, civilian pants, a shirt, and with what looked like a naval peacoat. He was a career soldier, and like Murphy an outdoorsman; a tough, capable soldier with immense reserves of strength despite his advancing years. His face was leathery, a legacy of his time spent in the outdoors, his sandy colored hair streaked with gray. Yet the piercing, dark brown eyes were still youthful, like those of a younger man, filled with intelligence. Fraser was an officer who missed nothing, which was just as well. He reported to Eisenhower's headquarters on the strengths and weaknesses of the German military machine, as well as the ability of the Allied armies to defeat the enemy.

He'd met Fraser while training in Scotland, and with their shared love of climbing they formed an instant rapport. They'd arrived together in France and both took part in the fight to get off the beaches. Fraser was officially a liaison officer between British and American forces, but he spent most of his time on other duties. Intelligence duties. Frequently behind the lines, and although he would've denied it, those who were aware of his activities would've called him a 'spy.' If the Germans caught him, he fervently hoped they didn't come to that conclusion, although the clothes wouldn't help.

He went across to Murphy and greeted him warmly. The two men shook hands, and Fraser demanded to know what he was up to. He told him about Evrecy, and the Brits eyes narrowed. "We were supposed to be driving through the gap to split the German lines. You're saying the Germans got there first?"

"That's exactly what I'm saying, Major. And they're not just any Germans. Most folks would call them a bunch of bloodthirsty savages. Major, what happened to your uniform?"

He shrugged. "I got wet when we were crossing a river on a temporary bridge the engineers had constructed, and it collapsed. My uniform was soaked, and this was the best I could find."

"Sir, I'd change back into uniform as soon as you can. If the Jerries catch you, they'll shoot you as a spy."

"I don't intend to get caught, but thanks for the heads up. As soon as I get a moment, I'll find something military to change into." He went on to describe the fate of the 9th Division soldiers whose corpses they'd come across, and the apparent slaughter of the four Rangers the Lieutenant had sent in. His eyes narrowed as he listened to Murphy, and when he'd finished, his expression was bleak, his eyes as cold as chips of marble.

"My friend, we're gonna deal with those people, but right now it'll have to wait. There're still no reports of the German heavy armor, and that's worrying a lot of people. Especially now that Evrecy is still in enemy hands. We must punch our armor through the German lines, and the one place we can achieve that kind of a breakthrough is Evrecy. You say they've stationed infantry and heavy artillery in the town?" He nodded, "Artillery could cause a big headache for our tanks, and we'll have to find a way to deal with it. We can't afford another debacle."

"Debacle?"

He explained about the action the previous day at Villers-Bocage. "Advance elements of the 7th British Armored Division reached Villers-Bocage and took up positions on Hill 213, a high point to the east. Several German heavy tanks commanded by an SS officer named Michael Wittmann hit them from an ambush. In less than fifteen minutes, the Brits lost fourteen tanks, two anti-tank guns, and fifteen transport vehicles. Some of the tank crews managed to escape on foot, but the rest didn't make it."

"Jesus Christ, it can't get much worse."

"Can't it? The previous night the enemy launched a new weapon on London, V-1 rockets. They're still assessing the damage, but it looks bad. We have to make a breakthrough, and Evrecy could be the key. We need to push those Krauts out of the town."

"Damn right, but it won't be easy. An airstrike could do it."

"Every aircraft we have is engaged in other missions, and even if they weren't, an airstrike may not be enough. By now the Germans could've hidden their vehicles and guns under camouflage, and if the aircraft don't destroy them, they'll be waiting for us when we go in."

"Tanks?"

"Tanks against entrenched heavy artillery, possibly anti-tank guns, could lead to another disaster. I'm sorry, Murphy, but it'll be up to men like you to go back in there and do it the hard way."

He nodded, but he was thinking something else. He wanted the name of the German officer in command, the head honcho. He had charges to answer, and Murphy wasn't thinking about capturing him for committal to a war crimes trial. He had something else in mind, a kind of frontier justice. The kind they used to practice in Montana, and probably still did in certain parts. There'd be no heated cell, three hot meals a day, and a panel of judges to weigh up the evidence for and against. There'd be one man, him. And he didn't need to weigh up any evidence. He'd heard the firsthand testimony of the dying American soldier inside the town, and that was enough for him. Whoever that German was, he'd make him regret it for the rest of his short and very painful life.

Montgomery and Shriver completed their swift tour of inspection, and he observed the difference between the two senior officers. Monty, short and wiry, always on the move, a fireplug, like he always looked in his frequent appearances in the news media; Shriver was the total opposite, tall, fleshy, with a pronounced paunch. His face streaked with tiny veins. The kind of thing you'd see in a man who liked his booze, eyes squinting out at the world, suspicious. His movements were more ponderous.

It's like he's unsure about something, but that can't be, can it? Not in a senior commander on which so much depends. Is this a man we can rely on, a general who makes sure he isn't putting the lives of his troops in danger? Or is he out of his depth?

Murphy reserved judgment.

He climbed aboard the Dodge Command Car, and their

convoy drove away. Major Fraser remained behind, explaining he had things to attend to. Bravo Company Commander Captain Robert Washington emerged from his dugout, and his staff and platoon commanders were with him. Lieutenant Carter Adams rejoined First Platoon, all nine men, and they clustered around him.

"We're going back to Evrecy, but this time it'll be the entire company, four platoons. We'll be going in on foot, and we'll be heading out soon it gets dark. That'll be in around three hours. If we keep it quiet, there's a good chance the enemy won't see us coming." Murphy didn't say anything, although Kelly gave an ironic cough that caused Adams to look up in irritation, "We'll sneak into the town and do what they trained us to do. Kill the enemy. We'll be carrying bazookas, and each man will carry grenades, as well as plenty of ammunition. Those Germans have a lot to answer for, and we're gonna make them answer. That's all. We assemble in two hours for final equipment checks. Get yourself some chow before we move out."

Two hours later, they were ready to go, laden with so much equipment if they stepped into soft ground, they were liable to sink up to their knees. Second, Third and Fourth Platoons carried a Browning BAR and a bazooka apiece, along with spare rockets. First Platoon was shorthanded, and because they'd covered the ground before, they'd be on point, so they'd just given them the BAR. Carrying several spare magazines, four grenades each, and their personal weapons, it was still plenty to carry. For most men, a sidearm, and a Garand, for Murphy, a Springfield 1903 instead of the Garand. In addition, he and Dan Kelly each hefted an MP-40, trophies of war slung on their backs.

The Lieutenant looked at Rooker. The Company was forming up to leave, and he opened his mouth to tell them to get them moving. The words never came out of his mouth. The noise of engines became a roar. The unmistakable roar of tank engines and somebody panicked and shouted, "Tigers!"

They scattered, some diving for cover, others running away. In minutes the organized chaos of a breaking camp became total chaos, with dropped equipment, half-dressed men pulling on a remaining boot as they hopped on one foot to get away. Murphy crouched inside a thick hedge; his Springfield unslung. He worked the bolt to put a round into the chamber, tucked the butt into his shoulder, and put his eye to the telescopic sight, waiting for a target to appear. The barrel of a gun swung into view; followed by the armored bulk of a tank. The commander's head and shoulders poking out from the turret were in full view. He prepared to take the shot and released the pressure on the trigger.

He jumped to his feet and cupped his hands. "They're friendlies. They're British!"

The tank rolled forward and stopped in the clearing, followed by five others. They were British Cromwells. Cruiser tanks, a new design powered by Rolls-Royce Merlin engines. The commander of the lead tank, a captain, climbed down from the turret and Captain Washington walked out from cover to meet him. The rest of the men emerged, Adams joined them, and they chatted for a few minutes. The Brits were smarting after the beating they'd taken the day before at Villers-Bocage. A single Tiger I had accounted for a half-dozen British armored vehicles.

"The German in command is a bastard by the name of SS-

Hauptsturmführer Michael Wittmann. I'd like to meet that bastard and shove a few shells down his throat."

After recovering from the scare when they'd believed Tigers were attacking, Adams had relaxed, but as the Brit captain described the German heavy armor, the blood drained from his face. "You're saying there're Tigers in the area?"

He nodded. "Tigers, Panthers, and self-propelled guns, STuGs. We've identified several panzer units in the region, including the 101st Heavy Panzers, Panzer Lehr, and the SS Hitler-Jugend. My advice to you is to steer clear. They pack a lot of firepower."

Washington nodded. "We'll be careful."

Adams' head bobbed up and down in agreement, but he hadn't needed the warning. No soldier in Normandy needed a warning about the danger of enemy armor, which had a certain reputation. The Cromwells drove away, and the Company started moving back toward Evrecy. Talk of the enemy armor had stretched their nerves like violin strings, and as they walked, they looked every which way. The narrow lanes were a mass of the high, thick hedges, the formidable Normandy bocage, and with every footstep they glanced everywhere, looking and listening in case a heavy tank was about to burst through the hedge and start blasting.

They didn't encounter any tanks. Halfway to the town, four fighters buzzed them, and someone shouted, "Messerschmitts, take cover!" Once again they scattered, and two men pointed a Browning M1919 into the air to start shooting. They held their fire, as again they were friendlies, this time American P-47s. They swept low to check them out, recognized them as Allied troops, and flew away. The men got back to their feet, looking sheepish at reacting to yet another false alarm. One man turned back to retch into the hedge, and they walked on toward Evrecy, trying to make light of the mistake.

"The scares are making me nervous," Kelly grunted as they walked.

"Me, too. But the Germans are everywhere, so it's no surprise, until somebody 'cries wolf' once too often. When it is the enemy, and if we don't react fast enough, some of us are gonna die."

He frowned. "Maybe you're right. Keep sounding off when we hear something because sooner or later it won't be a friendly."

One of the new replacements, PFC Sam Crockett, who hailed from Kentucky, overheard them. "The way I see it, we've got the Krauts beat. Most of them are hightailing it back to the Fatherland."

Nobody took much notice. Crockett was one of those guys who never made an impression on a man's mind. Anonymous, with no distinguishing features. When he stood with other men, it was like he became invisible.

"Those Tigers that shot up the Brit armor weren't hightailing it back to the Fatherland. There's still plenty of them around, so if you see anything or hear anything, shout it out good and loud."

He squinted at Murphy, and he was that kind of a guy. Short, sallow-skinned, runty, and bowlegged, and each eye never seemed to be looking in the same direction as the other. It wasn't difficult to imagine him sneaking through the forests, poaching game, and clutching his Kentucky long rifle, which would've been almost taller than him. "You think they're out there somewhere?"

"I know they are. Don't forget the guys they murdered in Evrecy. They're out there, so keep your eyes skinned."

They didn't experience any more alerts, not until they were three miles outside Evrecy. Crockett glanced up after he heard aircraft engines. He stayed relaxed, identifying them as the four P-47s they'd spotted earlier. He was probably right. They looked much the same, at least from a distance, and they sounded the same, from a distance. When they were less than a mile away, Murphy, who had the instincts of a natural-born hunter, stopped and squinted his eyes to see better. They weren't P-47s. He tensed.

They aren't P-47s!

"Enemy aircraft, coming in! Cover!"

Most looked uncertain. They'd had those two false alarms, and they still felt sheepish about running from their own guys. Crockett was sneering as if to say Murphy should've listened to his own words. "Are you kidding me? Those're our guys. No sweat."

He shouted louder. "For Christ's sake, get into cover! They're Germans!"

They scattered into cover, just as the four Fokke-Wulf 190s came boring in, cannons blazing, and it should've been a catastrophe. They were defenseless against the fast-moving fighters, and although the bocage hid them from the enemy, it didn't protect them from cannon fire. Two men, slower than the others died when automatic fire caught them in the open, and several had narrow escapes. But they were lucky. They'd been marching parallel to a half-filled drainage ditch alongside the road, and they threw themselves into the muddy water. The Germans flew past, banked over, and turned through ninety degrees, lining up their next attack run. They came back, and this time following the line of the ditch. The troopers were unprotected, with no place to go, no place to hide, and all they could do was lie flat half-submerged in the stinking water and pray they'd survive.

The Fokke-Wulfs didn't open fire. Not through choice, but because the P-47s that'd passed by earlier were still close, and they'd spotted four juicy targets lined up for the taking. They swooped, the eight .50 caliber machine guns mounted in each aircraft blazing, and they watched in considerable relief and satisfaction as the German attack literally fell apart. Including some of the aircraft. The first 190 went down trailing smoke and fire, boring into the ground where it fireballed. The second fighter was hit, and the pilot bailed out, leaving his aircraft to fly on pilotless, disappearing out of sight. They heard the explosion as it hit the ground a couple of miles away. The other two turned tail and ran. The P-47s caught one and shot it down, but the other managed to disappear into a patch of low cloud.

The P-47s hung around a while longer in case the German decided to make another suicidal attempt to shoot up the troops on the ground, but after a few minutes, they flew away, satisfied he wasn't coming back. Captain Washington signaled them to keep moving. They walked on, and a half-hour later, they were within sight of Evrecy. They stopped a mile outside the town, and Washington surveyed the buildings through binoculars.

He glanced at Adams waiting anxiously beside him. "It looks clear. Maybe they've gone."

"That's what they told us last time and look what

happened."

He nodded. "We have to know. Your men have been in there before, it'd be a good idea to send in a couple of men to take a look."

The Lieutenant didn't look happy. "Captain, that's what we did before, and I lost half my platoon."

"Dammit, Lieutenant, this is war. We can't sit here on our fannies all day while we wait and see. Get it done."

"Yes, Sir."

He strolled back and found the Sarge. "I need two men to recce the town. Make sure it's clear."

"I'll go."

"No, not you, Sergeant, I can't afford to lose you." Rooker flinched.

Who said anything about losing anybody?

"Send Murphy and Kelly, they're good men."

"They always get the shit assignments, Lt. We should send in somebody else."

"I don't agree. Do it, Sergeant."

"Yessir."

He spoke to the two men, who were standing close. "You heard?"

Dan Kelly grimaced. "What are we, Sarge? Disposable?"

He grinned. "No, you're not disposable. You two men happened to be good at what you do. Too good. Get moving. You know what to do. If it looks clear, give us a wave from the town and they'll send the Company in."

"What if it isn't clear?"

"We'll see you running away like crazy."

"Got it."

"Murphy, you ready for this?"

"I'm ready."

He nodded. "I'm thinking about those guys they executed. If those same Germans are inside the town, it'd be a good plan to avoid getting captured by those bunch of psychos. Know what I mean?"

"I think we get that." He looked at Kelly. "We may as well get this over with."

They started walking toward the town, and with no cover, they had to walk across a half-mile of open ground where they'd be exposed to the enemy, if they were still around. That was the question. They couldn't relax, waiting for the sniper bullet that would reach out to pluck the life from them. Or for the salvo shells that would bracket the ground they walked across, turning it into a hell of high-explosive and flying shrapnel. They made it almost all the way. They were within three hundred yards of the town, passing a tumble-down farmhouse; conscious it would've made a convenient aiming point for the enemy artillery, if they were still there.

The snipers didn't cause them any trouble. The artillery didn't cause them any trouble. The Fokke-Wulf 190 that swooped from a patch of low cloud caused them a shitload of trouble. The surviving aircraft, with a pilot crafty enough to wait around for the Allied fighters to disappear so he could come back and exact some revenge for the downing of three of his comrades. It came in, 20mm cannons blazing, punching chunks of stone from the wrecked farmhouse, churning up the broken stones into smaller fragments. They dismissed their first instinct to dive behind the remainder of the building for cover, and with no alternative ran toward the town. If the enemy was there, that was too bad. They could fight one enemy at a time, and right now, the enemy was up in the sky, rushing toward them at four hundred miles an hour. They flung themselves through the window of a bar on the edge of the town.

Just in time, they lay on the floor in a mass of broken glass as the cannon shells punched through the window, smashing through the wall to reach them.

It was madness, total madness. The cannon shells had churned the interior of the bar into a thick fog of dust and smoke, smashing the bottles displayed behind the counter, and the room stank of booze. Between the dust, the smoke, and the stink, the drapes on either side of the window they'd tumbled through caught fire. The fire spread, aided by the alcohol spilled out over the floor, and the room became engulfed in flames.

"Get out!" Kelly didn't argue. If they stayed inside, they'd fry for sure. If they went outside, it was a maybe. Maybe the enemy fighter would get them, or they'd run into a bunch of homicidal Krauts. A maybe it was better than a racing certainty, and they raced to the rear of the building and stopped. A squad of Germans lay fifty yards away, tucked behind the machine gun inside the doorway of a grocer's store.

"Out the front!"

"What about the plane?" Kelly shouted.

"We'd better pray he's run out of gas. Let's go!"

They ran back through the surging flames and launched themselves through the window, back the way they'd come. Thick smoke had engulfed the area, hiding them from the aircraft it was still there. He lost sight of Dan, but he had to assume he was right behind him. The smoke was their best hope of getting away, and he ran, heading back toward the Company.

After the first two hundred yards, he realized he was on his own. Dan Kelly was missing.

He looked back, but the smoke hid everything, and there wasn't a thing he could do. The Fokke-Wulf was still up there, and although he couldn't see it, he could hear the drone of the engine as it circled, searching for a target. He had no choice but to keep running, hoping Dan was also heading back through the smoke. He made another two hundred yards, and he was far enough away from the burning building for the smoke to clear, and that gave the fighter the opportunity he'd been waiting for. He came back in, engines roaring. Murphy was out in the open, with no cover, and no way to defend himself from the avalanche of cannon shells about to reach down to tear his body into little pieces.

The first salvo churned up the ground ten yards away, and he jinked away, hoping to spoil the guy's aim. The aircraft came in again, and he threw himself flat. He'd heard another engine, but this time much smaller. A vehicle, no, it sounded more like a powerful motorcycle. The Jerries used motorcycles, and he assumed they'd sent a man out from the town to make sure, except it was coming from the opposite direction. He looked up and saw the impossible. It wasn't a Jerry. It was an American motorcycle. A Harley Davidson dispatch rider's machine, but the guy riding it wasn't an American dispatch rider, he was a British officer, and he recognized Major Andrew Fraser. He was in for another surprise. Fraser wasn't alone. He had another person clinging on behind him, although he couldn't make out who it was until the motorcycle skidded to a halt next to him.

"Jack, get on."

A girl's voice, the voice of Clemence Delon, and he

couldn't believe it. "Clemence?"

"Get on!"

She didn't need to tell him a third time. She clung on behind Fraser, and he leaped up behind her, balancing himself on the rear fender, just as the fighter completed its attack run. The Major twisted the throttle and skidded away, veering a zigzag course, but there was no way they could escape the vengeful Nazi fighter plunging toward them. All they could do was hope and maybe pray. Whatever they did, it worked. The aircraft didn't shoot, and afterward, they concluded it was out of ammo, after having depleted its magazines in the fight with the P-47s, and the subsequent attempt to swat Murphy and Kelly.

The fighter flew away, and the powerful machine raced across the ground, making it back to the Company without coming under more enemy fire. Fraser expertly slewed the machine to a stop next to the dispatch rider, who looked pissed. "You're in trouble, Major. I was about to tell the MPs you stole my motorcycle."

"Borrowed it, Corporal. Just a short-term loan."

He grunted. "I have to get back to Battalion with a reply to their questions about Evrecy." He grabbed the handlebars, and as they climbed off, he swung aboard and roared off to the west.

Fraser didn't look concerned "That worked out, Murphy."

"It was close, but thanks. What made you do it?"

"I saw you were in trouble, and a dispatch rider had just arrived from headquarters, so I took his bike to give you a ride."

"Major, you're crazy. I know you don't mind taking risks, but you could've been killed."

"But we weren't."

He looked at the girl. "Clemence, what the hell are you doing here?"

A shrug. "I assumed if they were going into Evrecy they'd need an interpreter, so when Major Fraser said he intended to accompany Bravo Company into the town to gather intelligence for a possible breakthrough, I said I'd come with him."

"You shouldn't be here."

She smiled. "Probably not, but I'm here all the same. Where's Dan?"

Dan!

In his vast relief and euphoria at escaping the enemy aircraft, he'd forgotten. He gazed back toward the town, toward the smoke from the burning building, and there was no sign of him. He'd seen him get out, yet after that, nothing. His euphoria evaporated. "I don't know. You didn't see him?"

Fraser shook his head. "All I saw was you. I'm sorry."

They stared back across the open ground, and there was no sign of Kelly, dead or alive.

"They got him."

"Maybe, maybe not. He could've escaped, or maybe he's hiding somewhere."

"You don't believe that."

He shook his head slowly. "No. I fear the worst has happened. You have to face it, Murphy. He's gone. Kelly isn't coming back."

CHAPTER THREE

15 June 1944

They waited for fresh orders from Battalion HQ. He was chafing at the bit, desperate to get back to Evrecy and try to find Dan, if he was still alive. And if it wasn't too late. Lieutenant Adams shook him off, and he went to see the Company Commander, Captain Washington.

"If we hit the town now, Captain, there's a good chance we can get to Dan before they kill him. It'll be dark soon, and they won't see us coming."

His expression twisted into a frown. "That's not gonna happen, Murphy. The news from Battalion is bad. The enemy is still holding out at Cherbourg, and it's essential we take the town so we can use the port facilities to speed up bringing troops and armor ashore. It's critical we take it, and they're putting everybody back to join the attack. That means us, all except First

Platoon." He glanced up as the Lieutenant arrived and gave Murphy a sour look.

Whatever was on his mind, he didn't spit it out. "Captain, did I hear right? They're pulling everybody back to Cherbourg?"

"You did, everybody except your platoon. We know the enemy is still holding Evrecy, and our armor will need to get past the town to punch past the German lines, get behind them, and hit them from the rear. I want you to hold this position and keep the town under observation. When the dispatch rider returns, I'll order him to stay with you, and if you see the Jerries pulling out, you can send a message back to Battalion."

"You're leaving us here?"

"That's right. You'll be fine, just dig in, and watch the town. The moment you see them leaving, make sure you send the message, and we'll relay it to the tanks. Good luck, Lieutenant."

"Yes, Captain." He looked nonplussed, "Uh, we don't have anything to eat. This mission wasn't supposed to last this long."

He gave him an encouraging slap on the shoulder. "You'll find something, Carter, I know you will. Keep us informed the moment anything changes."

He rounded up the rest of the company, and the few men that remained from First Platoon watched them march away. Most wished they were going with them.

It was twilight, and they settled down to spend a cold, hungry night out in the open. Murphy kept shooting glances back at the town, across one mile of open ground, and he was thinking about his buddy Dan Kelly. If the Germans had captured him, they were like to butcher him like they had the others. If they hadn't, he could be hiding out somewhere, lying wounded and in need of help. Fraser was a couple of hundred yards away, surveying the town through binoculars and making notes on a pad. Clemence had also stayed and was attempting to conjure up something to eat, mixing their remaining few rations with roots and berries she'd foraged nearby.

She persuaded a couple of soldiers to build a fire in a natural fold in the woods where it wouldn't be visible to the enemy artillery, and she used a helmet as a cooking pot, to produce a stew that smelled more than good to hungry men. It wasn't enough, but it was better than nothing, and it tasted as good as it smelled. They sat around, feeling better with food in their bellies, all except for Murphy, who had one thing on his mind. Dan Kelly.

Orders or no orders, I'm not going to sit on my ass and do nothing while my best friend is in trouble. There's one thing I can do, and that's to go back and find him when it gets dark.

He didn't ask Adams because he knew he'd refuse. So he waited for the right moment to make his move.

* * *

Dan Kelly was in more trouble than he'd ever been in his life. A slice of metal had taken a slice from the fleshy part of his leg. At first, he'd bled like a stuck pig until he wrapped a dressing around the wound and staunched the bleeding. He could still walk, and although it hurt like crazy, he could run if that was what it took. The problem was he had nowhere to walk, and nowhere to run. When the bullet hit him, he thought the wound was more serious. Remembering the basement steps he'd seen when they went inside, he dived back into the burning building, tripped and fell, and tumbled down the stone steps until he hit the bottom hard. So hard, it knocked him unconscious, and when he came to, he guessed he'd been out for a couple of hours.

The fire had died down, and he heard the tramp of boots on broken glass, and German voices sounded from above. He wasn't sure what they were doing until somebody laughed, another man joined in, and it sounded like they were having a party up there. He recalled the squad he'd seen in the doorway opposite and guessed they'd entered the bar to search for enemy survivors and found none. Instead, they'd discovered a bottle of booze that'd survived the cannon fire and found it too much of a temptation.

All he could do was wait it out, and in the meantime, he explored the gloom of the basement. There were hundreds of bottles of wine arrayed in dusty racks, and he went further, finding a narrow track door that would've given access from the street for unloading fresh supplies. He went back to the bottom of the steps so he could hear what was going on, and they were still there. Still drinking, and with a sinking feeling, he suspected what was about to happen next. They had the taste of alcohol in their mouths. With most bottles behind the bar destroyed, the natural place to look for more booze was in the basement. Sure enough, he heard jackbooted footsteps heading toward the staircase, and they started to descend.

He looked for a place to hide. There was nothing else, no place to go, and it looked like he'd have to fight it out there, with only one possible outcome. They'd kill him; probably toss a grenade down after he'd killed that man who was coming down the stairs. He drew his M1911 and was about to cock the action ready to fire when he remembered the hatch. Could he get out into the street in time? It would be close, but what the hell, when a man is about to die, fear lent him wings.

He sneaked to the hatch, climbed up a rickety wooden ladder, and slid the bolt across. Opened the hatch, climbed out onto the narrow sidewalk and closed it. He was out in the open, and fortunately, it was almost dark, so maybe he could get away. He crawled on his belly, heading for a building opposite that was in darkness and looked like a private house. Thankfully, the front door was unlocked. He pushed it open, crawled inside, closed the door, and got to his feet.

The interior of the building smelled strange, heavily scented, a musky mixture of French perfume and booze. He decided it must be another bar, which was fine with him, providing there were no Germans inside.

"Hello, soldier."

He looked up, the deep red painted lips had parted in a welcoming smile, and it came to him in a flash. The makeup looked like she'd plastered it on with a trowel; the low-cut dress that clung in all the right places, showing more of her breasts than it hid. The hair, a brassy, artificial blonde, she was a hooker, and this was no bar. It was the kind of place where hookers hung out. The kind of place they call a brothel.

"Uh, Ma'am, I didn't mean to… well, not exactly, I mean, I didn't realize…"

"I recognize the uniform. You are hiding from the Germans."

"That's right. How come you're still here, you haven't evacuated the town?"

"Why should we? Our services are in demand no matter which army occupies Evrecy."

"Are there any Germans in here?"

"No, soldier, but last night half-dozen arrived seeking entertainment. Which naturally we provided. When your soldiers come, we will of course do the same."

"How many of you? I mean how many girls work here?"

"Just me and my friend. My name is Monique, and she is Evelyn."

"Uh, pleased to meet you, Ma'am. I mean Monique. You think they'll be back?"

"Yes, of course. We'll have to find somewhere to hide you. There is an attic. You can go there, and if you're quiet, they will not know you are in the building. Usually, they arrive at ten and stay until midnight." Her expression became more rueful, "The Germans are not as tough as they would like us to believe."

He didn't know how to respond to that. "Okay. Show me to the attic, and I'll wait in there until they've gone."

She led him up the staircase to the second floor, pulled out a ladder, and propped it beneath a hatch. He climbed the ladder, opened the hatch, and went inside the attic. She removed the ladder, and he closed the hatch, finding himself in almost total darkness. All he could do was settle down to wait, and he realized how hungry he was. He hadn't eaten for most of that day, and now he was able to relax for a couple of hours, his stomach began to rumble. There was nothing he could do about that, except take sips of water from his canteen, and try to think of other things to take his mind off his belly.

He didn't know what'd happened to Murphy. The last he'd seen, he was running from the burning building when he disappeared into the smoke. He may have made it, or he may not. He had to have made it. He'd always thought Murphy was indestructible.

Yet what if he didn't? My best buddy, and if they've killed him, I vow to take revenge, to kill every damned Kraut I come across.

His mind whirled with images of carving a bloody carnage through the ranks of the enemy. Until he heard the stamp of boots crossing the floor below, jackboots, and they were here. He'd have to wait it out, make sure he stayed silent, and hope the girls didn't give him away. They were French girls, true, and he guessed they had no love for the Germans. Except their somewhat precarious profession require them to make what money they could, and when they could.

Will they sell me out to the Germans? Dear God, I hope not.

* * *

Major Gottlieb Kreis was growing impatient. He had the guns, and he had the infantry. He knew the Americans were close. He'd seen them sending those two men to recce the town, which meant they had to be planning an attack, an attack that had to come soon. Which would be a chance for him to obliterate them and seize glory for the Reich. They hadn't entered the town. When that aircraft fired on them, he'd seen at least one man running back to their lines under cover of the smoke. He assumed the second had done the same, which meant they didn't know his force was still intact. Still waiting to fall on the enemy when they arrived, and yet something was holding them up.

He'd no idea what it was, but perhaps they were wary of his artillery, as well they should be. He had a plentiful supply of both armor-piercing and high-explosive shells, and when they came, he'd grind them into pulp. Yet he had to persuade them to come, had to tempt them into the town, and the idea came to him. If they were nervous about attacking into the teeth of his artillery, he would pull out. At least, pretend to pull out. It was almost night, and they'd hear the noise of engines as his trucks left. In the darkness, they wouldn't see they hadn't limbered up the guns, which would remain in place.

He smiled. There was no way they'd believe the trucks had pulled out abandoning the guns. Provided he got his artillery undercover, even aerial reconnaissance would fail to spot them, and the Americans would come into the town. At least a company of infantry, perhaps even a battalion. They'd likely send their armor. They had to be desperate to break through the German lines, and Evrecy was the most likely place for them to try.

He shouted orders, and his men got to work. They even tumbled several troopers from the town brothel, much to their disgruntlement, and they emerged half-dressed, buttoning their flies and stinking of perfume. It was too bad. One by one, they maneuvered the heavy 75mm PAK 40 artillery pieces off the street, smashing through the windows of several stores to make space for them to hide inside. When they'd completed the task, he ordered them to drive the trucks away, making as much noise as possible. When they'd gone, he dispersed his men to defensive positions close to the guns, telling them to stay quiet and out of sight.

Now it was a matter of waiting for them to come. And they would come. He had no doubts. The route that ran past Evrecy was essential for the enemy to take if they were to continue east. Let them come. The more the merrier, and he pictured lines of American soldiers advancing alongside their Sherman tanks. He pictured his guns opening fire, and the 75mm armor-piercing shells punching through the feeble armor of the Shermans. His high-explosive shells would explode among the infantry, and there would be a mighty killing in this place. A major victory that would halt the retreat of the German armies, and if they moved fast and called in the panzers, they could retake the initiative and push the enemy back.

He stood at a second-floor window, looking out over the street. As if he could already see the enemy soldiers stealthily advancing along the street, into the teeth of his guns. Of their tanks, rumbling past his hidden guns, and their surprise as the armor-piercing shells punched into their thinly armored rear. Evrecy would become the cemetery of Allied ambitions.

It's all there for the taking. And afterward, I'll be a hero. Major Gottlieb Kreis, Iron Cross First Class. No, when the Führer learns what I've achieved, the Knight's Cross with Oak Leaves will be mine.

He heard someone snoring from the back room, and he rushed to the soldier supposed to be watching the rear of the building, in case they came that way. He kicked him and hammered his Walther over his head, drawing blood.

"The next time you fall asleep on watch, I'll put a bullet in you. Clear?"

"Yessir."

"It better be," he growled, "We are about to write a page of history, and every man here will be rewarded with Germany's highest decorations."

"Yessir."

Although the soldier gave him a look that suggested he

was thinking something else.

They can chisel your history on your tombstone, Major Kreis. All I want is to go home, like the rest of us. We're beaten. Don't you understand that? The Reich is in ruins after the bombing. The Allies are pouring troops and armor ashore in such huge numbers we don't have a hope of holding them back. Their aircraft roam the skies almost unopposed by Fat Herman's Luftwaffe. Why don't you face it, Major? We're fucked.

* * *

His chances of making it improved when they heard trucks moving out of Evrecy, moving east. It looked like they were leaving, and in the gathering darkness of late evening he prepared to make a move. As the light faded, he was confident he could cross the open ground without them spotting him, and one man could search for his body. Either dead or alive, he had to find him. If he was alive, he could be a captive of the Germans, facing a bloody execution, making his rescue critical. Quietly, he prepared to leave, making sure he had plenty of ammo, and even camouflage grease to smear over his face. He gave some thought to which weapons he should take and decided to leave the Springfield. He'd be sneaking through the darkness into an enemy stronghold, not long-range sniping, and he persuaded Crockett to take care of it.

He wasn't so sure and gave him a suspicious look. "Why not carry the rifle? Is there a problem?"

"No problem, I just have an errand to take care of, and I don't want to be encumbered by the rifle." He decided to let on the charm, "Besides, the telescopic sight is fragile if it's not handled right, and I wanted someone I could trust, someone reliable to look after it."

"Yeah, I get it. Sure, I can do that. And I'll make sure nothing happens to the scope."

He thanked him and found a place where he could wait in the gathering shadows, sheltered by a clump of bushes. Now all he had to do was wait. He was satisfied nobody suspected what he was planning, and he tried to relax, psyching himself up for what was to come. The shadows lengthened, and he estimated he had about another hour to wait before it was time to go. He was thinking about what he'd be up against when a familiar, slim figure slipped in next to him.

"What's up, Jack? You're up to something. Tell me what you're planning."

"Nothing."

She snorted. "I know you, and you're planning on going after Dan, is that right?"

"I don't know what you're talking about."

"Bullshit. If you try it, they'll kill you. You should…"

She didn't finish saying what he should do. They glanced over as a jeep emerged from the evening gloom and halted close to the Lieutenant, who was talking quietly with Sergeant Rooker. They gave it a casual glance. The driver was an MP Sergeant, Duane Bishop, complete with a long, white-painted nightstick hanging off his belt. Adams and Rooker gave him an idle glance, and a second later they stiffened. The passenger was two-star General, Earl Shriver. He bounded out of the jeep almost before it stopped and tripped on a tree root. Rooker grabbed his arm and stopped him from falling.

"My thanks, Sergeant." He glanced at Adams. "I'm touring our frontline positions, seeing how things are, finding out if there's anything you're short of. A lot is happening, as I'm sure you're aware, and I want to be certain my units are all on the top line. If there's anything you need, tell me, and I'll make sure you get it."

Adams started to shake his head. "Everything is fine, General. No problems. There's nothing we need. We're…"

Shriver smiled, but the smile faded when Rooker interrupted. "Food, General. We need food. The men are hungry."

"Food, right, I'll try to get something sent up for you. Although I doubt you'll be here for long. Things may be changing mighty soon."

He drew them to one side and talked with them where they wouldn't be overheard. The MP, Duane Bishop, strolled around, looking at every man until he found what he wanted.

"Murphy, I see you're still alive."

"You, too, Bishop."

The eyes hardened. "It's Sergeant Bishop to you, and don't you forget it."

"What do you want?"

"I'm still investigating the circumstances of the deaths of Sergeant Abbott and Corporal Pérez, and I'm sure there's something you're not telling me."

Murphy thought back to their deaths in a desolate stretch of Normandy. At the time he'd been fighting a determined adversary, a German SS officer who'd been stalking Clemence Delon. When the Nazi discovered he was protecting Clemence, he went after Murphy, and it became a duel to the death. In the middle of a battle he took out the German, but Abbott and Pérez almost took care of him, seizing on his preoccupation with killing the SS man to ambush him; until Clemence took them both out with a German MP-40. She'd saved his life.

It wasn't unusual for soldiers to die in battle, and Allied soldiers found killed with German bullets, what could be more cut and dried? They were trying to kill him, and Clemence had stopped them. That piece of information would stay with him, and he would never implicate Clemence in what happened that day.

Yet Bishop had the instincts of a cop, and the vindictiveness of a bully. He'd known about the animosity between Abbott and Murphy, and because he was in the area, he came to the natural assumption Murphy had to be involved in their deaths. Like cops the world over, he'd decided what'd happened and set out to prove it. The truth was incidental.

"I told you everything, Bishop. There's nothing more to tell. Although I guess it won't stop you making it up."

He scowled. "You can't talk to me like that. I'm a sergeant, you need to show some respect."

"I show respect when it's due, Bishop."

His scowl deepened. "I ought to take you in for questioning. A few days in a cell, and maybe you'll remember a few things you forgot."

"Some of us have more important things to do, like fighting a war. Say, why don't you stick around, and maybe you'll see some fighting?"

His face was beetroot red, and his hand dropped to his side to snatch out his nightstick, but he didn't draw it out.

"What's going on here, Sergeant?" They both stood to attention as the General walked up to them, with Adams following, looking anxious. Shriver bellowed at Bishop, "What's this about fighting?"

"It's this soldier, General. I've put a few questions to him about the unexplained deaths of Sergeant Abbott and Corporal Pérez, and he's refusing to answer them. Threatened to attack me if I didn't back off."

He gave Murphy a narrow-eyed stare. "Is that right, soldier?"

"No, Sir. I've told him everything I know, but he keeps pushing. It's stupid. Those two men died in battle with the Germans. They were killed with German bullets, yet he's trying to pin it on me."

He looked at Bishop. "What do you have to say to that, Sergeant?"

"Look at that gun of his, General. It's a German gun."

Shriver nodded slowly. "That's true, and it's against regulations. However, that's beside the point. It seems to me you have questions to answer. My next stop is Battalion Headquarters, so why don't you calm down, get in the jeep, and you can help out Sergeant Bishop with his investigation."

He felt a surge of anxiety. His best buddy was a mile away, across that stretch of open ground in Evrecy. He could be hurt, or he could be a prisoner of a homicidal Nazi, awaiting a brutal execution. If he went with Bishop, he'd have no chance of getting him out.

"General, we're about to recce the town, to assess the strength of the German defenses. It's a vital part of our Normandy offensive, so this would be a bad time for any man to leave the front."

Shriver looked at Adams. "Is that right, Lieutenant?"

"Uh, not exactly, General. Sure, we're going in at dawn to

check out the town, but just before you arrived, we heard the trucks moving out, and my guess is the Germans have left. We'll just walk in, look around, and call it in."

"So we're not expecting any problems?"

"No, General."

He nodded. "Very well. Sergeant Bishop, take this man back with you and question him at Battalion HQ." He looked at Murphy. "Son, I appreciate your enthusiasm for wanting to get into the fighting, but it looks to me like it's gonna be a walk in the park. Get in the jeep."

He was desperate. If he went with them, it could be a death sentence for Dan Kelly.

"General, I think you're making a big mistake. Just because we heard a few trucks leaving, doesn't mean they've all gone. Those guns could still be in the town, waiting to ambush our guys when they come through."

I'm not sure if it's true, but it's the best I could think of on the spur of the moment. Then again, what if it is true?

"If they're there, they're gonna need every man."

"Maybe, but I don't see how one man will make a difference. Get in the jeep."

He hesitated, knowing he was between a rock and a hard place. And Dan's fate lay between a rock and a hard place. Knowing Shriver had lived up to the Rooker's assessment, 'By the Book' Shriver. A man who ate, slept, and shit military manuals. He didn't move, and Bishop repeated the order. He still didn't move, and the bulky MP walked toward him. General Shriver gave you an order, Private. Hand over your weapons and get in the jeep!"

Bishop held out his hand for him to give him his guns, but

the roar of a Harley Davidson engine interrupted him to announce the return of the motorcycle messenger with another dispatch from Battalion. He saw the General standing next to Lieutenant Adams and the MP, and automatically stopped next to them, switched off, and swung down the prop stand on his machine.

He dismounted and saluted. "Dispatch for Lieutenant Adams from HQ, Sirs."

He reached into his pouch and pulled out a flimsy folded message that he handed to the Lieutenant, who walked away to find a patch of moonlight to read the contents.

Bishop turned his attention back to Murphy. "Okay, Private, hand over the weapons."

He hesitated for another second, but he'd made up his mind. No matter what it took, he wasn't going to tamely submit when Kelly's life was at stake. He needed to get out of this fix, and fast. To find a way to get across that stretch of open ground to Evrecy, and find Dan. If he ran, they'd stop him before he got very far. He needed something quicker, and it was right in front of him. Bishop took another step toward him and made as if to grab him. He turned away, and as he came after him, he shoulder charged him, knocked him to the ground, and ran. Not in the direction of Evrecy, but the direction of the Harley-Davidson. He pressed the starter, and the 45 cubic inch engine was still warm, so it started immediately. He kicked up the prop stand, engaged first gear, and twisted the throttle to maximum. The rear wheel kicked savagely to one side and refused to grip, throwing up loose dirt and debris that showered the MP Sergeant, who was struggling back to his feet, spitting curses.

He threw up an arm to protect his face from the shower

of debris, simultaneously shouting at Murphy to stop. He didn't stop. He got control of the bike, and just before he rode away, he heard Bishop shouting, "Stop, or I'll shoot! You do this, Murphy, and you're a dead man." He was ten yards away when Bishop shouted, "You asked for it, buster."

Bishop had snatched out his Colt M1911, and he got off one shot that whined past Murphy before a command that sounded like General Shriver's voice ordered him to cease fire. Adams was calling for Murphy to stop, but they could go screw. He'd made up his mind, and he roared past the astonished troopers of First Platoon. He got out in the open, covering the mile of open ground toward the town. He kept the throttle grip twisted all the way back, and the powerful motorcycle was hitting sixty miles an hour, bumping and lurching over the uneven ground.

He forgot about Shriver and Bishop. When he got back, if he got back, they'd make him suffer for disobeying an order, stealing a dispatch rider's bike, and probably the MP would think of a score of other charges he could bring against him.

Fuck him! If I find Dan, it'll be worth it. And maybe he'll pin the deaths of Abbott and Pérez on me, but I couldn't give a shit.

He focused on the task he'd set himself and arrived on the outskirts of the town in just over a minute. He reached the bar where he'd last seen Dan and brought the bike to a stop. Propped it on the stand, dismounted, and went inside, but not before he'd unslung his MP-40. On balance, he thought the Jerries had probably gone. Why wouldn't they? They had to know they'd lost, and the most sensible course for any man to take would be to get out. On the other hand, it was better to be safe than sorry.

He charged a round into the breech, unsafed the weapon, and pushed into the bar. It was a blackened ruin after the fire that'd destroyed it, but he checked through the charred remains, searching for and dreading finding a body. To his vast relief, he wasn't there, and as a final check, he went down into the basement. He wasn't there either, and at least he hadn't perished in the fire. He returned to the street and started walking into the town, moving silently in case they were still around. But there was no sign of the Germans, and it looked like they were right when they surmised those truck engines meant the Germans had left. Which meant if he got back, at least he could give them the good news before they arrested him.

He went into an adjacent building, and it was empty. He walked up the street, heading for the center of town. He'd no idea where to start looking, and he decided the priority was to make sure the enemy had definitely left. He should've been more alert, but the worry of coming across Dan's mutilated body gnawed at his mind. He was about to walk on when he heard a faint noise, something moving, and he stopped, which saved his life. The shot that rang out was inches in front of his face, and he was already moving, diving for cover toward the nearest building, which happened to be a church. Or at least, it looked like a church. Oak doors, small leaded windows inlaid with sacred images, and he was fortunate the door wasn't locked.

He pushed it open, went inside, and slammed it shut, not sure they'd seen him. The place smelled of incense, confirming his first surmise. He was in a church. He put his ear to the door, listened, and at first heard nothing. Then he heard them, the tramp of boots. Jackboots. Guttural voices, German voices. They were out there, running along the street, but they went past, and so they hadn't seen him. He decided he'd wait inside the church until they were well past and then push on further into the town. But this time he'd be more careful now he knew there were at least some enemy soldiers still around.

A voice made him spin around. "Who are you?"

He whirled, instinctively bringing up his gun, but the voice was a female, and he lowered it. Which was the only sensible move to make, the female voice belonged to a nun. Dressed in the full regalia of a traditional French nun, complete with the elaborate formal wimple. It resembled the sails of a sailing ship from a previous century.

"Uh, I'm sorry, Ma'am. I needed somewhere to hide."

"You can't hide in here!"

"Say, this is a church. I thought you people were supposed to be more charitable."

"This is not a church. This is a convent. There are four of us sisters who live here. We do not allow men inside the building.

"I'm sorry, Ma'am. They were shooting at me. I didn't have any place else to go."

"It's Sister," she retorted. She paused, and when she spoke again her voice had mellowed at least a tad, "The Germans are shooting at you?"

"Yes, Ma'am, uh, Sister. I'm an American soldier."

"You're here to push the Germans out of France?"

"That's correct, Sister."

For the first time, she smiled. "You may stay here in the lobby until it's safe for you to leave. You may not go further into the convent, is that clear?"

"I got it."

"Good. You are on your own?"

"Yes, Ma'am."

"Very well. Don't forget, stay here, and leave as soon as you can."

She turned and walked away, and in her long, black habit and ornate wimple she looked almost ghostlike, riding along the gloomy corridor. She was about to disappear around a corner when somebody hammered on the door. It didn't sound like a friendly visit, and she turned back and looked at Murphy.

"You'd better get out of sight. Just in case." She pointed to a narrow doorway, protected by a thick velvet curtain, "There is a small chapel in there where you can hide."

He nodded his thanks, swept the curtain aside, and entered the chapel. It was tiny, two yards wide and three yards long. Unfurnished except for a small, carved wooden altar at the end containing a crucifix, and a prie-dieu for a person to kneel at when engaged in prayer. He didn't engage in prayer, didn't put his faith in prayer. He put his faith in something the Germans were more likely to respect, and he made sure to cock his machine pistol ready to fire. Safety off, he peered through the curtain as the nun opened the door.

She said something in French, but whoever was at the door either didn't speak French or wasn't interested. The heavy oak portal banged open, and a grim-faced soldier stormed into the hallway. When she protested, he pushed the nun to one side while he stared into the building, his eyes squinting to pierce the gloom.

When he saw nothing, he turned back to the nun. "Wer ist hier?" *Who is inside?*

She understood some German, or at least she understood

the tone of his voice. And he heard her trying to explain she resided here with three other nuns.

"Amerikanischer Soldat?" *American soldier?*

"Mais non, Monsieur. Seulement les soeurs." *No, Sir, just the sisters.*

He didn't believe her, and when his voice became harsher, and his questions became more demanding, Murphy understood they must've seen him go inside. He was tempted to jump the guy. After all, he was just one man, but he resisted the temptation. He'd seen that squad clattering down the street, and the chances were there were more waiting outside. The German barked another harsh question at the nun, and he heard her calling out in French. Several minutes later, three more nuns appeared from further in the building, and he grunted more questions, to which they all shook their heads in the negative.

He didn't believe them; that much was obvious. His voice became angrier and angrier until he was roaring at the first sister. Then everything changed, and he felt a roaring in his ears. He was frozen with disbelief when he saw the soldier pull out a pistol and point it at the nun. He roared a final question, and when by way of an answer she shook her head, he put the pistol to her head and squeezed the trigger. Inside the confines of the stone building the bullet was so loud, it sounded like a bomb had exploded, and the noise echoed along the corridor.

He had to fight back his first inclination, which was to go out there and blast the bastards, and it saved his life. The door slammed back, and three more soldiers burst in clutching machine pistols and looking alarmed. The soldier who'd just shot the nun, Murphy realized was an officer, snapped an order. The three soldiers relaxed, but the horror hadn't ended. He raised his pistol, with a wisp of smoke still curling from the barrel and shot a second nun. While the noise of the shot reverberated around the corridor, he squeezed the trigger twice more, and the remaining two nuns died.

He couldn't hold back, not a second longer. He erupted out of the chapel into the corridor and opened fire. The burst took down two soldiers in a matter of seconds, and he swung the barrel around to take down a third. He hadn't seen the officer move behind him, and before he could squeeze the trigger again, he felt a hard blow on the back of his neck. Followed by two more, and waves of dizziness took over. He cursed; he must've lost sight of the officer. The guy had been behind him, and he started to fall. Strong hands gripped him, stopped him from falling, and tore off his helmet. It wasn't an act of kindness. The weapon that slammed into his neck hit him square on the back of his now unprotected head, and the blackness engulfed him completely.

The first surprise was when he woke up. He'd assumed the homicidal bastard who'd killed the nuns would've killed him, and for the first few seconds, he tried to work out if he'd gone straight to hell. One thing was for sure; with his track record it wouldn't have been heaven. He was neither in heaven nor hell, but lying on a stone floor in a dark, cold room. His wrists were fastened behind his back, his ankles similarly tied, and he opined hell would've been better. He was a prisoner of the Germans, and not just any Germans. The prisoner of the men who'd slaughtered those American soldiers. Which meant he could anticipate the same fate, unless he could do something about it.

He shuffled around the room, moving awkwardly with such limited freedom of movement. Despite his hands tied behind his back, he felt his way around, looking for a way out. There was none, save a single door that was the only means of entering or leaving the room. It was locked, which was no surprise, solid and unmoving, so he continued feeling his way around in the darkness. Nothing. He tried the floor, in case there was a loose board, but the floor was rough concrete, with no way out. It was some kind of storeroom.

He gave up trying, got himself into as comfortable a position as possible, and settled down to conserve his strength. To wait for an opportunity to escape when they came for him, and that was a faint hope. He cursed himself for getting into this situation. He should've done it differently, should've abandoned the motorcycle halfway across the open ground and crept into the town. They would've heard the engine and knew he was coming. He'd fallen into their hands like a lamb to the slaughter.

What made him feel worse was the knowledge he'd got those nuns killed. Sure, he hadn't pulled the trigger, but if he hadn't been in their convent, they would have still been alive. It was a heavy burden for his soul to bear. He wasn't a religious man, not in any way, although he'd spent the first part of his life learning the Christian principles of decency and honesty. Stuff like you don't kill nuns.

He knew it was morning when beams of light poked through chinks in the roof of the building, and he assumed they'd come for him. They didn't come. Instead, they left him without food or water. They wouldn't see any need to waste food or drink on a man they were about to execute. The day wore on, and his thirst was a raging torment. It was a relief when the door opened. Two soldiers stepped inside, dragged him out, and flung him back down to the ground.

The officer who'd killed the nuns, a major, was staring down at him. A face creased into harsh lines of cruelty, thick lips twisted into a sneer, eyes pale blue and watery, the eyes of a Nazi fanatic, yet he didn't look the image of an Aryan superman. A stooped posture, belly with a bit more bulge than was healthy, and he looked more like a clerk than a fighting soldier. He was looking at a weak man, a total shit. But a dangerous shit.

"Tell me how many troops are getting ready to attack the town. How much artillery and armor, and when will the attack start? Tell me now, and I may be inclined to be lenient."

He stared back at him, unable to prevent his vitriolic hatred for this man from showing in his expression. "I'll see you in hell before I tell you anything, shithead. You're wasting your time."

The German grinned. "Perhaps, perhaps not. I would like to introduce you to another prisoner." He signaled to another soldier standing inside the doorway to one of the houses. He turned and shouted an order to somebody inside, and they dragged out a man who'd been savagely beaten. He was wearing civilian clothes, or what amounted to civilian clothes, it was certainly no uniform. Except for the peacoat he wore over his pants and shirt. Murphy gazed in astonishment when he recognized Major Fraser, although this was a vastly different Major Fraser.

"Major! What the hell happened to you?"

He returned his gaze, and his face was so badly beaten if he hadn't been so familiar with him, he wouldn't have known him. "These boys play rough. They're insisting I'm a spy."

He didn't need to ask what the Scots Guard officer was doing in the town. He was doing his job, snooping around, gathering intelligence, and they'd caught him out of uniform.

Shit, shit, shit!

"Christ, you're not a spy."

"I told them, but they didn't believe me."

"I'll damn well tell them." He looked at the officer. "Mister, this guy is a major in the British Army."

The thick lips twisted in a sadistic smile. "Is that right? In that case, where is his uniform? See, he is wearing civilian clothes, and that makes him a spy. Under the Geneva Convention, I'm entitled to condemn him to death."

"Which part of the Geneva Convention entitled you to murder those nuns?"

The smile broadened. "They were aiding and abetting the enemy. That makes them combatants, and I was legally entitled to execute them."

"That's bullshit, Mister, and you know it. What about those American prisoners you murdered? I guess that was you. Or is the German army full of homicidal psychopaths like you?"

He nodded to a man standing behind him, and he felt a heavy blow in the small of his back. As he went down, a jackboot kicked him in the ribs, and through the waves of pain, he heard the German continue to question him. "How many troops, how many guns, and how many tanks? What time do you plan to attack?"

"Fuck you, Mister. You're wasting your time."

"Is that right?" He pulled out his Walther and pointed it at Fraser's head, "Last chance, when does the attack come?"

"Go fuck yourself. Let this man go, he's a soldier."

He fired, and to his horror, Murphy saw the bullet hit Fraser in the center of the forehead, the force of the shot throwing him backward. He lay on the ground, with a trickle of blood and brains leaking out to form a pool around his head.

The German nodded in satisfaction and looked at him. "When does the attack come?"

He shook his head, unable to comprehend what was happening. First, the shock of seeing those nuns murdered, and now to see the Brit officer shot down in cold blood. It answered one question. He now knew what'd happened to Dan. He was dead, without a doubt. And soon, he'd be joining him.

The officer grunted he'd be next, snapped an order, and they dragged him back into the storeroom, where they flung him back down on the stone floor. He didn't know how long he had to wait for his execution, but it wouldn't be long. He'd screwed up, big-time, and now he was about to pay the price. The ultimate price.

CHAPTER FOUR

16 June 1944

General Eisenhower ended the call, and he had a lot to think about. He glanced at his secretary, Kay Summersby. "That was Churchill, and the Brits are in deep shit. We must speed things up. Get Lightning Joe on the radio."

He was talking about General Joseph Lawton Collins, in command of VII Corps in Normandy. She picked up the phone and arranged for the patch to Collins' headquarters in the Cotentin Peninsular. It was several minutes before Collins replied. "General, what can I do for you?"

I've just taken a call from Churchill in London. The Krauts have launched a heavy raid on London, and they're taking one hell of a battering."

"A bombing raid? I thought we had the Luftwaffe beat."

"Not to the Luftwaffe. V-1 rockets, the so-called Flying Bombs. Two hundred and forty-four hit London last night, and there could be hundreds more on the way. They're launching them from sites on the Channel coast, most in Northern France and Holland. The faster we reach those sites and put an end to these damned bombs, the better. If we're not quick enough, by the time we get there, London could be a mass of rubble. Joe, you need to get the lead out, hit them even harder, and get them running."

"We're doing everything we can, General Eisenhower."

"You have to do more," he snapped, "What's holding you up?"

Collins was quiet for several seconds while he thought. "Cherbourg is still holding out. They're putting up a tough fight."

"Sure, but they're not going anywhere. We desperately need that port to bring in more tanks and troops, but it's just a matter of time before we roll up the whole of the Cotentin Peninsular. What else?"

"We're still trying to make a breakthrough, get behind the German lines and swing around to take them from the rear. We identified a gap in their defenses and a town called Evrecy, but we still haven't assessed whether they're still holding out or they've abandoned the town. We had a report of German artillery in the area, but it's vague. I sent in a Ranger company, Bravo, and they're checking it out now. As soon as we know it's clear, I'll send a combined arms division of tanks and troops through the gap to hit the enemy from behind."

"Get behind them, Joe. The Brits are worried, and I'm worried. As soon as it's clear, move in behind the Krauts, hit them hard, and keep hitting them. I want them in full retreat, running back to Germany so fast they're tripping over their tails.

They'll have no choice but to evacuate those V-1 launch sites, and we can save London from a pasting."

"I'll get onto those Rangers right away."

"Keep me informed the moment you know anything, and I'll pass on to Churchill."

* * *

The German officer visited him during the morning, stood regarding his prisoner lying on the floor, arms and legs bound, and he bared his thick lips in a cruel smile.

"I trust you enjoyed a comfortable night, American. My name is Major Gottlieb Kreis, and I come to advise you I have sentenced you to death. This is in accordance with the Führer's Commando Order issued on 18 October 1942. The order states that all Allied commandos encountered in Europe and Africa should be killed immediately without trial. Even if in proper uniforms, whether they surrendered or not."

Through parched lips, and a tongue that felt like it was glued to the roof of his mouth, he managed to spit defiance.

Why should I give this piece of Nazi shit the satisfaction of thinking I care about anything he says?

"You're a worthless piece of scum, just like Adolf. Do what you want, you'll be in hell before much longer, and your lunatic Führer will be there with you."

He gave him a hard kick, and at his kidneys, but Murphy was so cold and stiff after so many hours unmoving, he hardly felt it. "That is for insulting me and the Führer. The sentence will be carried out at 18.00. In case you're wondering, there won't be a last meal."

He spun on his heel and stomped out of the room. Murphy heard the bolts on the door slamming closed outside, but even if they'd left it open, he was so stiff and cold, he wasn't even sure he could crawl out. He lay there for several hours, and he worked out it had to be around midday. He heard movement outside, and as if to torment him further, he smelled them cooking a hot meal. His stomach growled, and pangs of hunger wracked his body. The numbness had been overtaken by the pain shooting through his immobilized limbs, and right then, he considered a firing squad or whatever else they had in mind would be a better option than lying there. He recalled how Major Kreis had executed the nuns, and he'd probably put a pistol to his head, squeeze the trigger, and it would be all over.

He was dreaming. He had to be dreaming because he thought he heard Dan Kelly's voice. "Jack, give me a few minutes, I'm gonna get you out."

It was good to hear Kelly's voice again, even if he was hallucinating. "What's the plan, a slap-up meal when we get to Paris?"

A pause. "Whatever. Keep it quiet."

He didn't say any more, and he felt a sense of loss when the hallucination ended. He was still thinking about the meal the Germans were enjoying when he heard something outside the door. It was like a surprised grunt, and a clatter as something fell to the ground. A moment later the bolts slid aside, the door opened, and a man entered the storeroom. Sunlight had dazzled him, and he couldn't see him, but he assumed he'd come to take him out for the execution. They must've decided to do it sooner.

"Jack, can you move?"

The hallucination had come back. He was hearing Kelly's

voice again. "What gives, Dan? Did you book the table?"

"Buddy, I don't know what the hell you're talking about. I'm getting you out of here."

As his eyes adjusted to the sunlight, understanding flooded into his brain. He wasn't hallucinating, it was Kelly, and he was dragging the lifeless body inside the room.

"How… I thought you were dead."

"Never mind that now." He slashed through the rope on his wrists and ankles, "Are you wounded?"

"Negative."

"Can you walk?"

"I need a minute to get the circulation moving, but, yeah, I can walk. Dan, I can't believe you're still alive. What's that odor? It's like… a mixture of booze and perfume. How come you smell like a whorehouse?"

"No idea."

"Not that I give a damn, you're here, it's like a miracle."

"We're not out of here yet, Jack. Try to loosen up some, and I'll take a peek outside, make sure it's clear. You won't have to walk far. If there's nobody around, there's a vehicle parked around back we could take, one of those funny German jeeps, the Kubelwagen. Ride back in style."

He disappeared outside, and Murphy attempted to force movement into his numbed limbs. As the blood flow restarted, the pain came in waves, but there are some pains a man can put up with, can even welcome. Dan came back.

"We're clear. They're inside the large building across the street eating a meal. You ready to go?"

"Wild horses wouldn't stop me."

They emerged into the sunshine, and astonishingly the

street was clear of enemy soldiers. Although he could hear the rumble of conversation, shouts of men laughing and joking with each other. They sneaked around the back and emerged in another small square. Parked behind the storeroom where they'd held him prisoner was the Kubelwagen unguarded, which was good news. Equally interesting the open-fronted building looked like it had been a garage for motor vehicles. Hidden inside the spaces designed to accommodate cars and trucks were the guns, four 75mm PAK-37 artillery pieces, anti-tank guns, capable of firing armor-piercing high-explosive shells.

They walked toward the Kubelwagen, and Dan murmured, "The girls told me they have several more guns in another part of the town, all placed so they can roll them out and deploy them in a matter of minutes."

"Which girls?"

"Uh, just some girls I bumped into. Long story."

"Right. Dan, the quicker we get out of here and tell our people what we've seen here, the quicker they can do something about it."

"Sure. I'll drive. We need to get going before they discover you've gone."

"The moment they hear the engine start, they'll know. Drive like hell."

"You got it."

They boarded the peculiar-looking German jeep. He started the engine and accelerated away. Out of the town, he floored the gas pedal, racing across the open ground back to their lines. They were halfway across when the shooting started. It wasn't the Germans shooting at them; it was their own people. Murphy stood on the passenger seat, held the windshield, and waved his distinctive American helmet in the air, hoping they'd get the message.

They got the message, but not before a bullet pierced the windshield, fortunately in the center, and it whined past, midway between them. No further shots arrived, and Dan drove into the camp and halted the Kubelwagen. They stared at them, and when they recognized Kelly, men were backslapping him, asking him how the hell he'd managed to get away.

Lieutenant Adams didn't greet their arrival with such enthusiasm. "Private Murphy, you have some explaining to do."

He climbed out of the jeep with some difficulty, his limbs still numb after his long incarceration, and he almost fell until Rooker grabbed him. "You okay, son?"

"Stiff, is all."

Adams grunted. "I can tell you General Shriver is less than happy about you stealing that motorcycle and driving toward the town. The MP, Bishop, told him you were deserting, and he ought to write a warrant for your immediate arrest as soon as they catch up with you, but the General told him to hold fire. Said there could be another explanation. I'm waiting for the explanation right now, Murphy."

He explained why he'd done it, and how he'd hoped to find Dan Kelly. "Dead or alive, Lt, I figured he needed to come back to our lines. It didn't seem right, leaving him out there."

He considered for a moment. "I understand your sentiment, Murphy, but not your method. You should've gone with that MP, not stolen a motorcycle, and taken matters into your own hands. There is a way of doing things in this man's army, and what you did was plain wrong."

Rooker interceded. "We should consider the end result,

Lieutenant. He got Kelly out alive, and that's what's important."

"I guess so. There's the question of the motorcycle, it's the property of the United States Army."

"We'll get it back when we go into Evrecy."

"We'd better. Okay, it's good to see you back, Kelly, and because of the way it worked out, I'll try and smooth things over with headquarters, although that MP may not be forgiving. I take it you're innocent of killing those two soldiers?"

"I guarantee you I haven't committed any crime."

He nodded. "That'll have to be good enough for now. Sergeant Rooker, before they arrived, I had a call from Battalion, and Bravo Company is coming back. We must kick the Germans out of the town ASAP, and as soon as they get here, we're going back in. They've allocated three Shermans to join the attack, and they're due to arrive at midday tomorrow with additional weapons and ammunition. This time, we go straight in. We know the Germans are there, and we'll be carrying bazookas and machine guns to hit the artillery and take some of them out before they get a chance to take potshots at our tanks."

Rooker looked at Murphy. "You were in the town, what're we are up against? They sent in the Brit officer, Major Fraser to look around. Told him the Germans had left, but he hasn't got back, so we've no idea."

"He's dead."

He told him about Fraser being captured, and how Kreis had killed him. "He was wearing civilian clothes, and he shot him as a spy. Not that it would've made any difference."

Adams gave him a sharp glance. "How so?"

He told him what Kreis had said about Hitler's Commando Order. "He's using it as a legal entitlement to shoot anybody he feels like. Like they killed those prisoners we came across. Like those four nuns, and I saw him pull the trigger." He explained about the nuns, and how the homicidal German had gleefully executed them, "I was scheduled to be killed at 18.00."

He gave him a sympathetic glance. "Thank God you got out in time. Tell me about the guns."

"We saw four 75mm PAK-37s, and Dan said some locals told him there're a few more hidden under cover around the town. That's why our aerial reconnaissance has failed to pick them up. When they see us coming, they'll deploy the guns in minutes and get them into action. There's something else, Sarge. That officer in charge, Major Kreis, he's a psycho. Watch out for him."

"Kreis, uh? We'll keep an eye open for him."

Adams took over. "There's something else we need to consider. German armor. They're still in the region, but we don't know exactly where. The 101st Heavy Panzers, the Panzer Lehr Division, and there's this other outfit, the 12th SS Hitler Jugend. They're under the command of the guy who knocked out all that British armor at Villers-Bocage. If we run into them, we can call for air support, and they'll send in a few P-47s and British Spitfires and Typhoons to take care of them. But calling in an airstrike takes time, so we need to keep our eyes skinned. As I said, we'll have bazookas, so we won't be defenseless, but..."

Rooker interrupted him. "Lt, bazookas against Tigers? You have to be kidding."

"At least we'll have a chance."

"Sir, we'll have no chance. If we encounter heavy armor, there's only one way to defend ourselves."

"And that is?"

"Run like fuck."

He paused while he thought about that, and finally, he slowly nodded his head. "That may be a clever idea, Sergeant. Pass it on to the men." He glanced at Murphy and Kelly. "In the meantime, it's good to see you back. Even if you went about it the wrong way."

"Yessir," they acknowledged in unison.

"Very well. Dismissed, and get yourself something to eat. Before you go, what's that smell? It's kind of a mix of perfume and booze. Did it come from all the broken bottles in that bar when the aircraft shot it up?"

"That must be it, Lt."

"I guess the owner must've been selling perfume as well as booze."

"I reckon so."

A jeep had brought along cans of food from the Battalion cookhouse, and although the remains were cold, Murphy tucked into it.

To his surprise, Dan wasn't so hungry. "The place I was hiding, they gave me food. They were nice people."

"A local family?"

"Something like that. They were real friendly."

He waded through three mess cans of cold stew and swilled down a tin mug of cold coffee. It tasted like a slap-up meal, the best he'd ever tasted, and afterward, he felt his strength starting to return. The bruises on his face and body turned purple, and Kelly reckoned it looked like he'd been ten rounds with Joe Louis. Nicknamed the 'Brown Bomber,' he had a reputation as an all-around good guy. Until he got into the ring when his opponents discovered he had the capacity to be an all-around bad guy. As the German heavyweight Max Schmeling discovered to his cost in June 1938. Louis gave him a taste of what Germany could expect from American firepower. He knocked him down three times before Schmeling's trainer threw in the towel after a mere two minutes and four seconds. A stupendous victory for the Brown Bomber, having kicked sand in the faces of the Nazis who'd trumpeted their man's inevitable defeat of the black American.

They bedded down for the night, and he glanced up at the stars, hardly daring to believe he was alive and free. Hardly daring to believe the other reason for feeling so good, in the shape of a compact, trim and incredibly pretty French girl, Clemence Delon, who'd somehow managed to stay with them, despite the efforts of the U.S. Army to send her to the rear.

"I thought you were dead."

"I thought I was dead, but for all their reputation, the Germans aren't as efficient as they think they are."

"Be careful, Jack. They may not be all that efficient, but the Nazis also have a reputation for being murderous scum, and it seems to me they're living up to that reputation."

"I'll be careful."

"They're attacking the town again tomorrow, that's what I heard. I take it you'll be part of the attack."

"That's the way it goes."

"If you get killed, this could be our last night together."

"I won't get killed. I've made it this far."

"Nobody can say that. Jack, there's something I want to show you. Follow me."

He'd no idea what she was talking about. Maybe she'd found a supersecret armored vest he could wear when they went in, something to protect him from German bullets. She walked through the trees and stopped inside a thick tangle of bushes. He looked around, but he couldn't see anything, and he was puzzled. "What was it you wanted to show me?"

She unbuttoned her jacket and shirt, removed them, and unsnapped her bra. Her breasts were creamy white, smooth, and firm, and he felt the arousal building inside him like a volcano. "Me."

She continued undressing until she was naked, throwing her clothes on the ground, and Jack Murphy, never being one to pass up an opportunity, did the same. Tossed his clothes on top of hers in a heap to make a simple bed, and she lay down. He lay on top of them, and kissed her, tasting her warm breath, and drinking in the musky fragrance of her body. They made love; silently because they were so close to the other men, and when they'd finished, he kept his arms wrapped around her, pulling her in tight to his body.

"What was that for? A warrior's sendoff?"

"It was to remind you what was waiting for you when you get back. In case you are tempted to take any chances. I hope it was enough to make up your mind to stay safe."

He was impressed, his mind on cloud nine, and the hard place of war had receded, and somehow the Normandy battlefield didn't seem such a bad place. "More than enough."

They dressed and strolled back to the camp, and the sentry, Sam Crockett, nodded an acknowledgment as they walked past. He didn't ask them where they'd been, didn't ask for the password of the day. He didn't need to ask. The look on their faces was enough.

They slept apart, not wanting to remind Adams or Rooker

she was still around, and she found a spot several yards away, tucked out of sight behind a small clump of trees. At dawn, one of the rookies, PFC Les Anderson, a soldier who always managed to show more enthusiasm than sense, made a fire and warmed the remainder of the food. Anderson claimed to have been a Boy Scout, and Murphy had to stop him from spending an hour rubbing two sticks together to get the fire started.

"Uh, Les, these days we got Zippo lighters. It's quicker."

He was clumsy, despite his Boy Scout credentials. At nineteen-years-old he possessed a blunt face covered in freckles, always set in a puzzled frown. Always bumping into things, and he picked up the pot he'd knocked over. He didn't look happy like he'd been looking forward to demonstrating his outdoor skills.

"If you think so."

"Keep the two sticks for later, when we have more time. Like when the war's over."

He put the flame to the kindling and the fire blazed. He busied himself stirring the pot, and he made the best of what little they had. Enough to fill one mess tin for each man, and they gulped it down. He'd managed to sequester enough for Clemence, and they seated themselves in a circle around her so Adams wouldn't notice. Rooker couldn't miss her and sat with them to eat his food. "Try and keep her out of sight when the Lieutenant strolls past, that's all. He'll go ballistic if he thinks you've disobeyed another order."

He had an idea, and he scrounged up a spare uniform from the rest of the men after he persuaded them to empty the contents of their packs. She changed into khakis, pants, shirt, jacket, and helmet, although with no boots small enough to fit her feet, she retained her shoes. At a mere five feet tall, when she was dressed, she looked like a kid playing with her father's clothes, but it would hide her from a casual glance. It would also give her some protection if the Germans captured her, especially one German in particular, although Murphy determined to find him first and kill him when they went into the town. The memory of those nuns, and of Major Fraser, was a scar on his psyche, an itch he had to scratch. Scratch it with a chunk of American lead. It wouldn't be German lead, not unless he got his hands on another MP-40 to replace the one they'd taken off him, and he determined to make that another priority when they went into the town.

He retrieved his Springfield, cleaned the action, and polished the lens of the scope. Dan scrounged around and found him a spare Colt, this one in a shoulder holster, and he didn't ask him how he'd managed it. When he strapped on the weapon, he felt more normal, armed, and ready for what was to come. He talked to Clemence, and this time got her solemn promise to stay back when they went in. She saw sense and agreed, which made him feel better, and they waited for the arrival of Bravo Company. They came in just before noon, and they were something of a shock. They'd tangled with a retreating bunch of German soldiers who'd set up a rearguard action consisting of an MG-34, and they'd lost more men. Captain Washington was down to less than sixty soldiers, the equivalent of two platoons, and the men reassured themselves at least they'd have the tanks in support.

The tanks were late, arriving at 13.40, along with a truck loaded with weapons and supplies, and there was more unwelcome news. They'd lost one tank along the way, not to enemy action but to a breakdown, when the casing for the final drive cracked, the oil leaked, and brought the Sherman to a grinding halt when the gears seized solid. They had to leave it for the engineers to arrive to start work on fixing the problem. It would be at least two days before they arrived and completed the repair. Meanwhile, they had two Shermans, along with seven bazookas complete the spare rockets, and ammunition belts for Bravo's light machine guns.

It should've been enough if the town was lightly defended, but with anything up to ten 75mm artillery pieces, and as many as a hundred soldiers, it wasn't enough. Sure, they had two Shermans, but the Germans had armor-piercing shells, and when they opened fire on the American tanks, they were liable to blast them into scrap.

They met to discuss tactics before the attack started, and Rooker, Murphy, and Kelly stood close so they could listen in. The officer in command of the tanks was a junior lieutenant, Second Lieutenant David Blake, who looked too young to shave. More like an eager, first-year college boy, the kind of kid with the right answer to every question his professors put to him. Until it was time to put that knowledge into practice. Yet he was enthusiastic enough, raring to get to grips with the enemy.

The commander of the other Sherman was a three-striper, Sergeant Chris Davidson. He looked about the same age as Murphy, and like Murphy, he looked fit, and below-average height. Like many tankers, who fought their war from inside the steel cramped confines of an armored hull. Big, tall men didn't fit so well inside a Sherman. His skin was sallow and greasy. The result of so much time spent locked inside a steel container during the endless preparations for the invasion of Normandy, immersed in the stink of sweat, oil, and grease.

Second Lieutenant Blake was eager to make his mark, although as yet he hadn't fired a shot in anger. Sergeant Davidson was inclined to be more cautious, but Murphy doubted either tanker understood the risk they faced from the enemy artillery.

They listened to Adams' suggestion they attacked from the flank, but Blake wasn't impressed. He wanted to grab the glory. "What's the big deal? If we drive straight into town instead of pussyfooting around the outside, we'll catch them back footed. Attack head-on, that's always the best way."

Rooker, Murphy, and Kelly swapped glances, and they weren't impressed. Captain Robert Washington was the senior officer present, and he heard them out before he decided.

"We'll hit them from the flank. They're expecting an attack, so there's no way we can surprise them. The best we can hope for is to hit the town before they deploy their guns to face a flanking attack. And start shooting before they do." He checked his watch; "We jump off at 16.00 and approach the town from the north side. So make sure you're ready to go."

They dispersed to get their men and vehicles ready. Rooker glanced at his two men. "You've seen the Germans in the town, and you've seen the guns. How do you rate our chances?"

"They're shit!" Kelly exploded, "Jesus Christ, Sarge, they have those guns tucked out of sight, but they're ready to roll out at a moment's notice. The minute they hear the tanks approaching, they'll wheel them out, and when those Shermans get there, they'll be waiting for them."

He nodded. "I was thinking much the same. They may be a bunch of murdering butchers, but they know plenty about soldiering, and I don't rate our chances of surprising them. What we need is a diversion, some way to get them looking in the wrong direction when we go in."

"An airstrike would do it."

"Except the aircraft are stretched thin across the whole of Normandy, and I wouldn't rate our chances of getting them to cooperate. Anything else?"

They looked at each other and Murphy nodded. "It'd be useful if we could stage a diversionary attack from the south. They'll deploy their guns to counter it, and they'd be pointing the wrong way when the Shermans go in. Except we don't have another tank." He chuckled, "I was thinking about the preparations for D-Day when they established FUSAG, the First U.S. Army Group in Southern England."

Rooker nodded. "Yeah, they called it the Ghost Army. Fooled the Germans into thinking we were planning to land at Calais. It's just as well it worked. It diverted most of their troops, guns, and armor to the Pas de Calais region, opposite Dover. Without them, it would've been a lot tougher. They used inflatable tanks, as I recall, and vehicles and huts made from thin plywood. Except we don't have any inflatable tanks."

He'd been thinking hard, and he got to his feet to work through an idea. On the edge of the camp, they could overlook the town. The north side was open ground, and he was thinking if they were in position the German guns would murder the two Shermans before they reached the outskirts. Sure, they'd have the Rangers carrying bazookas right behind them, but a bazooka has a limited range. With the German guns firing a mix of armor-piercing to take out the tanks and high-explosive to tear the infantry into ruin, the chances of getting close enough to use them would be slim.

On the other side of the town, the south side, there was some cover. Clumps of trees, and stone walls that looked like they'd been built hundreds of years before to separate neighboring farms. Enough to hide an approach by a vehicle, especially if it was low-profile.

"We have the Kubelwagen."

They both stared at him. "It's a bit light to think about fitting a 76mm gun on that bucket of bolts, even if it would carry the weight, which it won't."

Rooker had a point, but that wasn't his idea. "I was thinking of something else. If we hacked off the muffler, wouldn't the engine sound more like a tank? You know what it's like when a car has a defective muffler, the noise is deafening."

"But it's not like a tank."

"Maybe not, but would they know that? They know we're gonna attack real soon, and if they hear the roar of an engine coming in from the south, what's the first conclusion they're gonna come to?"

He nodded slowly. "It's a tank. Damnit, Murphy, you may have something there. I'll put it to the Lieutenant, see if I can make him listen."

Adams was with the three other platoon leaders, talking with Washington, and he gave Rooker an irritated glance. "What is it, Sergeant, I'm busy."

"Murphy came up with an idea for a diversion, Lt. I think you should hear it."

"Not now, we…"

"Hear him out," Washington said. He looked at Murphy. "What is it, Private?"

He outlined what he had in mind. Although it might not work, the Captain concluded anything was worth a try. "Get it done. We attack in less than an hour, will you be ready?"

"We'll be ready."

They got to work on the muffler of the Kubelwagen, which unfortunately was tucked right at the back of the rear-engined jeep. They didn't have access to a hacksaw, but one of the tankers loaned them a pry bar, and they used it to wrench off the entire exhaust system. Kelly started the engine, and the result was impressive. It didn't sound like a tank, not close up, but from a distance, it would be enough to make the Krauts take it seriously.

Washington wandered over when he heard the noise, and he looked impressed.

"We have a half-hour before the attack goes in, so get moving now, and with any luck, the enemy will fall for it, and we'll have an easy run into the town. Good luck."

Rooker stepped up to him, and he was holding a Browning BAR. "Sir, if it's all the same to you, I'll go with them. They're gonna need a heap more firepower when they run into the Krauts."

He paused for a few seconds and nodded. "I agree. Lieutenant Adams, you'll have to manage without your platoon sergeant. It won't give you any problems?"

He didn't look happy, but he couldn't say no, not unless he wanted to look like he couldn't handle the platoon on his own. "Well…"

"Wait, I have another idea. Where's that MP? Sergeant

Bishop. Someone find him and order him to report to me. He can substitute for Rooker during the attack."

Murphy grinned. "With pleasure."

Bishop was dawdling on the far side of the parked Shermans. It may have occurred to him their armored hulls would protect him if the enemy decided to lob a few shells toward them. He grinned with satisfaction when he saw Murphy, but the grin faded when he told him to report on the double to the company commander. "You'll be joining First Platoon for the attack, Bishop. I hope you enjoy it."

"You're kidding me. Is this some kind of a joke?"

"The joke will be on you if you fail to report. I believe they call it desertion."

He returned to the Kubelwagen, and Dan was still in the driver's seat with the engine switched off, waiting for the order to go. Rooker was standing on the passenger side with the Browning resting on the windshield. He climbed into the rear seat, the engine started, and they drove away. Heading due south to approach the town from that direction, the air-cooled engine making so much noise it was enough to wake the dead. Dan steered toward the trees and threaded a way through, and within minutes they were approaching the outskirts of Evrecy. Everything depended on whether the Germans fell for it. They had to. If they didn't, they were fucked.

* * *

Major Gottlieb Kreis heard the noise of tank engines, but not coming from due south. The noise grew in intensity, and they were heading in from the south-west. A few survivors of Panzer

Lehr, the division having been shot up by squadron after squadron of Allied fighter-bombers. The once-proud elite unit of Hitler's heavy tanks had been decimated, split into isolated stragglers, and three survivors made it into Evrecy.

Two STuG IIIs, the Sturmgeschutz III assault gun was Germany's most-produced fully tracked armored fighting vehicle during World War II, built on a modified Panzer III chassis, the factory replaced the turret with an armored, fixed superstructure mounting a more powerful gun. The third vehicle was a much-vaunted Panther, equipped with the same engine as the Panzer VI, the Tiger, and mounting more effective frontal armor and a gun with better penetration than the Tiger's 88mm. Yet its lightweight hull made it faster than its heavier cousin, a lethal fighting vehicle. The Panther had been hurriedly thrown into production to counter the Soviet T-34s, and like the Tiger, it suffered similar headaches. The Panther was known for frequent breakdowns.

Kreis wasn't interested in breakdowns. What counted was the appearance of three panzers to augment his scratch force. The senior tank commander was a First Lieutenant, a subordinate, and he jumped down from the turret of the Panther and saluted.

"Leutnant Weber reporting, Sir. We're on the way to…"

"Leutnant, you're not going anywhere. You've arrived, and just in time. I'm ordering you to place your tanks under my command, and we're about to come under attack, so make sure you're ready." He stopped, listening to the noise of an engine, coming in from the south, "What's that?"

Weber listened for several seconds; his expression puzzled. "Sir, it sounds like a tank. Although not one I've heard before."

"Could it be the Allies have brought in something new?"

"Anything's possible, who knows?"

"Damn, I didn't expect them to come from that direction. Leutnant Weber, prepare to meet the attack coming in from the south." He shouted to his second-in-command, "Deploy the guns to cover the approaches from the north. No wait, they may decide to make a frontal attack, so we need to be ready for anything. Roll out the guns to cover an attack from the west, and I want you to deploy two PAK-37s just in case they come in from the north."

He smiled to himself. With the arrival of the armor, he had everything covered. He watched the tanks roll away to the south side of the town and heard his sergeants bellowing orders to the men to get the lead out and place the guns in position. He was satisfied he'd covered all his options, and with the additional armor, victory was certain. When they came, he'd give them a bloody nose, and make the Allies regret the day they'd landed on the Normandy beaches.

CHAPTER FIVE

17 June 1944

The plan was a disaster. They were less than four hundred yards from the town, making so much noise the Germans had to fall for it. And they did fall for it, just not in the way they'd expected. There was no sign of them rolling out the guns to repel armor. Instead, they were confronted by panzers. Two STuGs and the Panther, speeding out from the town to intercept them, and he shouted to Dan to change course and get away.

"Get under cover. When they start shooting, we're fucked."

The Kubelwagen went up on two wheels as he swerved to change direction, heading away from the town toward a clump of trees. Before they made it, the Panther fired a high-velocity shell that whistled toward them and slammed into a distant hillside. They'd fired armor-piercing ammunition, and there was no great explosion when it hit, but he shuddered to think what would've happened if that shell had slammed into the flimsy jeep. One of the STuGs fired, and this time they used a high-explosive shell. Again, it missed, but their shooting was good, and the chances were they'd score a hit real soon.

Rooker shouted, "Kelly, zigzag. They've got our range!"

He spun the wheel over again, and two more shells that would've bracketed them had they continued on the same course, or maybe scored direct hits, exploded against nearby trees. The Kubelwagen was steering a wild course, flinging them from side to side, and another armor-piercing shell scraped past the bodywork, smashing into the thick trunk of an oak tree that'd probably been standing for hundreds of years. It severed it, and the tree tilted over and began to fall. Their shooting was too good, and if they struck, they were finished.

Dan had the pedal to the metal, the jeep racing along at top speed. He crested a hill, threaded between two trees, and a moment later they were flying through space. On the other side of the hill there was no gentle slope, just a sheer drop of around ten feet to a shallow river gully at the bottom. The Kubelwagen splashed into the water with a sickening thump, and it was no gentle landing but a bone-jarring crash.

Rooker had been standing upright, and he bent his legs to absorb some of the impact. He managed to keep hold of the BAR, and he shouted at them to get out. They scrambled out of the waterlogged vehicle and threw themselves against the bank. Just in time, the Panther arrived at the top of the slope and stopped. The engine ticked over, and they heard the guttural German shout from the tank commander giving orders to his men before he climbed down to search for the fleeing vehicle. He gazed into the distance, and then looked down and saw the

Kubelwagen stranded in the water. He looked around for the soldiers who'd been riding in it. He didn't see the three Rangers, holding their breath, flattened against the bank ten feet below where he stood.

He shouted again, sounding puzzled. Probably not realizing the noise had come from Kubelwagen they'd seen approaching. Wondering about the whereabouts of the tank. They waited several minutes while he continued to look around, but he was looking for a tank, not three men. When he found nothing, he climbed back into the tank and shouted an order. The engine roared, and it backed away, the tracks throwing up clods of earth as they chewed into the soft ground. The noise receded as it drove away along with the two STuGs.

Rooker climbed up to the top of the low hill and searched for the Germans. They were heading east, maybe assuming the tank they believed they'd heard had gone that way, and he shouted at them to come on up.

"Where the hell did those tanks come from?"

They looked at each other, and none of them had any answers. Murphy shrugged. "There was talk of a battalion of heavy panzers, but that was no battalion."

He grunted. "Whatever it was, if they meet our two Shermans when they attack, our guys are in trouble. Their shells will bounce off the Panther's armor, and those STuGs have low-profile hulls, so they make difficult targets. Things are not looking good for Bravo Company. They have more tanks, more men, and they have the artillery. They may not know about the tanks. We need to get a message back to them."

"Too late." Dan was looking to the north, and the Shermans were rolling in toward the town, followed by the

Rangers following in two columns, "It's already started."

"In that case, we need to get in there and try to help them."

Kelly gaped. "Help them how, Sarge? We have a machine gun, two rifles, and an MP-40. That's not much firepower."

"Maybe not, but who wants to stand here and watch while our guys get slaughtered? Let's go, and we'll do what we can."

They sprinted toward the town, a lung-bursting run. Before they reached it, the Germans opened fire, although it didn't sound like they'd deployed all their artillery. More like two guns, and they spat shells toward the Shermans, scoring several hits. They were lucky, with the sloped frontal armor, none of the shells penetrated the hulls, but as they got closer, it had to be a matter of time. Where were the rest of the guns? They'd emplaced them elsewhere, expecting an attack on a different part of the town, but as soon as they realized the main threat came from the north, it wouldn't take them long to deploy everything they had against the American attack.

They reached the street leading into the town, alert for the first sign of the enemy, and they needn't have worried. There was no sign of the Germans, which meant they were busy elsewhere. Just before they reached the square in the center, they found them. Enemy soldiers, racing to deploy their guns, ten men moving artillery pieces to the north side of the town to repel the American attack. They weren't watching for further threats elsewhere, assuming the panzers had their backs. Rooker led them in behind the swarming German infantry.

Two guns had opened fire on the Shermans, but one gun had fallen silent, blasted by gunfire from the powerful 76mm main guns, but as soon as they got the rest of those PAK-37s into action, everything would change. Then there were the tanks to consider, the Panther and the two StuGs. The Sarge warned them to keep a lookout for them.

"They'll be here soon, and they'll murder our guys." He grimaced, "That's after they've murdered us."

"What can we do?"

"I dunno. But there has to be something. We can't sit on our butts and watch our soldiers turned into mincemeat."

"We could hit them from behind with the BAR," Kelly suggested.

"My estimate is they have around one hundred men, so that's not an option. We need something else, and we need it fast." He paused as several guns opened fire, "Shit, they moved a lot faster than I thought. We have to do it Kelly's way, the hard way, there's no time for anything else. Let's go get 'em!"

They ran toward the sound of the guns, and they found them positioned on the edge of the town. They were raining armor-piercing and high-explosive shells on the Shermans. They scored a hit on one, the shell smashing into the tracks, bringing it to a grinding halt. The crew bailed out, and they were down to one tank. The Rangers closed up to use the armored hull for protection, but it was a matter of time before the second tank took a mortal hit. Rooker sized up the situation in a matter of seconds. Each artillery piece had a crew of four men, and another twenty were rushing to fetch more ammunition to feed the guns. The rest of the soldiers had formed up in a line, waiting for the order to charge out and decimate the Rangers. The order would come when they destroyed the second Sherman, and it wouldn't be long.

"Lock and load!"

They glanced at the Sarge, and it looked hopeless. Murphy

carried his bolt-action Springfield, Kelly cradled his MP-40, and Rooker the BAR. He also had four grenades clipped to his webbing. He slid a round into the breech and unsnapped his pistol holster, so his Colt was ready to use, and he reckoned he'd need it. Rooker hesitated for a few more seconds, but there was nothing for it but to charge the enemy. And expect to die.

"Let's go! Give 'em hell!"

They ran, screaming curses and war cries, firing repeatedly. His rifle magazine emptied in the first few seconds. He snatched out his Colt and emptied all seven rounds into the mass of Germans, not stopping to reload, but snatching a grenade off his webbing. He pulled the pin and tossed it into the middle of the soldiers, who'd turned and were staring at them in disbelief. Like they were demons appearing from the depths of hell. The grenade exploded. He pulled another, Kelly and Rooker tossed grenades, and they kept running.

The Germans could've hit them with sheets of gunfire. They were a mere three men ranged against forty armed soldiers, with a further sixty soldiers clustered around the guns and boxes of ammunition. But panic does weird things to men during the battle, and they panicked. Half of them ran, leaving most of the guns unmanned. He tossed the last two grenades, and the other two Rangers did the same. The ground was a mass of dead and dying soldiers, all of them German. But it couldn't last. An officer who he recognized as the Nazi who'd confronted him when he was a prisoner rallied his men, bellowing orders, shouting at them to fight back, threatening them with his Walther. He even shot and killed one man who was running away.

His threats seemed to rally them, and they started to shoot

back. Rooker led them into cover inside a nearby house, and they dived to the floor as sheets of gunfire tore through the doors and windows. The Germans had regained the initiative and were reacting fast. Boots pounded on the street as they rushed toward the house, and Rooker led them out the back into the yard. They scaled a high wall and crossed into the next street. They were searching for cover and dashed into the doorway of a boarded-up store, but the owner had fortified it with thick balks of hardwood. No matter how many times they shoulder charged the portal, it refused to budge.

More Germans were appearing along the street, and they had seconds before they reached them, cornered them, and gunned them down like dogs. They crouched, backs to the door, guns pointing outward. They reloaded, and Rooker took a quick inventory.

"What do we have left? Any grenades?"

"I'm out," Kelly and Murphy responded together.

"Bullets?"

"Two magazines for the Springfield and two for the Colt."

Kelly snapped out the magazine of the machine pistol. "This is it, half-empty, around a dozen rounds. Plus one more magazine for the Colt."

"The Browning is almost empty. We do what we can, and it's all over. We may as well go down fighting. We know how these bastards treat prisoners." He shook hands with both of them, and Murphy offered his hand to Kelly.

"Dan, it's been good knowing you. I wouldn't have wanted to serve with anyone else. You either, Sarge, it's been an honor."

"That goes for me, too."

"And me. Heads up, they're almost here."

They should've died, but they didn't. Because of the chaos, they'd all but stopped firing. Which allowed the remaining Sherman commanded by Sergeant Chris Davidson to make it to the edge of the town. The solitary tank rolled into a shallow depression in the ground, enabling it to fire from a hull-down position. The Rangers of Bravo Company arrived with their bazookas, took up positions, and everything changed. They rained rockets on the enemy, and the Krauts who'd seemed they had the three men cornered had a nasty shock. Automatic fire and bazooka rockets sliced into their ranks, and the sergeant in command of the Sherman popped his head out the turret and got to work with the M-60.

The Major shouted orders, and the Germans rushing toward them changed direction and went back to deal with the Rangers coming in behind the tank. They were rushing to swing three of the guns around to take it on at point-blank range. It became a point-blank exchange of fire, and Murphy saw several gunners fall to American fire, but most sheltered behind the armored shields of the guns, protecting them from incoming bullets. Sergeant Chris Davidson in the Sherman kept up a high rate of fire, but again the Browning was unable to penetrate the armored shields. It was a matter of minutes before the shells smashed into the tank, and at such short-range, they'd turn it into a funeral pyre.

Smoke wreathed the entire town, and the Sherman had missed the target. Several shells had slammed into nearby buildings, two of which were on fire, adding to the smoke, chaos, and confusion. Bullets zipped every which way, and close to where the three Rangers crouched in the doorway, they found targets. Enemy targets, and three German troopers went down in pools of blood. Murphy seized the opportunity and raced toward the bodies.

Rooker bellowed after him, "Get back here. You'll get yourself killed!"

"Gimme a couple of seconds. There's something I need."

Two of the casualties had been carrying MP-40s, and he was kind of partial to that gun, even more partial when Gottlieb had seized his from him, and he wanted one back. He snatched up a machine pistol and removed the webbing from both bodies, webbing with long ammo pouches for MP-40 magazines. He almost made it back, but an enemy soldier had been lurking nearby, and he fired a single shot from his KAR-98K. One bullet can make all the difference to a man, and when it hits him in the guts, it makes a world of difference. It hit him, fortunately missing his guts, skimming his side, and he almost fell when the kinetic force of the bullet nearly knocked him off his feet. He steadied, raced back to join the others, and tossed one set of webbing to Kelly.

"Spare magazines, we're gonna need 'em."

He didn't take the magazines. "You're hit. It looks bad."

"It's worse than it looks, so forget it."

He checked the machine pistol and found the magazine was full. He searched for targets, and there was nothing close. Wherever the Germans were, it wasn't in the immediate vicinity. Rooker took out an ampoule of morphine and jabbed it into his belly. "It'll take care of the pain, but if we get out of this place, the first stop is the medical tent at Battalion. Take it easy while we see what we're up against."

He felt the warmth of the morphine course through his

body, and the pain receded. His mind was floating, and he dug his nails into the palm of his hand for the hurt to focus his attention. He had something on his mind, something that couldn't wait. Incredibly, they were still alive. They hadn't won, not by a long way. They couldn't win. The Krauts had them outgunned, out armored, and outnumbered. The attack had been a mistake. But they had them back footed, and they could cause them a deal of hurt before they had to pull back. Before that happened, he had something he needed to take care of. A something called the German Major Gottlieb Kreis.

He looked at the other two Rangers. "I'm gonna take a look-see around the town, see who's about."

The Sarge eyed him suspiciously. "What're you up to, Murphy?"

He didn't reply, but Kelly answered for him. "He wants to find that Kraut officer and nail his hide to a barn door."

"You're kiddin' me! This ain't over, and our guys are in a lot of trouble. They need our help. This isn't the time to go off on some personal mission of revenge." A fresh volley of shots echoed from several streets away, and he looked around to work out where they'd come from, "Over there, that's where we're needed. Let's go."

He led the way, and Murphy followed.

Rooker's right. This is no time to go looking for Kreis, even if I do have a heap of bullets with his name on. Bravo Company needs help. The murdering bastard will have to wait.

They raced along the streets and emerged at an intersection where a dozen Rangers were fighting hard against twice their number of enemy soldiers. The Germans had two machine guns tucked behind sandbagged emplacements, prepared defensive positions. The Rangers had almost collided with them and lost two men before they ducked back into cover. Not all of them made it. A man lay on the street, and he was still moving, still alive, but unable to crawl into cover without exposing himself to more enemy fire. He was dead meat, and Murphy pointed to him.

"If we don't get him into cover, that guy is toast. Hit them with everything you have, and when they're not looking toward him, I'll dive out and drag him back."

"You'd better be quick." His expression clouded, "Wait a moment! You're hurt. You can't do this. I'll go."

"No, Sarge, it's risky, but we can't afford to leave the platoon with just Adams in command."

"He's not so bad."

"He's useless, and you know it. Gimme a minute to get ready, then let them have it."

He dashed to the end of the street, to the corner where he could see the man lying at the mercy of the machine guns. He could make out the coalscuttle helmets of the Germans, crouched behind the sandbags. He waited. It was all up to Rooker and Kelly, and he waved for them to go ahead. They opened fire, the Thompson and the MP-40 firing on full auto. Fire and reload, fire and reload, and they hit the Germans with a storm of bullets. They wouldn't have been human if they didn't duck down, and it was his chance.

He sprinted out in the open, legs pounding, his body tense for the bullet from the unseen sniper that would snuff out his life, but none came. His side hurt despite the morphine, but he put it behind him and reached the fallen soldier. He was in for a surprise. The man was a sergeant, and an MP. Sergeant Duane

Bishop, who'd stood in for Rooker. There was no sign of a wound. He'd fallen and looked like he'd banged his head hard on the cobbles, or maybe twisted an ankle.

"Sergeant, we need to get behind cover, can you walk?"

He looked up, at first uncomprehending. "Who is this?"

His eyes were white with terror, and the normally cruel expression had vanished. He wore a look Murphy had seen before. Fear. The guy was in a blue funk, and if he didn't snap out of it soon, they'd both be killed when the Germans realized what was going on.

"Get up! We need to go."

He didn't move, and he was like a rabbit dazzled by the headlights of a truck. He did the only thing he could do and slapped his face. Hard. Slapped it again, and his brain snapped back into some semblance of normality.

"You can't do that. I'll put you under arrest!"

"Get the fuck up, Bishop. We're getting out of here." He dragged him to his feet, and finally, the MP snapped out of it and started to run, toward the machine guns, "Not that way, asshole! This way."

He grabbed his sleeve and pulled him back to where Rooker and Kelly were still expending ammunition so fast they couldn't keep going much longer. They rounded the corner, just as the Germans worked out what was going on, and volleys of machine gun fire zipped past where they'd been a second before. They rejoined the two Rangers, and Rooker gave the MP a friendly nod of greeting.

"That was a close one, pal. If he hadn't got you out of there, you'd have been a gonna."

He was starting to recover from the terror that had

overtaken him. "I was about to get out of there. I didn't need any help."

Rooker shrugged. "Whatever, but that's not the way it looked from here. What happened, did you get hit, pull a muscle, or what?"

He looked nonplussed. "Uh, wounded, yeah. No, that's not right, it was a fall. Maybe it was a bullet struck my helmet, knocked me out."

Kelly gave it the once over. "Doesn't look like a bullet hit it."

He shot him a vicious look. "Maybe I fell, I dunno." He looked at Murphy, and he was his old self, "You struck me, Private Murphy. That's a court martial offense."

Does this guy never give up being a sack of shit?

He sighed. He'd had enough and he decided to give it to him with both barrels.

"Bishop, you ducked out of the fighting, and you know it. You were plain scared. You're a coward, and you left your men to do the fighting."

He drew his lips back in a vicious snarl. "That's bullshit, and you know it. I oughtta run you in for striking me. Put you in a cell while I work out what happened with Abbott and Pérez."

Rooker had heard enough. "Mister, you're out of line. The platoon is still fighting, so if you're not a coward, why don't you join them and do what Captain Washington ordered you to do? Lead them in the fighting?"

"I…uh…yeah, I'll do that." He paused, "Except you're around, Sergeant Rooker, so why don't you do some fighting instead of wasting my time? Get on with it. I've got things to do."

They watched him stalk away, heading west, toward the edge of town in the direction of the place they'd jumped off from. Like his war was over. Like he had more important work to do, breaking heads, and fitting suspects up to match up with the suspicions he harbored in the darkest recesses of his mind. They forgot about him. The two machine guns and more than twenty soldiers just around the corner, not far away, had several Rangers pinned down, and in addition, those tanks they'd seen earlier would be back soon. They knew time was what mattered. If they didn't get out soon, they'd lose more men, and Sergeant Chris Davidson's tank would be shot into scrap by the combined firepower of tanks and artillery.

They could hear it still firing, dueling with a couple of artillery pieces the Germans had got into action, but if they waited much longer, the massive advantage in men, armor, and guns would slaughter them all.

Rooker tried to work out how many enemy soldiers they faced. "A two-man crew for each machine gun, and there'll be a lot more real close, no question."

Murphy shot him a glance. "How do you want to handle this?"

"Our only chance is to surprise them. Hit them where they're least expecting it."

"Attack them head-on? Sarge, are you sure about that? They're tucked in behind those sandbags with a solid wall behind them. Which means a front attack." He grimaced, "One thing's for sure, they won't be scared shitless when they see us coming."

"Maybe not, but there's no other way. If we don't do something, our guys will take one hell of a beating."

Murphy regarded what they were up against, and it was the road to hell. He looked every which way. Up and down the street in front of the German position, and those MG-34s poked out through slots in the sandbagged emplacements, waiting to devour their prey like hungry predators. His eyes roamed upward to the roof of the building protecting the German rear, and an idea came to him. It could work. It would work. It had to work. Anything was better than committing suicide.

"We can get above them."

They jerked their heads around, and he explained what he had in mind. They both grinned. "Yeah, I like it," Rooker grunted, "Men, there's no time like the present."

They ran back along the street, around the corner, and the German position was out of sight. They were staring at a building with signs in French, a hoist on the upper floor, a heavy pair of doors large enough to admit a truck, and a single pedestrian door.

Rooker lashed out with his boot, a massive kick, and the portal didn't stand a chance. They entered, and they were in some kind of a grain warehouse, almost empty with just a few sacks of flour piled on the floor. Above them, an overhead pulley fitted with a block and tackle swung gently from side to side in the breeze filtering through the gaps in the wooden wall of the building; a ghastly metaphor for gallows to underline the terrible death awaiting them if they fucked up.

They walked toward a creaking wooden staircase and started up. Not caring about the noise they made, which was blanketed by shots and shellfire. They ascended to the second floor and found a dilapidated ladder that led to the roof space and climbed into a gloomy attic coated with ancient dust. There was no access to the roof outside, so they carefully removed several shingles, creating a hole large enough to climb through. They wriggled through and peered down on the enemy.

They were arranged in front of them, the crews crouched behind the machine guns, and the rest of the soldiers sheltering behind whatever cover they could find. One man even knelt behind a postbox, not a bad idea. It was made of cast iron and tough enough to resist a burst from a .50 caliber. The Germans had no suspicion the enemy was behind and above them, and Rooker spelled out how they'd handle it.

"We can shin down that steel pipe bolted to the wall, but I count at least twenty of them, so we're a tad shorthanded." They didn't react to the understatement, "When we hit them, we do it hard and fast. Check out your ammo. Let's see what we have."

It wasn't good. Murphy had four magazines left for the machine pistol, and he handed two to Kelly. Rooker's Thompson was almost out of bullets, and when he checked the magazine, he was down to less than ten rounds. He frowned. "Some surprise this'll be. When they see us coming, we're dead meat. What we need is a smokescreen. Some hopes. All we can do is…"

Murphy had been thinking along the same lines, and the thought of dropping in on those Krauts with hardly enough ammo to take out a Boy Scout troop didn't appeal. Smoke would give them the element of surprise, and he happened to glance through the hole in the roof, back into the attic. The breeze circulating the building had stirred up the dust, and it wasn't black dust, it was mostly white. Flour leaked out from the sacks they'd stored in the building, white flour. He recalled when he was a kid, and they'd tossed flour at each other in mock battles with neighborhood kids creating dense white clouds.

Why not?

"If they can't see us, they can't shoot back."

Rooker frowned. "Yeah, like I said, a smokescreen, except we don't have any means of making smoke."

"Not so fast, Sarge. Gimme a minute." He descended to the first floor, picked up a sack of flour, and carried it back to the roof, "This should do the trick."

"Fuckin' A," Kelly grunted, wide-eyed, "Who'd a thought it?"

They rushed down, grabbed a sack of flour apiece, and climbed back to the roof. They used their combat knives to cut through the sacks and balanced them on the edge.

"Ready? Let them have it!"

They emptied the three sacks of flour, each containing over one hundred pounds of fine white powder, onto the soldiers below. Within seconds, they'd engulfed the enemy in a thick, white fog. Rooker went first, shinning down an iron water pipe, followed by Murphy and Kelly. Kelly just made it to the bottom, before the steel pipe rusty from lack of maintenance tore away from the wall, and slowly toppled like a felled tree. The heavy pipe collapsed on top of a machine gunner, knocking him unconscious. The other Germans tried to resist, but they were fighting in a thick fog. Fighting an enemy coated in fine white flour. Every man resembled a ghost; the only way to make out friend or foe was by the distinctive shape of their steel helmets.

Murphy and Kelly got to work with their machine pistols, and enemy soldiers fell before the sudden hurricane of fire.

Rooker emptied his final few bullets and snatched up the MG-34 dropped by the soldier lying unconscious or dead beneath the steel waterpipe that'd laid him out. He held it at the hip, holding down the trigger, and spewed out sheets of bullets until the belt emptied. There was no time to source fresh ammo, but several bodies lay strewn over the ground. They'd dropped their weapons when the surprise gunfire ripped into them. He found two machine pistols, tucked one under each arm, and he became death. Firing twin bursts into an enemy too demoralized to hit back.

Outnumbered, outgunned, they swept a beleaguered enemy before them, and it looked like they were going to win this one.

* * *

Major Kreis watched the action from the top of the church tower in the center of the town, and he fought back his anger. This couldn't be happening. He had a company of infantry, veterans of the Eastern Front. He had artillery and he had three tanks. He glanced at the lookout standing on the far side of the tower, watching through binoculars.

"Do you see the tanks?"

A pause. "Uh, no, Herr Major. I thought I saw dust, or maybe exhaust smoke, but it may have been mist."

"Three tanks, dammit, they can't have disappeared. Where are they?"

"I don't know, Sir."

"Find them, dammit! They must be here somewhere. How can three tanks disappear?"

"Yessir."

The Major continued to survey the town, watching his men scuttle into cover as the Americans continued to advance. They were so few, yet the ferocity of their attack was slowly pushing his men back, and the remaining enemy tank seemed to have a charmed life, despite one of his artillery pieces continuing to attempt to score a hit.

"Where are our tanks?" he muttered, not knowing he'd spoken aloud.

"They're here, Sir. Coming in from the south-east."

"You can see them? All three?"

"Nossir. Uh, Yessir."

"What're you talking about? Is it yes or no?"

"I see the Panther and the two STuGs, and there's more. I count eight, no, make that fourteen. More are following." He paused, "A total of twenty, the Panther, the STuGs, and seventeen heavy panzers. Several Tigers, three Panzer IVs, and the rest are Panthers."

Kreis gazed up at the heavens. It was a miracle. They'd arrived, the 101st SS Heavy Panzer Battalion, or at least, the remnants of it after the Allied aircraft had repeatedly attacked them. He raced down the narrow spiral stone staircase, rushed into the street, and ran toward the approaching armor. He shouted to several of his men to join him, and he met the advancing armor as they entered the town. The commander was seated with his head and shoulders outside the turret, and when he saw him, he barked an order into his microphone. The tanks slowed and stopped.

"We were delayed, Sir. What are your orders?"

"The enemy is attempting to overrun the town. Grind

them into the dust. Kill them all."

The commander of the first Tiger had dismounted and walked forward to join them. He wore the black uniform of the SS tank crews and an Iron Cross First Class on his breast pocket. Kreis gave it a swift glance. Soon, he too would possess such a decoration. Like Kreis, he was a major.

"What's the situation, Major…?"

"Kreis. We were in danger of losing the town, but if you act quickly, you can retrieve the situation. Enter the town and hit the enemy wherever you find them. I want them all dead."

"How many tanks do they have?"

"One."

"One! And you have a company of anti-tank artillery?" He raised an eyebrow, "Never mind, we will deal with this tank for you. What about prisoners?"

He lost his temper. "Prisoners? How can we take prisoners? We are faced with a tidal wave of enemy troops and armor, and we are fighting for our lives. Remember the words of the Führer, we must show no mercy if we are to prevail. No prisoners."

He shrugged. "We will do what we can, but I cannot face mowing down unarmed men who have surrendered."

He returned a glacial smile. "I will relieve you of that problem, Major. I will order my men to follow the panzers, and they will deal them."

"As you wish." He glanced at the Panther commander. "I will lead the advance. I will order half the panzers to circle the outside of the town to form a barrier to prevent them from escaping. The remainder will enter the town and drive them into the barrier. After that, it is up to this man," he nodded at Kreis,

"To do as he wishes."

He returned to his tank and climbed aboard. The engine roared, and the Tiger maneuvered past the Panther to take the lead. He gave an order, and the entire column rumbled forward.

CHAPTER SIX

18 June 1944

They heard the rumble of tank engines, and they were approaching from the south-east. It had to mean enemy armor, panzers, and Washington glanced around his remaining troops.

Everything has changed. We've gone from defeat to a possible, incredible victory, and now this. A squadron of enemy armor, and what do I have to fight back? A single Sherman and several bazookas, shit!

He glanced at Adams. "Lieutenant, I need two men to take a look on the other side of the town and see what we're up against. Get it done, and I mean now! If it's what I think it is, we're in the shit."

"Yessir."

He looked around, and his eyes found a single man from his platoon. The others were scattered elsewhere in the town. "PFC Crockett, get over there and find out what we're up against."

He was a rookie, but he wasn't dumb. "Sir, it sure sounds like tanks to me."

"I gave you an order, Private. Get over there and check it out."

Crockett shook his head and muttered under his breath, "The asshole must think I'm stupid." Just loud enough for Adams to overhear, the Lieutenant ignored it.

Rooker, Murphy, and Kelly heard the tank engines while they headed through the town, mopping up the occasional enemy soldier trying to continue the fight. They took out five, braver than the rest, who were cowering behind cover, and they rounded a street corner and spotted Crockett. Rooker shouted at him to stop.

"What's going on, soldier?"

He explained Adams' order, and the Sarge nodded. They had to know what they were up against but sending a rookie to carry out such an important reconnaissance wasn't the best way to find out. Chances are he'd get his ass shot off on the way.

"We may as well head that way so you can join us, but they're not far away. What I'm saying is be prepared to duck into cover the moment you see one of those big ugly mothers, before they shoot your head off with an 88mm shell."

"Keep an eye out for snipers," Murphy told him, "A bullet from a Mauser rifle will kill you just as surely as a shell or a burst of machine gun fire from a Tiger tank."

He nodded, grateful to have fallen in with men who seemed to know what they were doing. The four Rangers ran forward another fifty yards and halted. They'd come across a small park, fenced in with an iron railing. In the center was a children's playground, but it wasn't the playground that caught their attention, rather what was trundling toward it, an iron monster riding over the swings, slides, and teeter-totter. A Tiger tank, and the crew spotted them at the same moment. The machine gun roared, sending a hail of bullets toward them. They threw themselves to the ground and crawled into an adjacent building.

"Keep going. We have to get clear," Rooker shouted, "Get into the building and look for a way out the other side where they can't see us."

"They can't machine gun us in here. We should be safe if we say inside," Crockett grunted.

"We're not safe, not from that monster. Murphy, find a way out of here."

"I'm on it."

He raced to the rear of the building and found the door locked. He shoulder-charged the portal to get it open, but the timbers, locks, and ironwork were too solid, and he gave it a burst from the MP-40 that left the padlocks shattered. The door swung open, and he stepped outside into a rear yard surrounded by a solid wall at the back, about six feet high. He ran back into the building.

"I got it open and there's a way out. Let's go!"

They leaped to their feet, and if Crockett had been in any doubt about staying or going, those doubts disappeared. With a shuddering crash of falling masonry, the Tiger smashed into the front wall of the building, and they were just in time. The gunner spotted the movement, and the machine gun sent another long burst of 7.92mm bullets that lashed around them. The dust and smoke surrounded them with a smokescreen, enough to cover them while they raced out the back way. They reached the wall and took a flying leap to get over the top.

They jumped down the other side, but the Tiger hadn't finished with them. It fired a shell that smashed into the wall, demolishing the barrier between them and the tank. All they could do was sprint desperately across the street and dive into the next building. Further back, the roar of powerful engines had reached a cacophony, and Rooker frowned.

"There's more of 'em. It could be that SS Panzer unit they've been looking for. Too damned late for us to warn them, we'll be lucky if we get out of this alive. Shit! Keep moving. We'll find the Company and tell them what they're up against. It's time to get out of here, and I mean a long way out of here."

He charged through the building, and they followed, but the roar of tank engines and the clatter of steel tracks were all around them. Murphy found a staircase fixed to the side of a building, and it led up to a flat roof.

"Sarge, I'll go up and see if I can work out where they're headed."

"Yeah, do that. We'll stay here and cover you."

He raced up the staircase and cast his gaze over as much of the town as he could see, which was plenty. They were everywhere. He counted eight tanks inside the town, and another ten driving around the outside. It didn't take a tactical genius to work out what they planned. To cut them off, and they'd be trapped between more panzers than you could shake a stick at. German soldiers were emerging from cover now things had changed, and in the distance, he saw a team of men struggling to deploy a 75mm anti-tank gun. In a matter of minutes, the entire town would become a death trap.

Three hundred yards away he caught sight of Captain Washington and Lieutenant Adams, waiting in the street close to the square. They'd be waiting for Crockett to report back, and they wouldn't be aware of the steel jaws of the trap closing around them. It was too far away to shout a warning, and he raced back down to ground level to report what he'd seen.

"They're in serious trouble, Sarge. We're all in serious trouble. They're closing the net around the town, and Washington doesn't know what we're up against. We have to warn him."

He nodded. "Lead the way, get moving. Run!"

They ran like crazy, ignoring the danger from snipers, and when Murphy rounded one corner, he came face-to-face with four enemy soldiers walking toward him. He'd been running so fast he reacted too slowly, and they nearly had him as he fumbled with his machine pistol. Almost doesn't cut it, not in war, and Rooker and Kelly were right behind him. They cut loose with scything bursts of automatic fire that tore them into bloody corpses.

"Keep running. We have to warn them!"

They kept running, and Murphy's lungs were on fire, but finally, they made it. He stopped before the company commander, chest heaving with the effort of drawing breath. The others were in no better shape, but Rooker gasped out a warning between sucking in air to his depleted lungs.

He explained the situation in less than a minute.

"Panzers behind us, panzers in front of us, the infantry are coming back, and they're deploying the artillery. They got us in a trap."

"A trap? You mean…"

"I mean we can't go back, and we can't go forward. We're fucked. Sir."

The Captain cursed. "We have to pull back, and now. Where's that Sherman?"

Adams looked sheepish. "Uh, I forgot, Sir. They sent a message. They were on the other side of the town, and they saw enemy armor coming in, too many to tangle with, so they were pulling out to get reinforcements."

"How long before they get back here?"

"They said it all depends."

"Depends on what?"

"On whether we have other units available. If not, they'll request an airstrike on the enemy armor, but the flyboys are also tied up. Too many missions, not enough planes."

"So we're on our own? Jesus Christ, Lieutenant, you could have told me sooner."

"Yessir."

Washington scowled. "We're in a fix, and I don't know how to get out of it. Except to fight. We all know what happens when soldiers surrender in this town. The bastard who runs the German defenses doesn't take prisoners, so all we can do is fight. Fight like crazy."

"Tigers?"

"We have bazookas, so we'll do what we can with them." He looked around, "There's a building over there we could use to make a defensive position. Could be a bank, but whatever it is, that's where we're headed. Get everybody over there, and pray those walls are tough enough to stop an 88mm shell."

NCOs shouted orders, and the survivors of Bravo Company headed toward the bank. The stout main door was locked, and it looked like it could stop a medium-sized shell, but Rooker went around back and returned less than a minute later.

"Rear doors are not so tough; we can get in that way."

They sprinted around back, pushed past a rusty iron gate that had once protected the rear loading area, but now hung drunkenly off its hinges that were eaten away with rust. Rooker charged the door, and it was no match for the weight and strength of the veteran NCO. They filtered inside, and he waited until they were all in.

"With luck, they won't have seen us, but we're outta luck today, so we have to assume they know we're here. Find something to barricade the door, and make sure it's tough enough to hold out against anything they throw at us."

"Against tanks?" Adams said, "I'm not sure we can do that, Sergeant."

"It's either that, or we'll end up the same way as the other poor guys they murdered."

Adams whitened. "Make it good and strong."

Men piled desks and steel filing cabinets against the rear door. It might withstand a burst of machine gun fire, but not much more, and Murphy ran through the building, looking for steps that would lead up to the roof so he could search for a way out. There was no staircase, and he guessed because it was a single-story bank building, they'd built it like a fortress to withstand robbery attempts. Which was fine, except they wouldn't have built it to withstand German panzers. All they could hope was the enemy wasn't aware they'd taken cover in the building.

It was a forlorn hope. He was walking down a set of stone steps that led into the basement, just in case there was another way out. There wasn't, but he heard engines in the street above, and the worst fears of every Ranger in that building were realized when he heard the furious pounding on the front door. Before long they'd decide to demolish the building with shellfire, and there was no way to counter it. They were fucked.

He went further into the basement, which was the bank's strongroom, although empty of any cash. He stopped. To his astonishment, it wasn't empty. There were people in there, around twenty French civilians, men, women, and children. The women and children stared at him in terror, not realizing he wasn't a German soldier come to kill them, and he produced a smile.

"It's okay, folks, we're the good guys. Americans."

"Americans?" A man emerged from a door on the other side of the strong room, his face and clothing covered in dust and dirt, "You have defeated the Boches?"

"Nossir, I'm sorry, we haven't." He explained how they'd been carrying out reconnaissance, and the Germans had brought in heavy armor, "They've surrounded the town, and right now they're outside this building. It's all over. There's nothing more we can do.

Except go down fighting, but I doubt they want to hear that.

The man was elderly, thin, and wrinkled, with the lined, sun-darkened skin of a peasant who'd spent his life working on the land. He gazed at him for several seconds.

"Then what? You die?"

He paused, but they were entitled to know the truth. "Yessir, we can't hold them. There's not a damn thing we can do, and we're cut off, so we can't call in reinforcements."

"How long before they get inside the building?"

Murphy shrugged. "Not long, maybe ten minutes."

"Can you hold them for longer? We need twenty minutes at least."

There was something he didn't understand. He guessed they wanted to say their prayers before the Germans murdered them, and he sympathized. The Krauts wouldn't sympathize. "I don't think so, no. If you want to pray, you'll have to make it quick. Do you have a priest down here?"

"A priest? What would we want with a priest?"

"I thought you wanted to say a final prayer before the end."

"Monsieur, we're getting out. Why would we want to stay longer to say a prayer?"

"Out? You're inside a bank vault. There is no way out."

"There may be a way, but we need more time."

"Mister, why don't you tell me about it?"

He explained how around ninety years before they'd developed the town there'd been an attempt to dig a mine for copper. The idea was ill-conceived and based on the testimony of a land surveyor who'd insisted the townspeople paid him handsomely before he would divulge the place to dig. They paid up, and he disappeared with the cash. They brought in skilled miners from the south of Normandy, who dug straight down fifty feet, before starting to dig a long gallery that pointed to the west. After they'd dug for a thousand yards, and the tunnel emerged on the far side of a low hill close to Evrecy. The plan to find copper was a bust. Wiser heads prevailed, and the stunned townspeople faced up to the facts. They'd been conned.

They covered the entrance to the shaft with concrete to make it safe, and the place had remained empty until forty years ago when the local branch of the Banc Nationale bought the land to build a new branch for the burgeoning business. After that, the failed attempt to get rich with a copper mine was forgotten, except by the man Murphy was talking with.

"I used to run the local library, and I have a keen interest in local history. When the Germans came, it was too late for some of us to evacuate, and we took shelter down here. I remembered the mine, and we went out after dark to find picks and shovels to dig through the floor of the vault. We are almost there."

"How long do you need?"

He spread his hands in a typically Gallic gesture. "Who can say, but we are close, chipping through the last layer of concrete. Perhaps a half-hour, perhaps more, I don't know."

He nodded. "It'll go quicker with a few of our guys to lend a hand. Wait there."

He rushed back up the staircase, found Washington, who was busy working out where the Germans were likely to attack first, and Adams and Rooker were with him.

Washington was a beaten man. "We could be wasting our time. They have tanks out there, so they're sure to hit us first with a volley of shells. It don't make no difference, they'll tear this place into rubble."

Lieutenant Adams saw Murphy, and he gave him a hard glance. "What're you doing here, soldier? Don't you have a post to go to?"

"Lt, you need to listen to this." He explained about the basement strongroom, and the French civilians digging down through the floor to reach the abandoned shaft, "It means we have a chance."

He snorted. "You're telling me this shaft has been there for ninety years? Don't you get it, Murphy? In those days they used timber to shore up the tunnels. Timber rots, the roof collapses, and the shaft would've disappeared years ago. Forget it."

Washington wasn't so sure. "Carter, it could be worth a try. We're out of options."

"Captain, before I joined the Army, I was thinking about becoming a mining engineer, following in my father's footsteps. I spent my early years learning everything there was to learn about mining operations, and I promise you that shaft will be long gone. Those poor bastards down there are wasting their time."

They all turned as they heard something heavy hit the front door. It wasn't a tank shell, because the door would've burst open, along with half the front of the building. A soldier had been peering out through a gap in the shattered windows, and he shouted out they had a couple of guys out there with sledgehammers, trying to smash the door open. They were puzzled why they weren't shelling the building until Rooker supplied the likely answer. "Remember, this is a bank. I'm guessing they don't want to do too much damage, in case there're valuables inside. It gives us a bit more time."

"Time for what?" Adams choked in exasperation, "For Christ's sake we don't have time for this."

"Maybe, maybe not. Murphy, show me what you've got in the basement."

They went below, and the elderly French civilian came out to greet them. "You wish to see the shaft?"

"You got that right, pop."

"Follow me."

He led them past the women and children into a small chamber on the far side of the room. Four men were working away, hacking at the concrete with picks and shovels, and after a quick look, Washington nodded. "I'll get you some help."

He raced away and returned minutes later with four of his beefiest, strongest Rangers. "Take those picks and try to break through as fast as possible. We're all depending on you, especially the women and children. Get to it, and we'll try to hold them off to give you more time."

He climbed back up the stairs with Murphy, and he muttered, "If Lieutenant Adams is correct, they're on a hiding to nothing. I hope to Christ he's wrong, but I don't think he is. Murphy, you can shoot. Find yourself a place where you have a view through the shutters and see if you can pick them off when they get close. Forget the guys with the sledgehammers. It'll take them a month of Sundays to break down the door. Concentrate on the real threats. Those Krauts in the tanks are exposed, and if you can take down a couple of them, it may slow them down."

Rooker was standing close, listening. "Over there, Kelly found a gap to poke a rifle through without them seeing you. Do what you can."

He joined Dan, who moved aside to allow him to peer through the chink in the wooden shutters where the wood had warped. He saw the two troopers with the sledgehammers battering at the front door no more than ten feet away, but what was parked fifty feet away got his interest. A Tiger tank, and just like Washington had said, the head and shoulders of the commander were exposed, and the Kraut was talking to a man he recognized as Kreis. The butcher who'd ordered the murder of the prisoners and would've murdered him if he hadn't gotten away.

It was a tempting target, but he had to save it for later. The real threat came from the squat, iron monster, the tank. Shooting the commander wouldn't negate the threat, but they'd panic, probably reverse away while they worked out their next move. Which would probably mean returning to take revenge, demolishing the bank building, and grabbing the money inside. All it would achieve was to give them time, and time was what they needed.

Provided that shaft hasn't collapsed.

He poked the muzzle of his rifle through the tiny gap in the warped woodwork, and there wasn't enough room to use the accurate yet cumbersome telescopic sight. He'd have to use iron sights, although at fifty feet, it wouldn't present a problem. He removed the scope and tried again. This time, he had a clear view of the target, and he lined up the foresight on the notched rear sight, steadying himself to take the shot. Despite the short-range, he had to do it right, the first time. The sledgehammers beating at the door were a distraction, and he shut them out of his mind.

He wasn't snuffing out a man's life. He was immobilizing a massive Tiger tank. Fifty-four tons of toughened steel armed with an 88mm main gun, two MG-34 machine guns. Each vehicle carried a crew of five men, the commander, gunner, loader, driver, and radio operator. One small 30.06 bullet, and it didn't seem possible it could make a difference, until he squeezed the trigger and saw the bloom of red in the center of the tank commander's chest.

All hell broke loose a split a second after he pulled the

muzzle back inside the shutter. Men shouted, searching for the source of the shot, looking every which way, up to the roof of the bank, staring at the door and windows, looking at the sides. Some even looked up at the sky, as if an aircraft flying overhead had fired off a single shot.

The German had jerked backward with the force of the bullet, and he was lying half in and half out of the turret as the huge vehicle backed away, disappearing into a side street. Kelly had found a spy hole in another part of the shutter, and he nodded.

"Nice shooting, Jack. It'll take them a while to get over it, but they'll be back, and they'll have the hatches battened down tight. We won't get any more chances like that."

"You're right. We have one chance, and that's to find that shaft."

"And pray it's still there."

"Don't worry, I'm praying."

The enemy tankers recovered fast, pissed off by the death of their commander, and three more panzers appeared in front of the bank. Like Kelly had said, they were all battened down, and a voice shouted an order at the two men with sledgehammers, and they jogged away. The three turrets turned, the barrels of their guns aimed at the building, and Murphy shouted, "Run!"

They left their viewpoint at the shattered window just before the first shell smashed through the front wall, which collapsed in a heap of dust and rubble. There was one place to go, the basement strongroom, and Washington was already shouting at the men to get down there. They vaulted down the stairs. Some jumped from the top to land sprawling at the bottom in their haste, just as a second and a third shell hit the building. The basement entrance was unprotected by a door, and rubble and dust rained down around them. Women screamed, children cried, while the French civilians and the Rangers doggedly kept hacking at the concrete. More shells landed, and heaps of rubble tumbled down into the basement, forming a pile at the bottom of the steps that grew larger and larger each shell landed.

The inevitable happened, and the rubble filled the basement entrance. They were entombed, and still the shells smashed into the building above.

Washington ran to the men who were digging. "How much longer?"

The darkness was absolute until a man lit a candle, and two Rangers found flashlights. The dim lighting enabled the men digging the hole to resume work. They redoubled their efforts, soaked with sweat and choking on air that was thick with dust. They were cut off from the outside, which meant the crowded strong room was running out of oxygen and the air increasingly foul. They worked like demons. Swinging their picks, shoveling furiously at the rubble, and still, there was no sign of any opening.

The Rangers stood watching, crowded into the tiny, dark space, and every man had the same question. If the shaft was still there, how much further did they have to dig before they reached it? Shells continued smashing into the building above, and abruptly there was a jarring crash as chunks of stone fell from above. In their fury, the Germans had decided to bury the Rangers alive, in revenge for the killing of their tank commander. Tons of stone were falling through the roof into the basement. Soon the entire roof would give way and the dark, fetid space would become a tomb, burying them alive in hundreds of tons of broken stone.

There was nothing more they could do, except watch. Some of the women were fingering rosary beads, their lips moving in silent prayer. Others were trying to quieten and calm the children, and Murphy pitied them.

This isn't their war. Evrecy's a sleepy French town that just happens to be in the way of the Allied advance. They don't deserve to face a dark, choking death, don't deserve to face any death, and yet…

"The pick went through! We may be there!"

The shout came from Rooker, stripped to the waist to take a turn with the pick. Flexing his tough muscles, like the branches of an old oak tree, and smashing the steel tool into the concrete. Pitting his huge strength against the unyielding concrete, and his efforts paid dividends. Washington rushed over with a borrowed flashlight and shone it down into the six-inch hole that'd opened up.

"You're right. It's the shaft, and it's still there. We're nearly out of here!"

"We don't know about the tunnel, Captain." Adams had walked over to peer down into the tiny gap, "Like I said, there's next to no chance it'll still be there."

"Next to no chance is better than no chance, Lieutenant. Sergeant, give it everything you have."

Rooker swung again, and again. He was like a mechanical digger, smashing with the toughened steel blade, and against his onslaught, the concrete stood no chance. The hole opened, became a foot wide, two feet wide, and when it was three feet wide Washington called a halt.

"Somebody take a flashlight, get down there, and see what we have."

Murphy stepped forward and peered down the dark shaft. His familiar feelings of vertigo resurfaced, and he steeled himself to fight it off. It wasn't as bad as it used to be, since that time when he'd dropped down a deep shaft to get through to an enemy gun battery. It was still there, still a dark, invisible force nagging at him not to do it, but it was one of those rare times when you told your brain to get in line, and it obeyed. He was getting over the worst of his secret fear, and he felt a sense of exultation. If he survived, he could get these people out of this dark tomb. That was the trick. Survival.

"I can do it, Captain."

Washington peered into the hole, and he looked doubtful. "You'll need a rope. Sergeant, pass the word, somebody look around and find some rope."

It took less than a minute to explore the cramped, claustrophobic strongroom, and they came up with nothing. Rooker suggested removing their coats and tying them together, like a line of bed sheets kids used to fasten together to leave their bedrooms for late-night romantic assignations. Before they could start the rubble blocking the staircase began to move, sliding deeper into the room. Leaving less space, and people crowded closer together as it continued to move.

"Somebody loan me a flashlight."

Kelly handed him a flashlight, and he played the beam around the exposed shaft. There were no handholds and no ladder, which was no surprise. But the sides of the shaft had been roughly done, and over the years the ground had shifted, leaving cracks and imperfections in the wall he had to climb down. It was enough. It had to be enough. He swung down into the shaft, holding onto the rough concrete opening the Sarge had hacked out, searching with his boot for his first foothold. He found one that would hold him and let go one hand, dropped lower, searching for a handhold.

At first, the going wasn't too bad, but as he dropped lower, the walls of the shaft had crumbled and decayed, and his foothold slipped when the ground crumbled. He managed to anchor the other boot into a fissure, but his handhold slipped, and suddenly, the entire wall of the shaft was crumbling into dust. He estimated he was halfway down, grabbing and scrabbling for foot and toe holds as he fell. He managed to slow his fall, and at the last moment shone the beam of the flashlight down to see he'd almost reached the base of the shaft. He bent his legs at the knees, letting his body go limp to absorb the shock. Like he'd been trained for parachute drops when he joined the Rangers, but he still hit the bottom with a jarring thud that knocked the wind out of him.

"Murphy, are you okay down there?" Kelly's voice, and a moment later a weak flashlight beam pierced the darkness, "We heard a crash, thought maybe you've fallen."

"I'm good. Give me a minute, I'll take a look around."

He played the beam around the base of the shaft, and he found it immediately, the horizontal tunnel they'd dug in their fruitless attempts to mine copper. It was narrow and low, no more than three feet wide and four feet high, but enough for them to crawl through. They'd shored up the roof with timbers, and as far as he could tell, the timbers hadn't rotted enough to collapse, although closer inspection showed the growing decay. It wouldn't be long before they were like cardboard, and a roof fall would soon follow. So far, it hadn't happened.

He returned to the base of the shaft. "The tunnel is still there, and it looks passable. I think we can make it."

"Roger that."

It was Rooker who shouted the reply, and a moment later the improvised line of Ranger jackets reached him, all of them tied at the arms. He wasn't certain it would hold. Probably the kids and the other civilians, but the Rangers were bigger and heavier, which was no surprise. They'd eaten three square meals a day, while the French civilians had suffered from a serious lack of food. Courtesy of the Third Reich that had seized the greater part of their foodstuffs, crops, and animals, transporting them to Germany, "We'll start sending them down now."

"Send the civilians down first, and one at a time. It'll be easier on the line."

"I hear you, Murphy, but we're almost out of time up here. The rubble is sliding deeper into the room. I'm lowering the first one down now."

It was a young mother, clutching a baby to her chest tied in an improvised harness. The infant couldn't have been more than a few months old, and the woman was shaking in terror. He untied the line from around her body, and as it snaked back up to the top, he pointed her toward the tunnel. "You need to get inside. There'll be more coming down, and they'll drop right on top of you."

"It's dark."

"Be thankful, if you can tell it's dark, it means you're alive, Madame." He raised his voice, "Move it."

Already the next person was coming down, and one by one they lowered them down until the tunnel was filled with a long line of civilians, all of them reluctant to push deeper into the unknown. It was getting crowded, and he shouted at them to keep moving, feeling guilty at giving the terrified people a tongue lashing, but saving their lives was more important than sparing their feelings. The first of the Rangers reached the bottom, and it was Kelly.

"Dan, get those people moving along the tunnel. We have to clear space for our people. They're scared, so give them your flashlight. All they have is a candle, so maybe when we can see a bit more they'll keep moving."

"I have a better idea. I can get past them and reach the front, lead them through. Give them some encouragement."

"Go for it."

He wriggled into the tunnel and squeezed past grumbling and protesting people. Although the language was French, he had a good idea he was going on a crash course in how to swear in the Gaelic language. But it worked, he reached the front, and the line moved faster. Adams was next, and the rest of the Rangers reached the bottom of the shaft and followed. The last man down was Washington, and he gave Murphy a nod of approval.

"You did good, son." He pointed to the tunnel, "After you."

Murphy followed the long line of people crawling along the tunnel, and it was slow, much too slow. Too slow because the rubble from the collapsed building had reached the hole in the floor, and the first chunks of concrete fell to the bottom of the shaft just as Washington entered the tunnel. He jerked further inside as a cascade of dust and concrete showered down from above. He stopped, Murphy stopped, both men waiting to assess the danger from above, and the rubble continued to cascade down the shaft. The dust had entered the tunnel, swirling amongst the people crawling through, and when it reached the civilians, they knew there'd be a panic. Even worse if they discovered the truth, they were entombed in the dark, abandoned copper mine.

Washington shouted, "Pass the word to the front. Tell them there's nothing to worry about. And tell them to hurry."

Men called ahead, and the line picked up speed, but the improvement was short-lived. They slowed again, and Washington fumed with impatience. "I've got a bad feeling about this. There's some kind of a hold-up. Find out what's going on."

The word went along the line, but Kelly had already sent a message back, and it reached them less than a minute later. Apparently, some of the civilians spoke a little English.

"The tunnel's blocked. He said the roof has collapsed. There's no way to get through. We have to go back."

Washington told Murphy to pass on the reply they had to clear a way through. "Don't say we're trapped, they'll panic. Just make it clear to Kelly we have to get through."

He passed on the message, and the reply came back minutes later. "He says it's impossible. There's no way to get through."

He glanced at Washington, and Washington glanced back at him. They had to face the truth. They were entombed in this dark, stifling pit in the ground. Already it was hard to breathe after the blockage both ends had cut off the supply of air, and soon, people would start to fall unconscious.

For the first time the Captain looked beaten. "There's no

way out!"

CHAPTER SEVEN

19 June 1944

Washington looked like his whole world had collapsed around him. He was tough and he was clever, but he hadn't been trained to deal with this situation. To be trapped in a dark, almost airless hole deep underground beneath the Normandy battlefields, with no way out. They couldn't go forward, and they couldn't go back, leaving them with a single option. To stay there and die, gasping out their last.

Murphy didn't have the weight of command on his shoulders, but he had something maybe the Captain didn't have. Back in his hometown of Whitefish, Montana, he'd trained to rescue people. Okay, maybe not from holes in the ground. He'd been a member of the local Mountain Rescue, and he'd learned early on that saving life was paramount, and you didn't give up until all hope had gone. And even then, some men didn't give up. He was one such man.

"I'll go up there and find out what's going on. There has to be a way, Captain."

He nodded in acknowledgment, but he didn't look convinced. Murphy began to slide past the Rangers squashed into the tunnel, squeezing past the men, snagging on rifles and equipment. He left his precious MP-40 and the Springfield before he went further, knowing he'd never get through if they snagged on the tunnel walls. When he reached the civilians, they were close to desperation, and the panic was like a thick fog swirling around them. They were in a bad way, and if they didn't find a way out fast, they'd die even quicker as panic caused them to gulp in more oxygen, depleting the little they had left.

He fought his way to the front, and Kelly was there, stabbing at the thick earth with his combat knife. He nodded to Murphy. "I don't think there's any way through, but if they think we're going somewhere, they may not panic so fast."

He kept his voice low, so they didn't overhear him, and it made sense. He looked at the blockage, and at first sight, there didn't seem to be any hope. A solid wall of earth had fallen into the tunnel, and it could extend for a few feet or a few hundred feet. There was no way to know. He took the flashlight and played around the edges, attempting to find any indication of the length of the blockage. He looked at the sides, looked at the floor, and it was solid, packed earth and rock. He played the beam over the roof, and at first, he saw nothing. The second look, and still nothing.

Yet maybe he was wrong. There was something there, a dark shadow, and he put his head closer and found it was a fissure in the solid wall of earth and rock. He drew his combat knife and stabbed at the earth, and as it came away, the fissure widened. There was something there, a narrow gap, but he couldn't tell how much of a gap. Maybe inches, maybe more, but he kept stabbing with the knife, pulling away impacted clods of earth, ripping away chunks of stone, and the gap widened. Enough for a cat to get through, although he had no way of knowing what was left several feet further along the roof fall.

People's lives were at stake, and he kept going, stabbing, ripping at the blockage, while Kelly cleared away the debris he'd thrown behind him. Gradually, the gap widened, and he got further in, and then it narrowed again. He kept going, faster, using the knife blade, his hands, ripping away his nails as he pulled out stones that refused to budge, scrabbling around them, dragging away more debris, and he slowly advanced. But it was too slow, and the air was stale. From further back in the tunnel, he could hear the low moan of despairing, panicking civilians, and soon it would rise into hysteria. When that happened, there'd be no stopping them from becoming an out-of-control, heaving mob, and they'd suffocate and die sooner rather than later.

The minutes dragged by, and he lost all track of time. His hands were bloody and raw, and he had to work hard to suck in air, knowing the countdown clock was fast approaching zero, the moment when people would start to fall unconscious, and then they'd die.

"Hurry it up," Kelly shouted hoarsely, "They can't last much longer."

He didn't reply. He'd heard something. A noise. It was bad news. The sound of earth and rock moving, like the tunnel was about to collapse even further, and the gap he'd battled to widen would disappear in a choking avalanche of dirt and rock that would sound the death knell.

"What's up? Why have you stopped?"

"You don't want to know, Dan."

He wriggled close to him. Okay, keep your voice down and you can tell me now. I guess it's bad."

"Something's moving further along the tunnel. I think the roof could be collapsing even more. If there ever was a way through, it's about to disappear, and maybe the entire tunnel will collapse."

"You're sure? There can't be another explanation?"

"I can't think of one, although I wish I could. What else could be causing that noise? Something is causing the ground to move."

Kelly managed to crack a joke. "I never thought we'd complain about the earth moving, Jack. Is that supposed to be…"

"Never mind that, we may have minutes or even seconds left before it collapses, that's how long we have to work out our next move."

Kelly looked at him, and he didn't need to put it into words. What could there be to work out when you were trapped by hundreds of tons of earth and rubble in the black, airless hole in the ground? "I guess we wait for… you know what I mean?"

"I know."

He meant the end for both of them, the two Rangers who'd done everything together. Who'd become the best of pals despite their opposite backgrounds and outlooks on life. Who'd planned to keep each other alive and end the war together. Their war was about to end real soon. He thought about Clemence Delon, the French girl he'd met in Normandy and had fallen for a big way.

It hurts that I'll never see her again, like a knife in the guts, yet I have to accept it, and hope to Christ she survives the war. Maybe she'll find somebody else and make a new life.

His head jerked around as he heard more earth and rubble moving. He waited for the rumble that would announce a total collapse, but it didn't happen. Instead, a trickle of earth showered down from the gap he'd been working to widen, and to their amazement, a light shone through.

"Is anybody there?"

He couldn't believe it. No, he was hearing things. He thought about Clemence, and his mind conjured up her voice, like a disembodied spirit issuing from the depths, and he shook his head to clear it. He heard another voice, a male voice, an American voice, talking in low tones, like he was discussing something with another person.

Maybe I'm going crazy. It's the lack of oxygen, yeah, that has to be it. Hypoxia, isn't that what they call it? I learned about that in Mountain Rescue training, although it didn't make a huge difference in the mountains of Montana. More like the taller peaks, like Everest and the Eiger in Switzerland. Why am I thinking of mountains at a time like this? I'm going nuts. First, I thought I heard Clemence, then an American voice, and now I'm up a damned mountain.

Maybe it was the best way to go. With the face of a pretty French girl at the front of your mind, and at back the thought of scaling the tallest mountain peaks in the world to fulfill a lifetime ambition.

He heard the voice again. "Is anybody left alive in there?"

It was her. It couldn't be. Maybe she was dead, beckoning to him from the afterlife, and there were worse things to look forward to after death. So why not reply? "Yeah, I'm here. We're all here."

A pause. "Jack?"

What the hell's going on?

He was having a conversation on the very edge of the grave. "Yeah, PFC Jack Murphy, in the flesh. But not for much longer, I'll be with you soon."

"We've almost reached you. It won't be long."

The edge of an entrenching tool sliced through the tiny gap, more earth cascaded around him, and he was looking at a face. The burly face, covered in dirt, of a Ranger. A man he recognized as the Third Platoon NCO. "Charlie Briggs? Corporal Briggs? Is that you?"

"Yeah, it's me. We're trying to reach you. Give me a minute, and we'll get you out."

It was still hard to believe, impossible to believe. They should've been dead, and somehow, they were getting through to them from the other end of the tunnel, but how? The shovel pushed through the last of the earth, and Briggs cleared away a gap big enough to get through. Fresh air flooded in, and he sucked it into his lungs, hearing the gasps of relief from further back.

"It's wide enough to get through, but I don't know how long it'll hold, so you'd better get your asses into gear and get out while you still can."

Clemence was staring at him, her face also covered in dirt, and she smiled with relief. "I thought you were dead."

"You weren't the only one. But how?"

"Charlie said we need to get out fast, so we'll talk later."

They turned and began crawling back the way they'd

come, and he shouted to the people behind them they were getting out before he followed. They were within thirty feet of the entrance, and they crawled out of the hole with a sense of both celebration and disbelief. As soon as he was on his feet, he helped the civilians and waited until they were all clear before he looked for Clemence. She was standing right behind him.

"Okay, tell me how you knew we were in there?"

"We saw the German tanks and artillery shelling a building, and we worked out it was the old Banc Nationale. I guessed the survivors from Bravo Company had to be inside. After all, why would they shell an empty building? Which meant you were surrounded and trapped, and I found a local farmer who'd lived here all his life and who knew of the project to dig for copper. He said the shaft was buried below the bank, and I figured there was just a remote possibility you'd try to get out that way. He showed me where the old mine works emerged, and I persuaded Corporal Briggs to help me search it and see if it was still open. Charlie found the blockage, and he started to dig in case there were any survivors."

He was the right man for the job. Built like a tank and heavily muscled, like Sergeant Rooker, the kind of man who could go toe-to-toe with an earthmover and manage to keep up.

She grinned. "It worked, and I found you. It must've been terrible in that old tunnel. Those people who got out look real bad. Even some of the Rangers."

He thought back to the desperate escape from the ruined building, and the knowledge they'd got out of one fix only to be entombed in another. But they'd made it out, and he nodded. "Bad enough. When I heard your voice, I thought I was hearing things."

It took them a lot of time to recover. They were exhausted, all suffering from hypoxia, and many lay on the ground while they recovered. Or maybe said prayers of gratitude to their God. The French tended to be religious. He could have suggested they acknowledge how Clemence Delon and Charlie Briggs had helped God stage their miraculous rescue, but he guessed they already knew. As they emerged into the open air, most walked around to restore their circulation, while they sucked in the precious, life-giving oxygen. The mine entrance was out of sight of the town, hidden behind a low hill, which was just as well.

The Battalion had come up, and along with it a unit of Shermans, a total of sixteen tanks, and whoever was in command had decided they'd had enough of screwing around. The reconnaissance had been painful, but it'd proved the Germans were still defending Evrecy, and they had no choice but to go in and clear them out.

General Shriver had arrived and taken command. Major Danvers who headed up the Battalion didn't look too pleased. They needed to hit the enemy with a hard punch to shake them up, push them out of the town, and send them scurrying eastward. Shriver wasn't that kind of an officer. He was a man more inclined to make sure he'd covered his back before he made a move. Taken care to make sure his every move followed regulations and order his men to do it by the book. Lieutenant Adams seemed pleased to have what he regarded as a level head in command. Washington stayed chatting to Adams, and he wasn't so sure.

"When I told him about the German armor, he said the Shermans could handle it, but he hasn't seen those Tigers and Panthers in action. The way to take them out is to hit them hard where they least expect it. Shoot first, make sure you hit the target, and leave the bastards burning before you hit the next one. Give them half a chance, and they'll blast our guys with everything they have, and they sure have plenty. If they get it wrong, those Shermans will be heading for the junkyard. And the tank crews for the graveyard."

Sergeant Rooker was standing nearby, sipping at a chipped enamel mug of hot coffee, courtesy of the Battalion cookhouse. "Captain, aren't you forgetting something? The artillery. Do they know what they're up against? Those PAK-37s pack a powerful punch. We could be biting off more than we can chew."

Adams subjected him to a frosty gaze. "Sergeant, you're an NCO, and your job is to make sure the men obey orders, not dictate tactics to senior officers. I suggest you attend to your men and leave the serious stuff to those in the know."

Rooker threw up an immaculate salute. "Yes, Sir, at once, Sir. It's good to know the battle will be in the hands of General Shriver, a man with extensive experience of warfighting."

It was doubtful Adams understood the irony. The truth was Shriver had a reputation as a desk warrior. A man who fought his war is with military manuals, with orders in triplicate, arranging his soldiers like he was fighting battles in the previous century. Some men suggested he saw war in terms of lines of blue and gray-clad soldiers. Firing muskets and rifles throwing up clouds of blue smoke as they exchanged bodies and fell in neat ranks.

"Did I hear somebody mention my name?" Unnoticed, the General had strolled toward them, "I take it you were discussing the coming action. I've been thinking about the best way to handle this, and in my opinion, we do it by the book. A feint frontal attack toward the town, and I intend to split the bulk of our troops and armor into two groups. They'll hit the flanks where the Jerries least expect it. They'll be throwing everything forward to meet the attack, and that's when we hit them from both flanks. Take them by surprise, and we'll roll them up like an old carpet." He grinned like he'd already achieved a stunning victory.

Adams was nodding his head in agreement. "It's a sound plan, General. Right on the button."

"I think so. What about you, Captain Washington? You don't look so happy. Did you have something on your mind?"

Before he could answer, Rooker interrupted. "Begging the General's pardon, you could be making a big mistake. The enemy has heavy tanks and artillery inside the town, and when we go in there possibly will be waiting for us."

He replied slowly like he was explaining a simple fact to a child. "You obviously don't know anything about tactics, Sergeant. My way is the best way, believe me, it says so in the manuals."

"What if the Germans have read the same manuals?"

His lips tightened, and he glared back at him. "Those manuals are written by men with a great deal of military experience. The attack will succeed, no question." He glanced at Adams. "Don't you agree, Lieutenant?"

"Yessir, it's a sound plan."

"You, Captain?"

"I'm not so sure, General."

His expression darkened. "You'd better make up your mind, Washington. If you're not so sure, maybe you're the wrong man to lead Bravo Company."

"I believe I can handle this, Sir. I won't let the Company down. No matter what happens."

"You'd better be right." His expression relaxed, "I know you have worries, but here is something that may ease your mind. We have a guide who knows the area, and he'll show us the best way into the town. He's a man who knows the area well. He's a Brit, but he spent a lot of time vacationing in this area. His family used to own an old French château. His name is Major Cuthbert Lawson, and he also happens to be an experienced tank officer, so this is a guy who knows his way around. They sent him out to replace Major Fraser, the previous liaison officer, killed in action. If you have any questions about Evrecy, he's the man to answer them."

He gave them a satisfied look, as if the battle had already ended in victory, spun on his heel, and stalked away. Adams made some excuse about needing to attend to something, and he left. Both men glanced at a familiar figure walking toward them, a tanker. Sergeant Chris Davidson, the commander of the surviving Sherman that'd reached them in Evrecy, and then pulled back in the face of the overwhelming force of heavy panzers.

He stuttered an apology. "I tried to persuade them to hit them with an airstrike to knock out those tanks, but they said they were too busy elsewhere. I'm sorry, guys, I feel like I left you all in the lurch."

Rooker held out his hand to shake. "Forget it, it wasn't your fault. You can only do so much with that tin can of yours, and if you'd stayed, you wouldn't be here now talking to us, you'd be burned to a cinder inside the wreckage of your tank." He looked around and saw Murphy and Kelly standing nearby, chatting with Clemence Delon. "Guys, come on over here over. Look who's arrived."

They greeted Davidson and shook hands. I told Chris he had nothing to apologize for, but he wasn't listening. "Did I hear right; they're bringing in Loony Lawson?"

There was a silence, broken when Murphy replied, "What do you know about him?"

"He's the guy who ordered a regiment of British tanks to enter a town without prior reconnaissance. They ran into a bunch of Tigers and lost a dozen vehicles. He has a lot of military experience, but he learned it during the First World War. He acquired a reputation as a clever tactician, but toward the end, in October 1918, a shell struck his trench. They say he hasn't been the same since."

He grimaced. "You're saying we're in trouble?"

"What I'm saying is if they listen to Loony Lawson, we're in deep shit. There's something else General Shriver didn't mention. Gas."

"Gas?"

"That's right. So far, we haven't been able to capture Cherbourg, so they have to bring everything ashore from the Mulberry Harbors. They're working well, but we have a fraction of the gas we need to continue fighting the war. There's a huge shortage, and it won't end until they take Cherbourg. It's so bad General Montgomery has canceled a major operation to push through to Caen and split the German lines. We must take Evrecy to open up an alternative route, but the Germans have begun to realize its strategic value, and they aren't likely to give in just yet."

"Do we have enough gas to win this one?"

He gave them a wintry smile. "That's the sixty-four-dollar question."

* * *

"Major Kreis, we need fuel."

He gazed back at the SS-Hauptsturmführer Ernst Weber, the captain who took command of the Heavy panzers after the death of the previous commander. Killed by an American sniper position inside the bank building.

"Fuel? What do you mean?"

"Major, a Tiger tank consumes five gallons of gasoline for every mile it travels on the battlefield. Our tanks are running dry, and we can't last much longer."

He shrugged in irritation. "What do you expect me to do about it?"

He returned an insolent half-smile. "I understand you're a Wehrmacht transport officer, so you have a responsibility to make sure supplies of fuel get through to the front-line units. The frontline is here, and we need supplies of fuel if we are to fight and win the coming battle."

He stared back at him for several seconds and drew himself up to his full height. He was taller by three inches than the stocky Hauptsturmführer, and he stared down at him, his lips twisted in a sneer.

"We're holding a French town, besieged by overwhelming enemy forces. The defense of this town is paramount if we are to stop the Allies from advancing further. The Americans have become aware of its strategic importance, and if you're in any doubt, consider how hard the Americans have tried to take it.

The French collaborator who reported at least twenty Sherman tanks within one mile of the town has been back to confirm they are preparing an attack, and you can be sure it will come very soon." He raised his voice to a high-pitched shout, almost a scream. A trickle of spittle rolled down his chin, "Don't come whining to me about fuel! You're in command of the tanks, and if you fail to make arrangements to refuel your vehicles, I will regard it as a dereliction of duty, and have you shot! Do you hear me?"

Weber stared back at him. "Major, I have done everything possible to obtain supplies of fuel, but none exists. I have radioed for headquarters to send us a refueling tanker, and they replied they don't have enough fuel to fill the tank of General Erich Marcks' staff car. I take it you're aware the Allies have repeatedly bombed the Romanian oil fields and cut off most of the production?"

"I heard that nonsense, but I didn't believe it. It's enemy propaganda. The Führer would never allow the enemy to destroy our vital oil supplies. The Luftwaffe would've shot down any bombers who dared to approach."

Weber snorted. "I don't believe the Führer was at the controls of one of the aircraft sent to defend the oilfields. The pilots who did take part are dead or prisoners of the Russians. Major, it doesn't matter what you believe. There is no fuel. You are the transport officer, and it is your job to find some."

"How much do you need?"

A shrug. "A thousand gallons would last for a couple of hours. Say five thousand gallons to keep my tanks moving for the next few days, provided they see no more than a limited action."

He threw up his hands. "Where the hell would I get five thousand gallons of fuel? It is out of the question, Captain. We'll have to fight with what you have."

"In that case, you'd better hope the battle doesn't last for longer than an hour. Any more, and my tanks will grind to a halt."

He walked away, ignoring Kreis' 'Heil Hitler.' Leaving the Major to grapple with another problem. He called for the officer he'd appointed his adjutant, Leutnant Meyer.

"The trucks are still hidden outside the town?"

"Yes, they're still there, waiting for the order to come in and hitch up the guns when we need to retreat."

"Retreat! What the hell are you talking about?"

"But, Sir, our forces are retreating all across Normandy. I assumed…"

"Don't assume, Meyer. Get those trucks back into the town, drain the fuel tanks into cans, and advise Hauptsturmführer Weber he will have what fuel we can find."

"And if we need to pull back with the guns?"

"It won't happen if we defeat the Americans. Soon, we will have more fuel."

"Yes, Sir." He didn't look convinced, "From where?"

"Headquarters will send us fuel." He spotted a man trying to get his attention. A civilian, and he recognized the French collaborator who'd remained loyal to the Germans. In return for safe passage to the Reich, and a handsome reward should the war go badly, "Wait. I need to speak with this man."

He waved for the man to come forward. He didn't like him, didn't trust him. His name was Bernard Marais, and he'd worked as an itinerant farm laborer and handyman before the

Germans arrived. He'd offered them his services, spying on his fellow Frenchman, especially Jews, many of whom had been arrested by the Gestapo after he betrayed them.

Marais was thin, weedy, ferret-like, and he snatched off his greasy hat, displaying an almost bald head, with just a few wisps of sandy-colored hair remaining.

"General, I have information you may find useful."

He recoiled from the stink of cheap wine on his breath and sighed. No matter how many times he told him, the man was determined to jump him several steps in the promotion ladder. "Yes, yes, I know about the tanks, and you have been rewarded with a small bonus. Unless you have something else for me?"

His eyes narrowed and his expression became even more cunning. "I heard your tanks and vehicles might be short of fuel."

He cursed. It was true, but he worried this man should be aware of the problem. If he could sell information to the Germans, he could sell information to the Allies.

"Perhaps, perhaps not. What business is it of yours?"

He bared his lips in a ghastly semblance of a smile. "There is a village about seven miles from here, a place called Monts-en-Bessin. During the First War, in 1917, the French government built several supply depots across France, with hundreds of drums of fuel hidden underground in case the war went on for much longer. Armies were using more and more tanks and airplanes, and they understood the need to have reserve supplies of fuel they could bring up to the front at short notice. There is one such depot at Monts-en-Bessin."

Kreis fought to keep his voice calm. "How much fuel?"

"Hundreds of drums, around fifty thousand liters."

He did the math, and what this scruffy peasant had described was more valuable than gold. Ten thousand gallons of gasoline, enough to keep the tanks fighting for long enough to win the battle; "You can guide us to this place?"

"I think I can remember the location. A little money for me to buy food for my family would help."

Kreis was aware he didn't have a family, and it was hard to consider any woman agreeing to marry this man. He didn't care, what mattered was Marais had just handed him the means to win, to conquer the Allies. "I will arrange another bonus, Bernard. You're staying in the town?"

"There is a bar at the side of the square, L'Auberge. I thought I might find refreshment inside."

"Remain in the bar, and don't get too drunk. I will send a man for you when I need you."

"Yes, General."

He walked away, and Kreis swung his gaze back to his adjutant. "Leutnant Meyer, get the trucks. After dark we'll get that peasant to guide us to this village, load up with fuel drums, and bring them back here for the tanks. You can advise Hauptsturmführer Weber he will have his fuel."

* * *

The Brit arrived at midday; in the passenger seat of a peculiar tracked vehicle the Brits called a 'Bren Carrier.' Which was no surprise, because the tracked reconnaissance vehicle mounted a Bren gun for the passenger to pour fire on the enemy. The man gripping the weapon looked as if he'd give anything for the chance to show the Germans what he was capable of. He jumped out of the vehicle even before it lurched to a stop close to where Washington, Rooker, Murphy, Kelly, and Clemence were chatting with Chris Davidson about the insurmountable fuel problem.

He glanced at Washington, recognizing his rank tabs. "Are you in charge here, Captain?"

"That would be General Shriver, Sir. I command Bravo Company."

He looked at each of them in turn, and his gaze rested on Clemence for much longer. Which gave them a chance to size him up, and he didn't need to introduce himself as Major Lawson for them to know this was the replacement for Fraser, 'Loony' Lawson. The reason for the nickname was obvious. He was swivel-eyed. His eyes looked every which way, but not at the same time. He couldn't stop moving his tall body, twitching and jerking his arms, his stick-thin legs, and even his long, narrow face, as if continually jolted with bolts of electricity. His uniform was a mix of American khaki pants, a British battledress blouse, surmounted by a brown leather transport driver's jerkin.

He carried a British Sten gun cradled in his hands, and a belt fastened around his waist over the leather jerkin, with a holstered Webley service revolver.

His pale blue eyes regarded Clemence for a minute before he glanced back at Washington.

"What's the plan, Captain?"

"Sir, you really ought to talk to General Shriver. He's the senior officer."

"Shriver? I don't trust him. Met him once before, and the man's a fool. Deranged."

"I don't know about that, but like I said…"

"What's the fuel situation, Captain? I understand you're preparing to attack the town and create a gap to pour tanks and troops through to get behind the German lines. At least, that was the plan. I take it nothing has changed?"

A pause. "No, nothing has changed. That's the plan, and I'm not sure about the fuel. Maybe you should discuss that with General Schreiber."

He gave Washington a hard stare. "Dammit, man, I've been at Montgomery's headquarters, and I happen to know the situation is difficult all over the front, and it won't get any better until we capture Cherbourg. You must be running low on fuel, but I'm asking you how low? Do you have enough to complete the attack? To win?"

Washington made a decision. This Brit was on the same side, and there didn't seem any reason he shouldn't know the truth. "I don't know, Major. I just don't know."

But the tanker, Sergeant Davidson interrupted. "I know. We're almost running on fumes, and we need gas. The answer to your question is we don't have enough. There's heavy armor inside that town, and it's well defended. If we tangle with the Tigers and Panthers, I'd say we're fucked. Our vehicles will run out of gas, and we'll be sitting ducks for the enemy."

"So why not find some gas, fill up the tanks, and do it right?"

Davidson gave him a pitying smile, as pitying as he could make it to a superior officer. "Mister, if there was gas to be had, we'd have it. The fact is there is a severe supply shortage all over Normandy. If you've been at Monty's headquarters, you must know that."

He nodded slowly. I know, I know. But I needed to assess your particular situation. I may be able to help."

Davidson glanced at the Bren carrier. "What are you planning, to drain the tank of that crazy machine so we can put a few gallons into our Shermans. My guess is they'll give us around a gallon apiece, and that won't even take us a mile. Sherman burns two gallons of fuel for every mile, so to be exact one gallon will take us a half-mile. Unless you have any cleverer ideas?"

"What about ten thousand gallons of gasoline, neatly stored in fifty-gallon drums?"

The tanker grinned. "Yeah, and you're my fairy godmother."

Washington snapped a warning. "Sergeant, he may be a Brit, but he is a senior officer, so give him some respect."

He nodded, but Loony Lawson waved away. "Don't worry about it. We're fighting a war, and it's been hard. This man had seen his friends torn into shreds killed by enemy fire, and he'll take some convincing. I can convince him if you hear me out."

"Yeah, right. What're we talking about here, the Red Ball Express? I know about it, but there are twenty-eight divisions on Normandy, tanks, trucks, aircraft, and it'll take more than a few truck convoys to make up what they need. That's assuming the Krauts don't get wind of it and knock off a few on the way. Ten thousand gallons is a lot of gas, Major, and there'll be other units competing for their fair share."

The Brit didn't change his expression, which was no less crazy and manic. "The fuel is about eight miles from here, stored in fifty-gallon drums. It's a holdover from the last war, and it's just waiting for somebody to happen along and take it."

Washington shook his head. "Now hold on. I'm aware you're familiar with this area, and I don't doubt it was there last time you were here, but aren't you forgetting something? The Krauts have been in the driving seat since June of 1940. That's four years, and in that time, they must have located it and seized every gallon. It won't be there, Major, that's for sure."

"It's there. The French military lost all records of it during the 1930s, and the only man who also knew about it was a Frenchman, a laborer, and a handyman who did odd jobs for my family. A man by the name of Bernard Marais."

"Suppose he's sold out to the Germans?"

"Bernard? No, I don't think so. He's a drunk, but we always looked after him, so I believe he'd remain loyal. Besides, I doubt he even recalled it was there. Gentlemen, the fuel is there. Find a way to transport it, and it's all yours. It's outside a small village called Monts-en-Bessin."

They glanced at each other. It was a big break, an unbelievable break, if they could get the fuel. "We don't have trucks," Washington pointed out, "And no way of getting them here. Even if we had trucks, we'd never get through the roads, they're so snarled up with traffic. We'd never get through in time."

"Tanks."

The Captain looked at Murphy. "What was that you said?"

"Tanks. We have twenty Shermans, twenty-one if we include Sergeant Davidson's vehicle. We could load the drums on top of the hulls. Not all of them, but enough to fight their way into Evrecy."

He shook his head. "Shriver will never agree to it."

"Does he have to know?"

"Well, uh, I'm not sure we could…"

Loony Lawson guffawed. "Of course he doesn't have to know. I met General Shriver when he came to Monty's HQ, and he's too cautious by far, nothing like General Patton. Now there's a man I respect. He's a soldier's soldier, a fighting man who's set his sights on defeating the enemy. Not pussyfooting around like 'By the Book' Shriver." He saw their puzzled expressions, "That's what some American officers call him. They say the pen is mightier than the sword, but in Shriver's case I'm not so sure."

Washington still didn't like it. "We can't detach the entire armored force and send it careering off into the countryside, leaving the Battalion without armored support."

"How about using half the tanks? Say ten vehicles, which leaves eleven to face the enemy if they hit us."

He still didn't like it, but Lawson pointed out they had limited choices. If the enemy attacked in strength, the Shermans would quickly run out of fuel, and they'd be stranded, sitting ducks for enemy fire. He agreed to give it a shot, and Davidson said he'd talk to the tankers.

"They won't be a problem. They've been worried for a couple of days how the fuel shortage could be their death sentence. You'll have your ten tanks, Captain. What time do you plan to strike out for this place?"

"Late evening, when it's getting dark. Major Lawson, you're sure you can find this place?"

"I can find it."

"God help us if it's not there. We'll have used up vital fuel for nothing."

They dispersed, while Davidson went to talk it over with the tankers. Murphy climbed the low hill with Clemence to look over the town, and to spend some time with her.

"I'd like to come with you. I know this region."

He gave her an emphatic shake of the head. "Not a chance. We don't know what's out there, and if there's any fighting, I don't want you to be hurt." He took both her hands and stared into her eyes, "You mean everything to me, and I want to know you're safe. Stay here, or better still go back to the rear and find a place to keep your head down. No matter what happens here, there's gonna be a major battle. Both sides have realized its importance, and they're gonna fight like crazy over it. Get out of here before it starts."

She considered for several minutes, and he waited her out. "Very well, I will do as you say. But come back to me, Jack. You say you don't want to lose me, well, I feel the same way."

"I'll be back."

The sky had blackened, and a few drops of rain fell before it became a squally shower. They rushed to find the cover of a nearby stand of trees, and while they waited for the rain to ease, Murphy saw a shadowy figure walking toward them from the town. He tightened the grip on his machine pistol and waited until the man, who proved to be a civilian, was close enough for him to intercept him.

He recoiled before the powerful smell of alcohol on his breath. "Hold it there, Mister. Who are you, and where do you think you're going?"

He didn't understand a word of English, and Clemence translated. "He says he had important information to sell to the Allies. Something about fuel."

"Fuel?" He recalled what Lawson had said about one man who shared the knowledge of the fuel dump, "What's his name?"

"He says he's Bernard Marais."

"Marais? That's the guy who worked for Lawson. He needs to know about this."

He took his arm, keeping a firm grip on his greasy sleeve, and trying not to inhale the unwashed stench. They found Lawson in the camp, where he was cheerfully regaling Dan Kelly with a tale of some exploit he'd been involved in, although it wasn't clear if it was the current war or the last one. His swivel eyes did overtime when he saw Marais, who didn't look so pleased to see the Brit.

"Bernard? What are you doing here?"

He spoke in fluent French, and Clemence translated the conversation.

"He told him he has information about a fuel dump. He wants money."

Lawson talked with him for several minutes, at first keeping calm, but he became angrier and angrier. Clemence explained he'd asked the Frenchman what he was up to in Evrecy. He didn't seem able to give a straight answer, and he…oh, shit."

Loony grabbed the hapless Frenchman by the throat, and in a move, so swift they almost missed it, he produced a sharpened stiletto as if by magic and pressed the point at his throat. "He's asking him how much he told the Germans, and what they paid him."

"Yeah, I guessed he wasn't talking about old times."

The truth came out, and it was all over. "He told them

everything," she translated, "They need fuel as much as we do, and he sold the information to them for money."

"So we're fucked. They'll be on the way to grab that fuel, and there's not a damn thing we can do to stop them. Shit, shit, shit!"

188

CHAPTER EIGHT

She translated further, and it was all bad.

"He hoped to sell us the same information. If Loony hadn't been here, we'd never have known. Jack, we're too late. The German trucks have already left for the fuel dump. They're desperate to get their hands on that gas."

Washington grimaced. "They won't be short of fuel for much longer."

Lawson had been listening, and for once his eyes seemed to stabilize. "Captain Washington, I'm not sure about that."

"Major, we're too late."

"No, we're not. Trucks have to use the roads, but tanks can travel cross-country. There's a chance we can head them off and beat them to it. What do you say?"

"Dammit, you're right. Sergeant Rooker, get over to the tank park and tell 'em we're leaving. Now, dammit! Get the lead out. We're in a race, and there're no prizes for the losers."

The Sarge raced toward the tank park. Minutes later, the peace of the night disintegrated as ten Continental R975 9-cylinder radial engines roared into life. He briefed the crews about the need to make it snappy before some nosey senior officer decided this was more than a routine engine check. The tanks clattered over the ground as they started to move and picked up speed.

Lawson shouted, "Get aboard the leading tank. They'll need to know where they're going."

"What about Marais?"

He shrugged. "He's a traitor, and we still have the death penalty in Great Britain."

He was still holding the knife, and in a casual gesture, like he was just cutting up his evening meal, he slashed it across the Frenchman's throat, tossed the body aside, and sprinted toward the fast-approaching Sherman. For an older man, he was impressively fit. He leaped on the hull and gripped a steel stanchion to stop him from being tossed off the lurching and pitching vehicle. Washington followed, and they went after him, until they were safely on top of the hull, clinging onto any handhold they could find. Loony shouted directions to the tank commander, who didn't seem too surprised he had company. It was Sergeant Chris Davidson, and he warned them to keep a tight hold.

"It's rough country, and I don't want you falling off and landing beneath the tracks of the vehicle behind us."

Murphy made sure he was secure and looked around to see if the rest of them were okay. He nearly let go and fell off the hull. "Clemence, what the hell!"

"You may need a translator, so I thought I'd best come along."

She wore the American helmet and khakis she'd acquired earlier, and in the darkness, it wasn't obvious she was a civilian and a female. When it became daylight, he wasn't so sure, but it was too late to do anything about it, and he accepted the inevitable as the line of ten Shermans raced toward Monts-en-Bessin.

He was concerned about the whereabouts of the Germans. If they were as desperate for gas as the French traitor had told them, they'd either be on the way to the fuel dump, or they'd already be there. He pictured them manhandling the drums onto trucks and driving them away to refill the thirsty panzers. It was bad enough to contemplate American armor facing the formidable German tanks, with their thicker armor and more powerful guns. Having to fight a major battle with insufficient fuel was a nightmare scenario. A scenario with one outcome, and he didn't want to think about that.

They approached the village just before 03.00, and everything was in darkness. He felt a sense of relief. They'd beaten the Jerries to it, and Loony Lawson positioned himself next to the turret, giving directions to Sergeant Davidson. They swung wide of the main street and drove along a muddy farm track. He heard Lawson shout the fuel dump was behind a cluster of buildings about four hundred yards ahead.

He was smiling wolfishly. "We've beaten them to it. I suggest we form a defensive line in case they arrive. We can take out a few of their trucks while we're grabbing the fuel. A win-win."

Davidson nodded uncertainly. "I hope you're right, Major.

We need that gas."

He spoke into the microphone, and half the Shermans fell back to guard the entrance to the farm. His lead tank led the way past the buildings, and Lawson pointed to a dilapidated, timber gate. "It's through there. As soon as we…" He stopped, and he didn't seem so certain, "That's strange, the gate shouldn't be open."

"Why not? It looks rotten, I'd guess a strong gust of wind could've blown it open."

"No, it only looked rotten, so people wouldn't think something valuable was on the other side. The rotting wood is a disguise, a thin cladding over a toughened steel frame. The locks are also toughened steel, military specification, and this means somebody's opened it."

"You mean…"

"I mean they're here. Sergeant, warn your men." At the same time, a Panther tank appeared in front of them, the noise of its approach blanketed by the rumble of the Sherman engines, "Enemy in sight! Engage!"

The shell whistled past them and slammed into the third tank in the line. A direct hit, and the armored vehicle became a ball of flame. The Rangers were already leaping off the lead tank, finding cover on either side of the track, and they found more than cover. They found the enemy. German infantry had deployed behind cover and were just a few yards away. The Panther fired again, and the shell slammed into Davidson's tank, but the sloped frontal armor deflected the worst of the impact, and the round failed to breach the hull. But they were in trouble, a lot of trouble. They'd no idea what they were up against, whether it was one Panther, a whole company, or even a battalion of enemy armor. How many troops they faced, was it a dozen, or were there enough to swamp them?

Loony Lawson was shouting at the men to hit the Germans head-on. "Get them, kill the bastards!"

They ignored him. Sergeant Davidson ordered the surviving tanks to swerve off the track and work their way around the flanks until they knew what they were up against. Washington led the Rangers at a tangent away from the Germans, heading for a stone barn where they could find some cover. Lawson ran for several yards, and by a miracle he survived the bullets whistling around him. Until he realized he was on his own, and he darted aside, rolling into a shallow ditch at the side of the track. It wasn't a shallow ditch, it was a sheep dip, and he fell into the rank, stinking water. He went beneath the surface, which saved his life. He emerged several seconds later spluttering and cursing.

Lawson joined them, soaking wet and stinking, but he was alive. They were safe behind the stone barn, at least for a few minutes, and Washington counted numbers. "Did we lose anybody?"

Rooker made a quick assessment, and although it seemed unbelievable, they were all there. "Just the guys in that Sherman. What's the plan, Captain?"

"Plan? The first thing we need to do is find out what we're up against. We'll have to leave the Shermans to take care of the Panther. If the enemy saw us reach the barn, they'll be along any moment. There could be a lot of them, who knows? We need to go forward and find that fuel dump, see what's going on, and how many soldiers they have. If there's just a few, we'll hit them hard and fast."

"And if there's a lot, Captain?"

He looked at Kelly. "In that case, Private, we'll need to make a plan."

"Is that the plan where we run like hell?"

"Not a chance. Or have you forgotten we're Rangers? We don't run, not from anybody, not from a bunch of Krauts. If there're a lot of them, we'll beat them. It'll just take a bit longer. Move out, men, they could get here real soon."

The Shermans were dueling with the Panther, swapping shells. Flames and sparks lit up the night as the shells impacted toughened armor, but they had no time to watch the fireworks.

They sneaked through the darkness for several hundred yards and almost walked into a German sentry. He was gazing toward the pyrotechnics thrown up by the tank battle, and he didn't see the dark figures moving through the gloom. Neither would he see anything else, not when Washington pounced like a leopard hunting its prey and wrapped a strong arm around his neck. He choked off his air supply, simultaneously stabbing into the man's heart with his modified First World War bayonet. He lowered the body to the ground and looked cautiously ahead.

"There could be more, so I want you, Murphy to take Kelly with you and go forward another hundred yards. There's a clump of bushes in front of a fence, and I think I see movement behind it. Don't make a sound and show yourselves. We need to take them by surprise."

They nodded in acknowledgment, and Murphy jogged forward with Kelly following. They reached the timber fence, climbed over, and pushed through the bushes. They'd found it. A line of trucks, ten in all, and a swarm of German soldiers were busy rolling steel drums up a narrow ramp from underground.

Too narrow for the trucks to drive down, and so they sweated and heaved the heavy drums toward the trucks. When they reach them, they sweated and heaved even more hauling them up onto the cargo bed. They'd already loaded three trucks and were busy loading a fourth.

There were more soldiers than you could shake a stick at. They counted around twenty men on guard, which together with the twenty or so loading the drums, was a lot of soldiers. If the Shermans couldn't get past that Panther, they were on their own. In the shit, unless they could handle them themselves, and that meant killing them all. They'd seen enough, and they raced back to where Washington was waiting with Lawson. They described what they'd seen, and Lawson was all for charging in, guns blazing, but they managed to persuade him it might not be the best idea.

"Major, we have eight men, and they've just told us the Germans have forty. That's bad odds. If we're gonna do this, we have to do it right." He frowned, "A pity we don't have any machine guns. What about grenades?"

Murphy supplied the answer, and it wasn't what he wanted to hear. "Sir, are grenades a good idea? I mean, they're loading drums of gasoline? Last I heard, grenades and gasoline don't mix."

He grimaced. "You're right, dammit. I didn't think. Okay, we have a situation. It's just us. Without the tanks, we have to find a way to take them without destroying the gasoline. Does anybody have any ideas?"

"I do." A female voice, and their eyes swiveled in surprise to Clemence, who they either hadn't realized was along or had elected not to notice, "I can distract them, tell them I'm a local farmer, and make up some story. While they're looking at me, you can attack them from behind."

Washington chuckled. "Ma'am, you don't look like a local farmer. Not in that uniform."

"The uniform? I will take it off. I have civilian clothes underneath."

"I don't think so, but thanks for the offer. Murphy, Kelly, you've seen how the land lies, what do you think?"

They glanced at each other, and it was Kelly who came up with an idea. "Captain, she's half right. We need to get them looking the other way, although we need to find another way to do it. I was thinking what Murphy said, about not using grenades because they'd cause an almighty explosion, kill us all, and destroy the gas. What I'm saying is, they're sure to know that."

"Yes, yes, of course they know that. What's your point, Private?"

"Suppose me and Murphy worked our way around to the side and came at them with grenades." He held up his hand, "No, hold it, hear me out. I'm not suggesting we use them. What I'm saying is we could scare the shit out of them. If they think we're about to lob grenades in the middle of those fuel drums, they're gonna get the fright of their lives. If they think we've pulled the pins, they won't shoot, but sure as hell, every man will be staring our way. They won't be doing any shooting in case we drop the grenades and they detonate. Do it right, and you can be all over them before they know what's hit them."

Washington glanced at him for several seconds, thinking it through, and he nodded his head. "You know, it might just work. Provided some trigger-happy jerk doesn't start shooting before he realizes the danger. I could lose both of you."

Dan frowned. "I don't intend for that to happen. What do you say?"

"Get to it. We'll move as close as we can so we can see when you make your move, and we'll jump them."

They jogged away, and when they reached the fence, instead of pushing through the bushes to reach the other side were careful to keep an eye out for more sentries. They worked their way between the fence and the bushes until they were one hundred yards away from the hive of activity, and they got themselves ready. Took out two grenades apiece, and they sneaked in closer. They were in luck. One of the drums had rusted so badly it was leaking, and the area stank with the pungent aroma of gasoline. Another reason to be terrified should grenades detonate close enough to cause the entire fuel dump to go up in a cloud of flame powerful enough to kill them all.

They shouldered their weapons and walked forward with a single grenade in each hand. They stepped out in the open. At first, the Germans were so busy loading the trucks and staring at the explosions coming from the battle still raging along the track, they didn't notice the two Rangers. Until one man happened to glance around, saw them, and stiffened.

He shouted a single word, "Achtung!"

More heads jerked around, rifles came up, and they heard the rattle of bolts as they prepared to fire. Since he'd been fighting the Germans in Normandy, he'd heard enough German words shouted by the enemy to fill a dictionary, and a few had lodged in his memory. When he was close enough to use a grenade, he'd heard them shouting a warning, "Granate!" He'd also heard them shout, "Nicht schiesse!" *'Don't shoot!'*

He made use of them now and bellowed, "Granate! Nicht schiesse!"

Somebody got the message. An NCO shouted an order, and they held their fire. He chatted to another man who nodded and walked forward. A junior officer, a lieutenant, and he stopped ten feet from the Rangers.

"What do you want? If you throw the grenades, you will kill yourselves as well as us. I doubt you have come here to die."

"I doubt you have either. Here's the deal. You back off. The fuel is the property of the French government, which means what you're doing is theft. I want you to put it back."

His eyebrows rose in astonishment. "Back? You cannot be serious? I have fifty armed men, and you cannot hold us up forever. Sooner or later, you will have to leave, if you want to live."

"Negative. Put it back, Mister."

He was watching the stealthy movement behind the Germans. Fifty men and fifty pairs of eyes fixed on him and Kelly. Terrified to open fire, terrified to make a move, in case it was the wrong move and they died in a blazing conflagration. The officer hesitated. He was in a fix. He couldn't stand down, that was ridiculous, but neither could he attack. Stalemate, and Murphy watched his eyes, knowing when he'd worked out what to do. The first indication would be in those eyes. It was always in the eyes, the mirrors to a man's soul. These men had come from Evrecy where they'd carried out a bloody execution of American soldiers. He almost willed the man to make a move. He'd want to see them suffering a terrible punishment for what they'd done; except he'd die, Dan would die, and they'd lose the gas. He did the one thing he could do and waited. Waited for the Rangers to get close enough. The German officer opened his mouth and started to turn around to shout something to his men.

Washington's men needed a few more seconds, and he shouted, "Lieutenant, listen to me. We can work this out."

He turned back. "How?"

"What I'm saying is this, how about you take half the gas, and put the other half back." It was the stupidest suggestion he could make, but all he could think of on the spur of the moment, and he couldn't believe the German almost went for it, "There were two hundred drums, and so far we have removed almost a hundred. I will leave the rest, but in return, you must surrender the grenades. Replace the pins and…"

He glanced at the grenade Kelly held in his left hand, and his eyes went wide. They'd held them so it wasn't possible to see the pins were still in place, but Dan's grip had moved, and the plan was very much in evidence. "What's going on? You weren't…"

The area exploded into action. Washington led his men into the attack, a half-dozen Rangers against fifty, but he'd planned it well, and they went for the sentries first. They went in with guns blazing, and some carried automatic weapons like Rooker's Thompson. Washington was similarly armed, and Lawson carried the British Sten gun. They took down a dozen Germans before they were aware they'd come under attack.

Murphy jumped the lieutenant, slammed a fist into his face, and used his weight to throw him to the ground. The officer tried to snatch the pistol from his holster, but the Ranger got there first and hammered the muzzle of his MP-40 on his wrist. As he recoiled in pain, he snatched out his Colt, and put a bullet in his head. The NCO was looking at the battle that'd come at them from the night, then staring back to see what'd happened to his officer, and he was undecided. Kelly made up his mind by blasting him with a short burst, and the two men ran.

They didn't run to join the fight, but to reach the soldiers who'd been loading the drums onto the trucks, and they weren't fighting soldiers. They were transport troops. Men who'd assumed their war would consist of driving, loading, and unloading trucks, with the greatest risk from fighters roaming the skies. Now the risk had come to them, in the shape of two men who were fighting soldiers. Two men who'd worked out if they gave them time to recover, they could unsling their rifles and do plenty of damage given the time to join the fight.

They shot down half-dozen men milling around the back of a truck, and another three took off and ran. There were four men on the truck, manhandling the drums, and they made up their mind their best chance of survival was to fight back. All four unslung their rifles, all the cumbersome KAR-98K, and they worked the bolts to chamber a round. They were wasting their time. Murphy vaulted onto the back of the truck and scythed them down with a burst from his machine pistol. One man got away, leaped off the side of the truck only to almost fall on top of Dan Kelly, who was running alongside it to check the cab. He cursed and swung round to put a bullet into his belly.

"Bastard, jumping out on me like that. I could've been killed."

A half-dozen soldiers were racing up the ramp from the underground fuel store, and they'd had time to recover from the surprise attack. They opened fire, and the Mauser KAR-98K rifles spat bullets at them. Both Rangers dived behind the truck for cover, and the Germans made a fatal mistake, assuming they'd run. They hadn't run, and when the Krauts raced around the truck thinking to see them fleeing into the distance, they went down in a hail of bullets fired from the two machine pistols. With no other enemy soldiers left, they ran to join the fight, which was going badly. Washington's force had lost two men, and the remaining four were fighting like lions. But they were losing to the overwhelming enemy strength, and as they ran toward them, Murphy saw another figure step out from the shadows and start shooting with a handgun. He recognized Clemence Delon, and he shouted, "Shit," as he ran even faster.

"Don't shoot until we get close," he shouted at Dan, "We need to hit them like a bolt from hell, so hard and fast they don't have time to recover."

"I hear you, pal. Say the word."

They were within ten yards, and he shouted, "Now."

He squeezed the trigger and emptied a magazine into the Germans, who were pushing the Rangers backward. Washington's men had no choice but to hit the deck to make smaller targets. For Murphy and Kelly, it was fine and dandy. Those men who were on their feet were the enemy. Those lying on the ground were friendlies. They held the MP-40s at the hip and let rip with full magazines, sending a hail of bullets into the enemy ranks. They stopped going forward and some turned to face the new threat. They fell into total confusion, and the Rangers kept up a steady rate of fire, giving them time to insert fresh magazines into their machine pistols.

They fired again, and the Germans had no answer. Clemence added to the confusion, standing in full view, firing single shots from the heavy pistol, and it was too much. Men began throwing down their rifles and raising their hands, and the shooting came to a stop. The Rangers advanced toward them and began frisking them for weapons. An eerie quiet had descended on the area, and that meant the battle between the Panther and the Shermans was over. He glanced in the direction he'd last seen them, wondering what'd happened. Yet the silence was ominous. He had a terrible premonition the German tank had knocked out all five Shermans and had taken off.

He glanced at Washington. "Captain, I'd like to go back there and see what happened to our tanks."

He nodded tiredly. "Yeah, why not? As soon as you know, get back here."

"Yes, Sir."

He took off, jogging along the track, and he came across the last thing he expected to. It didn't seem possible, yet the tanks were all there. The four surviving Shermans and the Panther. The American tanks had surrounded the stationary German armored vehicle, and they'd all switched off the engines. Sergeant Davidson was holding a gun pointed at five Germans, the tank crew. He glanced around as Murphy approached.

"You're just in time. They surrendered. How're things back there?"

"We're good, but..." He stopped as he heard engines starting, and in the distance, he saw two trucks racing away, driving across a field, and they were laden with fuel drums. They'd failed to check the truck drivers, and now they were getting away. More importantly, getting away with precious supplies of fuel, fuel that would keep their heavy tanks fighting when they attacked Evrecy, "Sergeant, stop them!"

He gave a half-smile. "Not a chance. We're almost out of fuel, and we switched off a few minutes ago to save gas when the Panther surrendered."

"Why did they surrender?"

"A mechanical problem, it's common with the Panthers. The final drive unit was poorly designed, and they keep breaking down. Which is just as well, we thought he'd get a few more of us before we knocked him out. I'm sorry about those trucks, but they got away. By the time we get the engines running, they'll be out of sight. They've gone."

"Shit. Okay, we've captured a few more Krauts. They may as well join the others."

"Did you get the gas? I hope they didn't get away with all of it. I doubt we have enough to get back."

"We got plenty of gas."

He walked back to rejoin the Rangers, and they were pushing the prisoners toward the underground fuel store. There were still plenty of drums of fuel underground, and Washington put them to work bringing up the rest and continuing to load the trucks. They kept a close eye on them, their guns held ready to shoot, but the prisoners had taken enough. They worked to finish bringing up the last of the drums, loading them on the trucks. Washington was trying to work out what to do with them when Loony Lawson came up with an idea that wasn't at all loony.

"Put them in the underground storage chamber. We can lock them in and call headquarters to come and collect them when they're good and ready."

He grinned. "Major, that's a damn good idea. Men, push

them down that ramp, and when they're all inside, close and lock the doors. As soon as we're done, we're heading back. We have a battle to fight."

Sergeant Davidson's voice shouted to them from the darkness. "Before you go, I'd like to lighten the load. My vehicles need some of that gas."

"You're more than welcome."

He took three full drums of fuel to top up the tanks of each of the thirsty Shermans, and when they'd finished, the armor formed up in front and behind the trucks. They drove back in a long column, and by the time they reached Battalion Headquarters, it was almost light.

They ran into a shitstorm. General Earl Shriver stalked out of a mobile command post he'd had brought up so he could personally direct the coming attack. Lieutenant Adams was with him, and both officers stood hands-on-hips. Shriver's face was as red as a prize beetroot. He waited until they came to a stop and made a deliberate gesture of counting the tanks. He waited for Washington to approach.

"General, we got the fuel."

"Where's my tank? Captain, you took off without orders, and persuaded an NCO to sequester ten of my Shermans. I need them all, and you've put the entire plan of attack at risk. You'd better have a damn good reason, Mister."

"Sir, like I said, we got the fuel. Without gas, those tanks would've had a hard time, but now we have enough to keep them going, at least for long enough to kick the Krauts in the ass."

The Rangers were standing around, watching and waiting. They had eight trucks, each weighed down with fifty-gallon drums of gasoline, and it had to count for something. Didn't it? Washington deserved a medal. Shriver didn't agree.

"I asked you a question, Mister. Where is my tank? You took ten Shermans, and I count nine. What happened to the other one?"

Murphy noticed the Lieutenant was smirking at his Captain being in the shit, and if he'd disliked him before, he hated him now.

"We lost it in battle, General. The crewmen are all dead."

He spoke slowly, carefully pronouncing each word. "You lost it in battle? You're telling me you took off on an unauthorized operation and cost this man's army a valuable armored vehicle?"

"We got the gas, General."

"I don't care about the gas! I'm in command around here, and you don't make a move without my say so. Call out the MPs. Captain Washington, I'm placing you…"

It was like an attack by a hungry lioness. Clemence Delon had been listening to the exchange, and she strutted up to Shriver, head held high, staring straight into his eyes.

"You stupid man! If they hadn't done what they did, your tanks would've gone into battle so low on fuel I doubt they would've made it to Evrecy, and no way did they have enough to fight the battle. Captain Washington made the right decision, and if he hadn't done it, you'd have been staring at the wreckage of the entire Battalion, as well as the loss of every tank. How can you be so stupid? He saved your ass, General!"

He opened his mouth, but no words came out, just a choking noise as he started, unsure whether he should shout back at her and order her arrest or was there an alternative course of action he could take. Like order his men to put her in front of a firing squad.

"I…uh…" He still couldn't work it out, and he became even more confused when Loony Lawson walked toward him, his expression calm, but his eyes were icy.

"General, the action to secure the fuel was carried out professionally. We were short of fuel, and Captain Washington took steps to address the shortage. I intend to contact the headquarters of General Montgomery and report what I regard as a failure of command within this unit. He'll pass it up to General Eisenhower, who will make up his mind about who to send in to replace you."

"You can't…"

He still hadn't recovered his balance, and he was like a punch-drunk boxer recovering from one blow too many. "I can't tell Eisenhower what to do, no, but everything I've seen here will get back to him. On the other hand, now you have gasoline, would it be a good idea to make sure all your Shermans top up their tanks ready for the coming battle?"

He finally got the message and nodded. "That's exactly what I was planning to do. Men, get those tanks gassed up. We're about to go into battle."

The camp was a hive of activity. Men rushed to unload the drums of gasoline from the trucks, and the tankers found hand pumps to transfer the fuel into their parched tanks. Infantry and Rangers prepared for the coming attack, and Shriver put the lessons of his sacred military manuals to good use. He sent in a small reconnaissance party to check out the approaches to the town. They were back within the hour, and the news wasn't good. The Germans had refueled their tanks with the drums from the two trucks that'd got away, and the Tiger, two Panthers, and two STuGs were already maneuvering into position.

The enemy wasn't stupid. They'd have their own reconnaissance out to observe what was going on in the American positions, and they'd know what was coming. It was going to be tough. Although Shriver's force had more tanks, the panzers had the benefit of thicker armor and more powerful guns. The STuGs had the advantage of a lower profile, making them difficult targets, and had the artillery. Every man in the American camp was less than happy with what they were about to tangle with.

Murphy was cleaning his MP-40, and he glanced up as Kelly strolled toward him.

"It's gonna be a tough one."

"Oh, yeah. Shriver at his best."

"I hate generals. Waste of space."

He grinned. "Amen to that."

"Dan, I'm down to my last magazine, how about you?"

"The same. Say, about that German, didn't you say his name was Kreis? What's the plan?"

"He's no dummy, so he'll be a tough proposition to take down. I get the impression he's one of those officers who wants to make a name for himself. Get the Iron Cross, or maybe some higher decoration, whatever they give them in Germany. He wants to be Hitler's blue-eyed boy."

"As I recall, he does have blue eyes," he grinned, "But I reckon Adolf has other problems. We're coming for his ass, and the Russians are coming in from the east for his ass, so Kreis can forget about some Iron Cross. It's a pity Hitler's generals don't bump him off. It'd save us all a lot of trouble. They should've done it years ago."

"You ask me, those Kraut generals are a bunch of lily-livered cowards."

"Worse than some of our generals, and that's saying something. You're not well disposed toward generals, Murphy, are you?"

"You got that right. Dan, when we go in, I want to be upfront, and when I see him, he's mine."

Kelly grimaced. "Aren't you forgetting something? They're not gonna throw up their hands and surrender. They have heavy tanks, and they have guns, as well as a lot of infantry. We don't even know if they brought up reinforcements over the past twenty-four hours, now they've discovered the importance of the town to both sides."

"Does Shriver realize that?"

"Do the Krauts realize that?"

* * *

While they were talking, General Shriver had called his unit commanders in for a briefing. He was all smiles and wore a self-satisfied expression. "You men may be pleased to note I've postponed the assault for twenty-four hours."

They gaped at him, and Washington couldn't stop himself before he'd blurted out, "That's crazy! We're giving the enemy time to stiffen up their defenses. We need to hit them now before they have a chance to make things harder for us."

"Hear me out, Captain. Our forces are still looking for a gap to pour troops and armor through to get behind the enemy.

With this in mind, I've called in reinforcements. Three infantry companies from the 105th were supposed to be shipping out to the Pacific, and I managed to get them diverted to the Normandy theater of operations. They're due to arrive later today, and I have no doubt these men will make all the difference. Worth waiting twenty-four hours to give our attack more of a punch, now what do you say?"

"You said they're infantry? Have they seen combat?"

"Negative, there're just out of basic training, but their regiment was part of the New York National Guard before the Army inducted them into Federal service. They're good men, and they possibly will give us a powerful edge to roll over the Germans. I know they have tanks, but our tanks outnumber them, and we have plenty of fuel."

"So do they," Washington murmured beneath his breath.

"There's something else you should know. I've requested an airstrike to target the guns and the tanks. The planes are gonna hit at the exact moment we jump off for the attack. By the time we get there, they'll be in no shape to offer much resistance, so we'll just walk in and take over." He looked even smugger, "That's it, men, a twenty-four-hour postponement, and if you have any doubts, the extra men and the airstrike will take care of them. Continue preparations for the attack, which I've timed for 07.00. Until then keep everything under cover. The Germans won't know what we're up to, and I want to keep it that way. That's all."

He walked away, and nobody said anything. What was there to say? If he didn't want the Germans to know what they were up to, he could forget it. The Germans knew exactly what they were up to. They had eyes, and they had ears. There was also the scrap at the fuel dump, or had Shriver forgotten about that? Washington walked back to his men and looked with misgivings at their depleted numbers.

They're good men, combat-hardened, and they'll do everything asked of them. But will it be enough? If the Germans are waiting for us, those tanks and guns will hack into us before we even reach the town. I hope to Christ they aren't waiting for us. I've lost enough troops in this man's war, and I don't want to lose any more. I have a strong suspicion we'll be walking into a trap.

CHAPTER NINE

Major Kreis fought back his fury. He was speaking to a mere captain at Field Marshal Gerd von Rundstedt's headquarters, explaining the situation at Evrecy. The strategic importance of holding the town, and how he needed more tanks and troops to counter the clear threat of an imminent Allied attack.

"Major, we have other priorities," the officer replied smoothly, "Of course Field Marshal von Rundstedt is sympathetic to your requirements, but we are fighting on many fronts, and we have nothing available."

"You have to make something available, Captain," he snapped. He was a major in the Wehrmacht, engaged in a major operation to hold back the Allies, and this junior officer wasn't listening to a word, "I need more tanks, and I need more troops. The enemy has at least twenty tanks. When they come, I have to have the means to defend the town. If it falls, we could lose the battle for Normandy."

The officer continued in the same silky tones. "Major Kreis, Field Marshal von Rundstedt has every confidence in your abilities to make the best of the situation."

Kreis stamped his foot, maddened by the man's obduracy. "I doubt the Field Marshal even knows who I am, Captain. Don't bullshit me!"

"Major, he knows exactly who you are. You're a logistics officer in command of a transport detail you diverted without direct orders. You also diverted a unit of artillery and commandeered those tanks. When he found out, he considered having you arrested for disobeying orders, and it's fortunate your actions prevented the Allies from taking the town."

Kreis understood he'd had a narrow escape, and he calmed down. "They will still take the town unless you get me those reinforcements. Captain, there must be something you can send."

He heard a long sigh the other end. "Perhaps there is. We have a small unit of tanks heading your way, with orders to push back the enemy and relieve Cherbourg. It may be possible to divert them to Evrecy to stiffen your defenses. When you have fought off the attack, they can continue on their mission."

He grunted a reply. The Wehrmacht was desperately short of armor, and they were scraping the bottom of the barrel, throwing every obsolete vehicle into the fight to stem the Allied advance. Czech tanks, Polish tanks, and he'd even heard of a regiment of Russian T-34s pressed into service for the Third Reich. As far as he was aware, none had distinguished themselves in battle.

"What tanks are these, Captain?" He listened to the reply and smiled to himself. The battle was as good as won, "They'll do nicely."

* * *

They sat around in the early afternoon, enjoying the summer sunshine after the improvement in the weather. They were trying to digest their almost inedible rations, washing them down with almost undrinkable coffee. It was the right color, a kind of muddy brown, and it was lukewarm. But the resemblance to real coffee ended there. He tossed away the unfinished java and grimaced.

War is hell.

He was chatting with Clemence, Kelly, and Rooker, and they were all seated on ammunition boxes in place for the coming attack. He gave her a firm glance.

"You shouldn't be here. You know we're about to attempt to assault the town, and that means there's gonna be a major battle. I'm talking big, real fireworks, and it's gonna be tough. I'd appreciate it if you went to the rear where there's plenty of work for you. They've taken thousands of prisoners, so they'll be desperate for an interpreter."

Rooker nodded his agreement. "He's right, Ma'am. This is no place…"

"Don't call me Ma'am," she snapped, "It's Mam'selle."

"Whatever. But you shouldn't be here. You know that. Neither should you be wearing that uniform. When the battle starts, it'll make you a target."

She looked from one to the other, and she knew it was no go. "Very well, I will remove my clothes."

A soldier walking past gave her a hard glance, and he

stopped a few yards further on, looking back in case he was about to be treated to a free show. He was in for a disappointment. After she'd removed the helmet and khakis, she still wore pants and a shirt, and the hoped-for striptease wasn't about to happen. Murphy had seen him, and he grinned at the guy's obvious disappointment.

"If you go to Shriver's mobile command post, there's sure to be a jeep heading back to Army HQ, and you can hitch a ride." He put his arms on her shoulders, "Clemence, I don't want to lose you. Please, do this for me."

"I don't want to lose you either, but I'll do as you say." She gave him an impish smile, "Just this once."

She said farewell to Kelly and Rooker and walked away. They saw her disappear behind Shriver's command truck, and Murphy felt a sense of relief. He could concentrate on the coming fight, without having to worry about his girlfriend getting hurt. Or worse.

Toward the end of the day, the reinforcements arrived. A dozen trucks crammed with troops, so overloaded many were down on their axles. They began to disembark in full view of anyone who happened to be watching until Washington bellowed at them to get out of sight. They ducked low and scrabbled for the nearest cover. The trucks parked a few hundred yards back, and they saw him grimace. The damage had been done, and that was too bad. The enemy would have to be blind to miss it.

The camp was restless during the long night as men made their preparations for the next day. The new arrivals tried and failed to make themselves comfortable as if they were in a Boy Scout camp, rather than the front line of a major offensive in western France, involving hundreds of thousands of men. Murphy was trying to get some shuteye when the first shells arrived. It looked like the Germans felt the need to remind them what they had waiting for them, dropping a score of high-explosive shells into and around the camp before they ceased fire. In that time, they'd done the damage, killed several men, wounded many more, and the biggest wound of all was to their morale. So far, the rookies had only ever seen practice rounds fired during training, and the rain of high-explosive came as a severe shock. After the shelling, nobody slept. Maybe that was the German intention.

Kelly paced around, fidgeting with his Colt automatic, as if he was looking for someone to shoot, like one of those Kraut gunners. He came back to Murphy. "You awake?"

"I woke up when those Krauts opened up. I guess they couldn't sleep, so they decided to wake us as well. Bastards are uncivilized."

"You never said a truer word. You know they'll be waiting for us when we go in? Despite what that mad bastard Shriver thinks, we may as well have taken a front-page advert on the Berlin Daily News, or whatever they call the newspaper. It's gonna be tough."

"I reckon."

At 05.00, one hour before dawn, enemy artillery fired again, and men dived for cover as more shells landed. This time the barrage was more intense, and he counted as many as one hundred shells hit in or around the camp before the shooting stopped. The sky began to lighten, and he glanced up as if to see the fighters heading in to give Jerry something of what they'd given them. The sky was empty of aircraft. But not empty of something else, and he felt chilled. Thick clouds were scudding in from the east, leaving a low ceiling he estimated at less than one thousand feet. The clouds were moving overhead like a pale gray blanket stretched over the town.

He saw Loony Lawson talking with Washington, and they didn't look happy. They walked past where he stood with Dan Kelly, and he overheard the conversation. He wished he hadn't.

The Brit was saying, "They can't fly, not in this. We can forget the airstrike."

Washington frowned. "It can't be easy with such a low cloud ceiling, but surely it's not impossible. They can just fly low."

"Captain, it's not that easy. Have you ever flown aircraft?"

"No, I haven't."

"I guess not. There're many problems to overcome, including navigation, which means finding where you're going. I'm looking to the east, and it appears to me the clouds are coming in thicker and lower. I doubt they'd be able to find Evrecy, let alone attack it."

"Without an airstrike to soften them up, it'll be even tougher. Thank Christ we have the tanks."

"And they have tanks. Not so many, but the Tiger and the Panther are pretty tough."

"You're forgetting something, Major. We have more troops, three companies of infantry."

"Three companies of rookies. Pitted against tanks and artillery, they won't be much more than cannon fodder."

"You don't think this'll work?"

"Let's just say I don't believe General Shriver is the best man for the job."

"I guess not. But we don't have any choice but to follow orders."

Loony Lawson had a peculiar look in his eyes. "Perhaps. Perhaps not."

They walked out of earshot, and Murphy couldn't help but wonder how different things would be with a good man in command.

Generals, who'd give them houseroom? One thing's for sure; you can rely on men like Shriver to make the same mistakes. Again and again and again.

He was thankful the girl had gone to the rear. If things went badly, who knew what would happen? The Germans could've brought in reinforcements after they'd realized the strategic importance of the town. If they brought up reinforcements, more troops, and more armor, there was an outside possibility they could not only beat off the attack, but they could counterattack, and this entire area would be under threat. It wasn't unheard of. There had been several counterattacks already in the Normandy theater of battle, and the Germans had a reputation for being clever and skillful at it.

He wondered about Lawson's comment about them having to follow orders.

Perhaps, perhaps not, what did he mean?

They crouched low, keeping down until the last moment before they had to expose themselves to fire from the town. Despite what they'd told them about the difficulties of mounting an airstrike, he couldn't believe they'd call it off. There was a lot of open ground to cover, and the Germans could blanket it with so much shot and shell it would become a death trap. Sure, they had the tanks, and the last he'd heard they'd lead the advance.

The infantry would follow, protected by the armored hulls, but if they hadn't knocked them out, emplaced anti-tank artillery could take a fearful toll on the Shermans.

He looked up at the sky, and he was starting to worry. Lieutenant Adams appeared at 06.45, coming from the direction of Shriver's command post, and he shot a glance at Rooker.

"Sergeant, is everything ready for the attack?"

"We're all set, Lt. Waiting for the airstrike, and praying they give them a good pounding."

A pause. "It's canceled."

"The attack?"

"The airstrike. The cloud base is too low."

"So, what's the deal? How're they planning to soften up the target? Are they sending in mobile guns to give them a pasting? Not so good as an airstrike, but it'll give them something to think about."

"There won't be any mobile guns, Sergeant. We go as planned. The Shermans will lead, and we'll follow."

He stared back at Adams for several seconds. "Lieutenant, if we go without artillery or air support, we're gonna take serious casualties. Men will die unnecessarily."

"Sergeant, this is a war. Men die in war, and this battle will be no exception. I admit it's not ideal, crossing that open ground without softening up the enemy first, but that's the job they'd given us, and that's what we're gonna do." He looked at his watch, "The time is 06.50. We jump off in ten minutes. Make sure they're ready."

He stalked away, and Rooker glanced at the platoon, down to just seven men. "You heard the man, ten minutes."

They exchanged glances, and there wasn't a damn thing

they could do. Except wait for the Shermans to roll across the open ground, and they'd have no choice but to follow.

Kelly grunted, "It's like the fucking trenches in the First World War. If the Germans are ready, they'll murder us."

Rooker shrugged. "Orders are orders. Maybe the Krauts won't be ready."

"They'll be ready."

"I guess."

He fingered his Thompson, removed the magazine, checked, and replaced it. They'd seen him do the same thing several times in the past hour, just one of those rituals that men do before they go into battle. Murphy ejected the magazine from his Colt, took out the bullets, and replaced them, one by one. He'd checked his machine pistol several times since their rude awakening after the German artillery hit them in the night, but he'd managed to locate his Springfield, and he did what he always did. Polished the lens of the scope to make sure no dust or dirt would obscure his vision. Patted his pockets to make sure he had spare stripper clips, and he ejected the shells, wiped each bullet, and reinserted them. Wiped the metalwork with a clean, lint-free rag, and dry fired the rifle. It was fine, and he worked the bolt to chamber a round. When he needed to shoot, he couldn't afford the extra split second it would take to work the bolt and load the round before he fired.

The engines started with a massive roar, and the Shermans drove forward to the start line. They were still out of sight, invisible to the enemy guns emplaced inside the town, but when they drove out into the open, all bets would be off. General Shriver was there, and he wore a beaming smile. As if the master plan he'd put together was about to succeed, expecting them to salute him as some kind of military genius. Murphy doubted it would happen, except in his wildest dreams, his fevered imagination. He'd been inside that town, seen what they were up against, and he had severe misgivings.

Those PAK-40 anti-tank guns were mean mothers. Sure, they had more tanks, but the enemy armor he'd seen in action was no pushover. The Tiger, the Panther, and the STuGs were formidable, proven in battle, and more than a match for the Shermans. Shriver's troops should outnumber them, now he'd brought up the three companies from the 105th, but what if Kreis had also brought in more men? They could be facing a crack SS outfit. Nazi fanatics who'd fight with savagery the rookies would find difficult to combat.

The Shermans nosed out into the open, and Washington waved his company forward. The three platoons moved out, and it didn't look like many men. The rookies followed, around three hundred troops, and they walked slowly, looking terrified. Kelly was right. It did look like a throwback to an earlier war, and once again he looked up at the sky, hoping against hope they'd found a way to send in the fighters to suppress the enemy, but the sky was empty of everything. Except fucking clouds.

He found the platoon was walking behind Sergeant Davidson's tank, which gave him confidence. Chris was good people, and he'd handled himself well when the shooting started. Which it did, right there and then. Shells whistled over, and the bastards had got it just right. Kreis had divided his guns into two sections, with one firing AP, armor-piercing shells, and the other HE, high-explosive. The effect was devastating, and although they ducked low to avoid the metal fragments showering around them, several shells fell in the rear. A few of the newcomers fell, some wounded, and some beyond help.

Washington shouted up to the turret, "We need to pick up the pace. It's too slow. We're making it easy for them."

Davison nodded, spoke into his microphone, and the tank went faster. The Rangers broke into a jog to try to stay close behind, but the fast-moving vehicle was outstripping them. Every man stuck out into the open was relieved, for as they got closer to the town, the Germans switched tactics. All the guns were firing AP, taking their toll on the lightly armored Shermans. Two tanks took direct hits. The crews perished in explosions of flame and smoke, but their deaths gave some respite to the others, as roiling clouds of black smoke rolled over the open ground. Now it was the turn of the Americans to get in some licks. They'd pinpointed the locations of the guns shooting at them and opened fire at the stationary targets. Their shells crashed into the buildings over the gun emplacements. The men on the ground couldn't see them through the smoke and confusion, but they saw three massive explosions as the shells smashed into their positions, destroyed the guns, and ignited the munitions stores.

One Sherman broke down and came to a stop. The hatch opened, and the crew climbed out and ran back. The men following clustered behind the seeming protection of the steel armor, until an NCO screamed at them to keep moving. "It's a sitting duck for the Kraut guns. They'll possibly hit it with everything they have. If you want to live, keep moving!"

Davidson's tank was firing repeatedly, shell after shell into the enemy positions, and Murphy realized much of the smoke wasn't from burning tanks. They'd been firing smoke shells to give them a screen, and his estimation of the Sergeant's skills went up a notch. Smoke wouldn't stop bullets, but it would stop them from becoming sitting ducks for the enemy. They were two hundred yards before the town when everything changed, and it wasn't for the better. Over the thunder of the guns, the roar of the tank engines, the chatter of machine guns, and the hundreds of rifle shots from either side, a new sound reached them. They came in from the right flank, enemy armor. The Tiger and the Panther, and their fire was both accurate and lethal.

The Shermans automatically turned to face them, so their thick frontal armor would give them better protection against the 88mm main gun of the Tiger, and the higher velocity 7.5cm KwK 42 gun fitted to the Panther. Both guns were more powerful and capable of better penetration than the Sherman's lower velocity 76mm gun, and they scored three hits in rapid succession. From the moment those panzers appeared, everything started to unravel. By turning to face the new threat, the Shermans had exposed their lighter armored flanks to the PAK-40s, and the battle became little more than a slaughter.

Two more tanks exploded, and half-dozen Shermans turned to duel with the anti-tank guns, but it had become a rout. Already, the green troops who'd hung back at the rear had started to edge away, and a few were crawling back to the start line to escape the hell of hot metal and high-explosive swamping the battlefield. Rooker was still going forward, and Murphy and Kelly had stayed with him. But when everything fell apart, he looked for the Lieutenant, who was a few yards behind them, walking with the more numerous men of Second Platoon.

"Lt, you have to talk to Washington and call a halt. We're going nowhere with this."

"Negative, Sergeant. We have our orders, and we'll carry them out."

Rooker glared at him. "You're wrong, Lieutenant. I'll talk to Captain Washington."

"Sergeant, you will not go over my head to the company commander. Do I make myself clear? You do that, and I'll have you arrested for insubordination."

He stared back at him. "Lieutenant, you're a horse's ass."

He didn't say it too loud, and it was fortunate that a fresh barrage of shells landed at the same time, close enough to make it difficult to hear. Adams pretended he hadn't heard what he'd said.

Murphy grinned to himself. If he did hear, he took no notice.

I guess he knows he's a horse's ass.

The Shermans popped more smoke, and a thick fog descended over the battlefield, screening them from enemy fire. They worked their way back to the start point, and when they made it over the low rise out of sight of enemy fire, men threw themselves down, surrendering to the total exhaustion that'd overtaken them. The kind of exhaustion that comes from the sheer terror of knowing you're going to your death, and the sheer relief and pleasure of knowing you'd survived. A feeling of total euphoria, mixed with the guilt experienced by survivors when men they have bunked down with, have eaten with, and have fought alongside, hadn't been so lucky.

The last of the Shermans rolled over the rise, and they were out of sight, although enemy artillery continued firing shells over their position, some landing too close for comfort and causing more casualties. One man fell with blood pouring from a gaping wound when a chunk of metal sliced through the muscle of his leg. Murphy and Kelly rushed to help him, and they fastened a tourniquet to stop him bleeding to death, applying a dressing over the wound.

He nodded his thanks. "I survived all the way out there and all the way back, and now this. I guess I'm lucky it wasn't my neck that got hit."

"We're all lucky, pal. It was sheer murder out there, and the guy who gave the order to go up against those guns should have his brains examined."

A voice snarled, "You're out of line, soldier. If you'd done what I ordered you to do, we'd have taken the town and kicked the Nazis out."

Murphy glared at General Shriver, and he couldn't stop himself from speaking his mind.

"General, the attack was a disaster from start to finish. We had no air support and no artillery support. You should've called it off until we had the means to finish the job."

"That's crap. What I needed was men with guts, is all. I'm not standing here to argue with a private soldier. I'm ordering them back in. Dawn tomorrow."

He stalked away, and Murphy struggled to contain his disbelief. The word went around they'd be doing it all again, and the atmosphere through the rest of the day was poisonous, talk of men refusing to obey orders. It was close to a mutiny until wiser heads like those of Captain Washington and Sergeant Rooker prevailed, talking to the men, and explaining they'd do what they can to make him see sense. When they came back from meeting with the General, their faces were dark.

"He said we go again. Dawn tomorrow, same time."

They glanced at Rooker. "Air support?"

"The cloud base is still too low for air operations, so we can forget it."

"What about artillery?"

"Nothing, he said there's nothing that can get here in time."

"So why not wait?"

He shrugged. "No idea, but my guess is they're putting pressure on Shriver to make a breakthrough, and he's one of those guys who hates to say no to Eisenhower. In the manuals, it says to follow orders, and if those orders tell you to do something, you say yes, and jump to it."

"And get your men killed."

"If we don't do something different, yeah, it's likely."

"Different like what?"

A shrug. "I don't know, but the Captain was talking with Loony Lawson, and maybe they're cooking something up. All we can do is wait and see."

They waited and saw nothing, except the rain. To add to their misery, the skies opened up into a Midsummer storm, and the pelting rain soaked into their uniforms. Men shivered, knowing they would spend a miserable night under their flimsy waterproof ponchos, which were worse than useless when you were already soaking wet. In the early evening, Washington and Lawson found them, and they drew Murphy and Kelly to one side, along with two other Rangers.

"You men have been inside the town, and you know how the land lies, yes?"

"That's correct," Kelly nodded.

"Sergeant Rooker, as I recall you had to dig your way out

through that tunnel that started beneath the bank."

"We did. It was either that, or we'd have been buried alive. You may recall they dynamited the building above the entrance to the tunnel, and it's buried beneath tons of rubble."

Lawson took over. "Would it be possible to get back in the way you came out?"

Rooker shook his head emphatically. "Not a chance. Not without a team of mining engineers, and some heavy equipment."

"Suppose there was a way through. I've had several experiences with collapsed buildings during my time as a soldier, and things are not always as tough as they look. Masonry falls in peculiar ways, and there are often gaps where a man can wriggle his way through."

"When we came through, we were more concerned with avoiding our own funeral. What're you saying, Major?"

"I'm proposing we send a squad back into the town through that tunnel, armed with grenades, explosives, and maybe a bazooka or two. Try to break through into the remains of the building and come out behind the enemy. If we can destroy the guns, we're on our way to winning this one. Without the PAK-40s, our tanks will have more of a chance against those panzers. What do you say?"

Murphy replied. "How about you get General Shriver to lead the operation? I'd like to see that bastard in action, see how it feels."

Loony Lawson grinned. "I don't think so, but you haven't answered my question. Will you do it?"

He thought about that long crawl through the abandoned mine, a dark, spine-chilling tunnel that threatened to collapse and bury them at any moment. All that kept them going was the knowledge every yard they covered was a yard nearer the safety of their own lines. And now Loony was proposing they went back into the cauldron of enemy-held Evrecy. No wonder they called him Loony.

He looked at Washington. "What do you say, Captain?"

"It's up to you men. Sergeant Rooker, Kelly, yourself, and the others who made it back through that tunnel. If you say it's not possible, it's not possible. We'll just have to hope things don't go as bad tomorrow as they did today. If it makes any difference, I'd be coming with you. First Platoon is shorthanded, and I'll bring along a few men from Second Platoon to make up the numbers. They reckon they're hotshots with the bazooka, so they can take care of that side of things. I reckon twenty men should be enough. Any more, and we'll make a traffic jam inside that tunnel. Oh, yeah, there's a man in Second Platoon, Corporal Miguel Hernandez, and he's built like your Sergeant Rooker. He'll help out with the digging."

"You can count me in," Lawson grinned, "I wouldn't miss this for anything. Get behind Jerry, take him by surprise, and give him a good kicking. There's something else. One of the French civilians who came up with you, he used to have a keen interest in local history and archaeology. I think I can persuade him to come along."

"As long as he's not like the last two-timing bastard."

"No, no, I guarantee it. He's more than grateful you got those people out, and I think he'd be happy to repay the favor."

He nodded. "It looks to me like you have it all worked out. We may as well do it, anything rather than another disaster like what happened today."

Loony smiled. "I thought you'd see it our way. If General Shriver gets wind of it, he'll put a stop to it, so we need to keep it all quiet. Captain Washington, if you'd get the men together, and we'll assemble at 23.00 outside the tunnel entrance."

"We'll be there, and I'll make sure we have everything we need. Grenades, bazookas, spare rockets, and a couple of BARs. When the enemy finds out we're there, we're gonna need one helluva lot of firepower. Murphy, can we get all that gear through the tunnel?"

"It'll be a struggle, Captain, but if we don't take it with us, we'll be wasting our time. We're gonna need every bullet, every grenade, and every rocket. We have to get it through."

During the evening, the atmosphere in the camp was somber. Every man knew they were going back into disaster the next day, and there was nothing they could do about it. When a General said jump, the grunts had to jump. Or else.

At 22.00 they made their way through the darkness to the tunnel entrance. The black hole gaped menacingly, and it was like looking at the entrance to Hades. Corporal Hernandez arrived. He was almost a twin to Sergeant Rooker, except a bit bigger, taller, around six feet four inches, and as broad. Muscles more pronounced, and he looked like he'd spent most of his life laboring in the construction industry, which proved to be true.

"If you need any digging, I'm your man," he told them cheerfully. He had a thick, Mexican accent, although his English was easily understandable and more important, he carried the tools of his trade. A spade and a pick, and they looked both high quality and well used, "I found these abandoned in a builder's store, so I brought them along, thought they might come in useful. You can forget army entrenching tools. These'll cut a tunnel to hell if necessary."

Rooker grinned, and it was obvious the two men had formed an immediate liking for each other. "Miguel, that's where we're going. To hell."

Washington and Lawson arrived last, and the Captain nodded to Rooker and Hernandez. "It's up to you guys, time to make a start."

They dived into the tunnel, and Murphy followed. The speed the two NCOs made along the darkened passage was nothing short of incredible. The earth flew back from their picks and spades as they carved away through the earth partly blocking the route. They made good time, and when they reached the blockage that'd threatened to prevent them from getting through, the two men chewed through it like a knife through butter. Within a half-hour, they were digging through the rubble blocking the entrance to the strong room. Their progress slowed, but it didn't stop. It took them two hours, but they made it through, finally emerging into the even more cramped space beneath the old bank building.

There wasn't room for all twenty men to emerge, and they had to wait in the tunnel until they'd cleared more of the rubble. Murphy watched them digging, astonished at the speed they worked. When they emerged from the tunnel, they'd stripped to the waist, and both men's huge bodies glistened with sweat as they hacked away at the rubble, and then Hernandez held up a hand for them to stop.

"I see something. There's a gap."

They had a bad moment when Rooker was helping him pull out a huge, heavy slab of masonry that must've weighed a quarter of a ton. They slid it out of the narrow excavation they were digging to reach the first floor of the building when the rubble moved. The entire mass of masonry, hundreds of tons, began to shift. Murphy froze. If it came down, the place would become their tomb for all eternity, like those Romans when Mount Vesuvius erupted and buried the city of Pompeii under a solid mass of ash and lava.

They hurriedly shoved the slab back into place, and after a few seconds, the movement stopped. They paused, looked at each other as they worked out their next move, and Rooker glanced back at Murphy.

"Better tell them to stay in the tunnel until we've worked this out."

"Yeah, that sounds like good advice."

He passed on the message to Kelly, who was waiting in the underground chamber. When he looked back to check the digging, the two NCOs were prowling around with flashlights, looking for another way through. They found it and continued working, although this time they were slower and more careful. The rubble could shift at any moment, and they picked at it piece by piece. Where there was any doubt, they used small pieces of stone as props to make sure there were no repeats like what'd happened when they moved that slab. The process went even slower, but he wasn't inclined to argue. Better to make it a bit later. Better than a premature burial.

They continued working, and he checked his watch. The minutes were ticking past, and the hours were ticking past. It was already 03.00. There was no doubt General Shriver would launch the attack at 07.00, just like the last one. He didn't know if it said that was the right way to do it in the manuals, but he doubted it. At least, not since the last war in the trenches, when the generals had ordered their men to make repeated attacks. Walking through the mud into the teeth of enemy machine guns, attempting to fight their way through over the hundreds of corpses of those who'd gone before.

It was 03.30 when Rooker buried his pick into the next solid mass of rubble and met no resistance. He glanced back. "I think we're through. Keep it quiet. We don't know who's out there."

He worked even more slowly, clearing a space large enough for a man to climb through, and at last he emerged into the open. He looked back down and grinned.

"We're in the clear. Out in the open, and I can't see any soldiers around, but keep the noise down just in case. Get them up here, and we'll work out our next move.

By 04.00 they were standing amid the mass of rubble that had once been a solid bank building. It'd taken time to drag the heavier weapons through, like the bazookas and the Browning Automatic Rifles, but they'd made it. Now they needed to work out where to hit the enemy, and for the first time, Murphy noticed the civilian, an older guy who spoke good English and told them to call him Marcel.

"We're close to the center of the town, and I understand the Germans have sited the guns on the west side. There is a way to get through without being seen. Follow me."

They followed, and Marcel led the way, threading through narrow lanes. Once they walked through the front door of an imposing building, he told them had been the Mayor's residence, out the back way, and across the rear yard. When they emerged, he told them they were two streets away from the edge of town.

"I imagine the guns will be close, in the next street or the last one. I cannot get any closer."

They thanked him, and at a nod from Washington, Murphy crept forward. When he heard a noise behind him, he saw Loony Lawson was following.

"I need to see where they are," he murmured.

"Keep it quiet," he hissed, "They're close."

He didn't reply, which was sensible. At least the guy had enough sense to take the advice of another man, even when it came from a private soldier. He heard a noise in the next street and crawled into a house, up the staircase, and he was staring out the back window. Staring at the guns, five in all, with the crews starting to stir. Some were already up and dressed, smoking and drinking coffee, chatting with each other. They looked relaxed, without a care in the world. Why should they be concerned? They'd seen an amateurish attack launched the previous morning and had fought it off with ease. They were bound to have a low opinion of the guy in charge of the American troops, and they looked like they were preparing for a repeat.

He was about to pull back when he saw more troops appear from another street to the south of the town, and there were still a lot of them. They were carrying machine guns, MG-34s or MG-42s. Yet more carried belts of ammunition. Scores of belts of ammunition, and it looked like they had access to a supply convoy of munitions. The guns had shells stacked around them, plenty of shells. Each piece was protected by sandbagged emplacements, reinforced with chunks of stone they'd torn from nearby buildings, forming an additional three or four feet of protection in front of each gun.

They'd be a tough nut to crack. He couldn't be sure a

direct hit from a Sherman 76mm would be enough to smash through the sheer mass of stone and sandbags to the guns. Neither could he be sure how many of the Shermans would survive the first barrage of anti-tank shells.

"I make the gun crews around twenty men, and the soldiers who just arrived number forty or fifty. Four machine guns, and they have plenty of ammunition."

Loony Lawson grimaced. "If they fire first, our men will take a hammering."

"So we'd better make sure we fire first. Major, we need to bring up the rest of the men, take up positions behind them, and be ready to fire. If we hit them when the attack starts, an instant before they start shooting, they'll be thrown into confusion, and they won't know what the hell's going on. While we're keeping them busy, you can shoot first, and I'm kinda hoping our guys can shoot straight. We'll be in the path of our own shells, and I reckon it's gonna get kind of hairy."

Lawson nodded. "They'll fire ranging shots first, which shouldn't be too much of a threat to the tanks, but they'll give away their positions. That'll enable our guys to locate the targets."

"So we let them each fire a single shell before we throw down on them, and then we get out of Dodge before our guys cut loose, is that what you're saying?"

Lawson opened his mouth to reply, but he closed it a fraction of a second later. They'd heard a boot scrape on the staircase. Somebody was climbing up toward them. One of ours, or a Jerry? They brought up their guns ready to fire, but if it was an enemy, a single shot would bring alert the Germans. They'd swamp them with troops, and when they'd killed Murphy and

Lawson, they'd wonder where they'd come from. The next move would be to search the town, and they had to find the rest of the guys.

He prayed it was one of theirs. It wasn't. The soldier appeared wearing the iconic coalscuttle helmet appeared, saw them in the same instant, and pointed his machine pistol. "Hande Hoch!" *Hands up.*

They lowered their weapons to the floor both raised their hands. Murphy breathed, "We're fucked."

CHAPTER TEN

He didn't look like a rookie. A hard face screwed into a savage smile, the eyes squinting at them, and everything about him looked like he'd seen plenty of action. Like the machine pistol, scratched and battered. His uniform, splotched with dark stains, and Murphy had seen plenty of stains like that before. Bloodstains. His face was badly scarred, peppered with ingrained black spots that could only have come from munitions that'd exploded too close. Shells, bombs, or hand grenades. This was a man who'd been in battle, and the fact he was still alive proved he knew how to handle himself.

The guy spat a long stream of questions at them in German, and they both shook their heads to indicate they didn't have a clue what he was talking about. All they managed to do was make him even more pissed. The narrowed eyes reddened, the lips tightened with fury, and he looked about to gun them down for the mere offense of not understanding German. It was no surprise. The Germans gunned people down for a lot less than that, and Murphy was trying to work out how to get the drop on him. He lowered his eyes; looking for a chunk of debris on the floor he could tap with his boot and send it to the other side of the room. If he averted his eyes for long enough, he could drag the Colt from the holster, but he considered it likely the guy was too experienced to fall for a simple ruse.

His eyes fixed on a chunk of plaster that'd fallen from the ceiling, and he lined it up, flicked it away with the toe of his boot, and it flew across the room to clatter against the wall. The German didn't fall for it, and the thin lips formed a smile. He said something they didn't understand, but it didn't sound promising. He tapped the gun into his shoulder, and Murphy tensed, ready to jump and launch himself at the soldier in a last desperate move to take him down before they both died.

He didn't jump. An American helmet appeared around the doorway. The owner of the helmet took one step into the room, and he was clutching a combat knife. Dan Kelly wrapped an arm around the guy's neck and stabbed the knife into his throat, while another man, Marcel, the French civilian deftly relieved him of his machine pistol.

The German was struggling and threshing to draw breath and to fight back, but he was dying, choking on his own blood. Unable to suck air into his lungs, Kelly gently lowered him to the floor without making a sound.

"What kept you?"

He glanced at Murphy and chuckled. "I stopped at a bar for a cold beer."

"Next time try to get here a bit quicker." He gestured to the window, "Take a look. They're all out there, no more than forty or fifty yards away."

He explained the plan to start shooting after the attack started, just before they opened fire, "The trick's gonna be avoiding our own shells. Before those Shermans start throwing munitions at the guns, we need to be anywhere but here."

Kelly nodded. "That makes sense. Maybe Marcel can point us toward the best route out of here."

"Except when they see the guns destroyed, the Germans will likely be running in the same direction." He thought about that for a second, and he could see Dan and Lawson thinking the same thing. He grinned, "Ambush."

They brought up the rest of the men and deployed the bazookas two streets behind. There was still the question of the panzers. They wouldn't be far away, and when they discovered what was going on inside the town, they were certain to appear in record time. Washington positioned the Brownings across the estimated route the enemy would take if they were fleeing from devastating enemy fire. The rest of the men took up position in the houses overlooking the street where they had the guns in clear sight.

He checked his watch, and the time was 06.05. Fifty-five minutes before the attack started, and they watched and waited. The Germans seemed relaxed, and that was good. If they were relaxed, they wouldn't be expecting any big surprises. He glanced out the window, as far as he was able without showing himself, and everything looked good. There were five artillery pieces, the machine guns, and the German infantry lounging close to small barricades they'd prepared to duck behind and hide from incoming fire. Nothing they couldn't handle. When they started shooting, the soldiers would wish they'd made those barricades more substantial, with protection from the rear as well as the front.

Too late for the Krauts, if this came off, they were toast. There was no reason why it shouldn't come off. The shock of the attack from behind, the crash of exploding grenades and bullets whining through the air, were bad enough. Until the tanks started shooting, and they'd hammer them from both sides. The Rangers would fall back behind the Brownings they'd positioned across their escape route, and they'd hose them down like rats in a trap. If everything went well, the Shermans would take out the guns, they'd take down most of the soldiers, and…

He looked at Washington. "There're five guns down there."

"That's correct."

"Last time I counted, they had nine."

"Maybe we took some of them out during yesterday's attack. We had to have hit something."

"Did we? Captain, what if we didn't? What if they have those other four guns positioned elsewhere?"

"Like where?"

"We know this Kreis guy who's in charge around here is no dummy. A butcher and a Nazi war criminal, sure, but he's no fool. If he's expecting an attack to come in like it did yesterday, wouldn't he position his guns just the same to hit our guys in the flank where the tanks are more vulnerable?"

"You mean to the north the open ground they have to cross?"

"That's exactly what I mean."

He squinted out the window to the north, as if he was expecting to see an array of four artillery pieces, neatly lined up, and all pointing to where they expected the Shermans to happen along any time soon. "I don't see anything."

"Captain, that's because they're out of sight, hidden behind camouflage of some sort."

Lawson came up beside him and gazed around. He also found nothing.

"Captain Washington, what he says is a possibility. If we didn't destroy those guns in yesterday's attack, they could be out there." His expression was bleak, "And there's not a damn thing we can do about it. We're too late."

The noise of engines broke the quiet of the early morning, and down below, the gun crews ran to their stations. The noise of the tank engines got louder as they came nearer, and the Rangers tensed, waiting for the moment when the artillery fired ranging shots.

He jerked his head around and looked at Washington. "Where're the tanks?"

"The tanks?" He pointed out front, "They're there. Can't you hear them, coming straight toward us?"

"They're ours. I'm talking about the enemy tanks, the panzers. They had four, a Tiger, a Panther, and two STuGs. They can't have gone, not if they knew we were preparing another attack. They must be close. But where?"

They both looked every which way, and there was no chance the enemy would see them. They were concentrating on what was coming toward them. Preparing their guns to fire those first all-important ranging shots. Waiting for the Shermans to get close enough so they couldn't miss.

"Where would they be?" Washington looked at Kelly, his forehead lined with worry.

"What was that?"

"I said where would they be?"

He looked at Kelly, and what he'd heard was the most sensible answer. Where would the Germans position their armored vehicles to be in the best place to take on the expected attack? They'd positioned four artillery pieces to the north so they could hit the Shermans in the flank. The answer was obvious.

"The south. Where else?"

They glanced at each other, and the terrible truth hit them like a punch in the belly. If they knew what was coming, and they had to, classic military doctrine dictated the best defense would be to hit them from the flanks. Which meant when they started shooting, there'd be carnage out there. Even if the American armor managed to destroy the guns on the edge of the town, enemy tanks and artillery on both flanks would savage the Shermans, and they could be facing yet another rout.

"What can we do?" It was Rooker who shouted the question. He was standing next to Miguel Hernandez, the big guy who'd stood shoulder-to-shoulder with him, shoveling their way through the rubble to get them into the town.

Hernandez had the answer, and it was simple. "Say, what about the bazookas. It was damned hard getting them through that tunnel, and I've been kinda hoping it wasn't all for nothing."

Washington grinned. "Corporal, you're a genius. Consider yourself promoted to sergeant when this is over. Murphy, Kelly, get yourselves back to the bazooka crews and tell them to haul ass to the south and locate those panzers. They'll be there somewhere, and when they see them, tell them to shoot the shit out of them. The machine gun crews can stay right here along with us. We'll be needed when the enemy falls back."

They raced away down the staircase, and as they emerged into the street, they heard the first ranging shots crash out. A moment later all hell broke loose as Washington's men lobbed grenades down onto the guns, and the soldiers clustered around them. The Shermans fired, and those ranging shots had given them their targets. Shells crashed around the PAK-40s, and soldiers screamed as the high-explosive and metal fragments sliced into them. Washington led them out of the building, and they raced back to the machine gun positions. Just ahead of the German infantry who were streaming back in panic.

Murphy and Kelly hustled the bazooka crews to grab their gear and get moving, and they took off, helping them carry their spare rockets. They raced through the town until they reached the southern outskirts, in time to see the blunt, thick frontal armor of a Tiger appear from a dip in the ground where it'd been hiding. The 88mm gun fired, sending a massive shell toward the American tanks that narrowly missed. They didn't wait for the next shell to hit, and they fired. The first rocket streaked out from the tube to impact on the heavy frontal armor of the Tiger.

"It's no good targeting them there. We need to hit them in the side or the rear," Murphy shouted. He dropped flat as the machine gun mounted on the turret sent a stream of lead toward them. Bullets ripped up the ground around them, and a bazooka crewman dropped the launcher and fell with his chest torn open with a volley of bullets, "We have to move. Now!"

He scooped up the dropped launcher and they snaked away, threading through empty buildings, searching for a way to get behind the enemy tank. The Tiger moved out the open, and the massive main gun opened fire, sending another shell whistling toward the Shermans. The Tiger was moving further away, and when they reached the edge of town, it was already out of range of the bazookas. Which left them with no choice but to race out into the open and chance the machine gun. The Tiger rumbled on, increasing the distance, firing on the move, and they had to cut across a stretch of flat, open ground to get into a good position to open fire.

That's when the STuG struck. They'd gone unnoticed, tucked into a fold in the ground, almost invisible, with just the 75mm main gun poking out from cover. They'd camouflaged the barrel with branches and foliage torn from nearby bushes. The secondary 7.92mm machine gun spat bullets, churning up the nearby ground, and they dived behind a rusting trough filled with rancid, algae scummed water. The water was a barrier that protected them, but the bullets tore holes into the thin metal, and the water began to drain away. He worked out they had less than ten seconds before the trough emptied, and the metal would give them no more protection than a sheet of parcel wrapping paper.

"We're moving out, now. If we're gonna hit the Tiger, we have to take out that StuG first."

"This is fucking suicide!" the corporal clutching the other bazooka muttered, "I didn't sign up for this."

"Neither did those guys in the Sherman. Bring the launcher, we're leaving."

He scooped up the bazooka, catapulted to his feet, and ran out into the open. He'd seen a chance to reach the German assault gun. It would mean a detour back into the town, racing between half-dozen buildings and emerging into a field protected by a stone wall. The field ran partway toward the position of the StuG, close enough for the bazooka.

The Germans chased them with another stream of machine gun fire, and they dived behind a house a split second before the gunner found the range. They ran through the streets in a desperate race against the clock to help the Shermans. They nearly lost the race when they ran into a bunch of soldiers. German soldiers who'd retreated after the storm of fire that destroyed the artillery. Ten men had bunched together, looking like they didn't have a clue where to go, whether to fight or run. Murphy made up their minds for them. They were still carrying grenades they'd brought through the tunnel, and as he ran, he unhooked a grenade, pulled the pin, and threw. He launched a second grenade and shouted, "Cover!"

They swerved aside, crashing through the plate glass of a fashion store, driving past a display of cotton frocks on manikins, and both grenades exploded. Soldiers screamed, and when they peered back out through the broken shards of glass, three bodies were lying in the street, while the survivors dragged away two wounded men. Murphy sent them on their way with a quick burst from the MP-40, and the last thing on their minds was fighting a rearguard action. They sped away like the Four Horsemen of the Apocalypse were chasing them down, and they disappeared around the corner.

He slung the machine pistol on his back, grabbed the bazooka, shouted, "Let's go!" and ran back out onto the street. Dan was still with him, and two of the bazooka crew climbed out behind him. One had gone missing. He opined he'd run. It was too bad, but they had both bazookas, and he was counting on them to do the job. They raced out into the open, doubled over to stay below the top of the wall. They ran to the end, peeked over, and the STuG was one hundred and fifty yards away. Although it would fly further, the accuracy of the rocket was lousy at any distance over one hundred yards. But they didn't have a choice. If they went out into the open, the machine gun would chew them into blood and gristle. They crouched behind the wall, with the launchers poking out over the top.

He glanced at the bazooka crew. "What're our chances from here?"

A shrug. "I've scored from this distance, but it's tough. Maybe one chance in three."

"We have two bazookas, which gives us two chances out of three. Better than average. You take the first shot, and we'll see how it's done."

He nodded and muttered something to the other guy. Probably telling him they were wasting their time, but he took aim, squeezed the trigger, and the rocket soared away.

The rocket missed. He estimated the error was infinitesimal, maybe a few inches, but a miss was a miss. It exploded against a tree several hundred yards away, and they'd given away their position to the enemy. The 7.92mm machine gun opened up, and bullets smacked into the wall. They had to duck low and wait for the volley to end. It was the worst thing that could've happened. They'd got so close to the assault gun, yet given away their position, and now the enemy knew they were there. They had to do something, and he came up with a possible solution, the only solution. He shouted at the other bazooka crew, who'd ducked so low they were lying flat.

"You have to take another shot!"

The corporal looked up; his expression incredulous. "Pal, you have to be kidding me. The moment we put our heads up, that machine gun will blow them off. Forget it."

"It's the only way. We'll move a hundred yards further along the wall, and while they're targeting you with machine gun fire, we'll get in another shot."

"I told you to forget it! I already told you, we're not here to commit suicide."

"Okay, we'll take the shot. Move further along the wall, about a hundred yards should do it. The wall runs at an angle, so the range should be about the same. When we pop up, they'll start shooting. That should give you a chance to line up another shot. With any luck, the next one will score a hit."

He muttered something to the other guy, who shrugged, and he nodded. "Okay, okay, we'll do it. Give us a minute."

They ran doubled over to a new position a hundred yards away. He signaled they were ready, and Murphy glanced at Dan. "We don't need two men for this. If I need to reload, I'll duck back down where you'll be ready with a spare rocket."

"For Christ's sake, Murphy, remember you're just taking a decoy shot. No heroics. Pop up, squeeze the trigger, and get out of sight."

"Roger that. Be ready to reload. If I need to shoot again, I'll have to move like greased lightning."

"Greased lightning, gotcha. Go for it."

The machine gun had stopped firing, and he leaped to his feet, pointed the bazooka over the wall. The rocket left the launcher, to miss by several yards. The enemy responded fast, faster than he would've believed. A bullet glanced off his helmet before he got back behind the wall. He shook his head to clear the ringing noise, but it persisted, like a swarm of hornets had got inside his head. He took off his helmet to explore the damage. The bullet had forced a deep dent in the steel, but it hadn't penetrated, which was why he was still alive.

"Remind me to find out who made this thing. I owe him a vote of thanks and a case of beer."

Dan grinned. "Amen to that." He shoved in a new rocket, "Locked and loaded."

"Roger that. I'll wait for the other guys to fire, and who knows, maybe we won't need to shoot again."

The other bazooka fired. The rocket whistled toward the StuG and exploded.

"He got him!"

They popped their heads up. "He missed."

The rocket had impacted on a pile of logs fifty yards before the target, and the explosion had ignited the timbers, so they were belching smoke. Murphy had the bazooka ready to fire again, but the smoke obscured his vision to target.

If I can't see them, they can't see me.

"I'm going out there."

"Forget it! You won't stand a chance."

"I reckon I can make it." He forced a grin. There wasn't much to smile about, but what the hell, every man had to die sometime, "I'll see you in hell."

He launched himself over the wall and ran through the smoke. A slight wind had come up, and the smoke was starting to thin. The hull of the StuG was a gray, dark shape that was becoming clearer every second. He'd already estimated how close he needed to get to fire the bazooka, and it'd be less than one hundred yards. More like eighty yards to be sure of a hit, but he still hadn't made it to where he wanted to be when they saw him, and the machine gun clattered.

He dived to the ground, and the gun switched aim as the other bazooka crew took the opportunity to stand and launch another rocket. Another miss, but the heat was off him, at least for a few seconds. It was now or never. He catapulted to his feet and ran. Another fifteen yards, and he'd be where he needed to be. Ten yards, and the gun had stopped firing. Five yards, and the bullets whipped around him. Almost there, and he leaped the final three yards, landing heavily, but he was alive. They fired another bazooka rocket that missed but made them pause to work out which target to aim for. Which was the greater threat?

He made up their minds for them. Pointed the bazooka while lying prone on the ground and fired. This time there was no mistake. The rockets leaped from the launcher, and it traveled the short distance to the StuG. It tore into the side armor, penetrating thick steel like a hot knife in butter, and the vehicle exploded. Dan leaped over the wall and stood in the open like he'd just won a gold medal for the one hundred-yard dash.

"Fuckin' A, you did it. Shot the shit out of the bastards."

"Dan, get down!"

The other StuG had appeared, pushing its way out of a building on the edge of town where it'd been waiting to ambush the Allied tanks if they got that far. It was coming out behind them, and they hit the ground as the mobile assault gun rumbled toward them. The machine gun fired, but not at them. They'd spotted the other bazooka team, and the 7.92mm MG-34 chattered, spitting out a hail of bullets. All that saved them was they were climbing over the wall to check out the wreck of the STuG, and the burst of fire smashed into the wall where they'd been crouching. They flung themselves flat, and Murphy shouted at Dan to load another rocket.

He got it done in record time, and now the target was close, still coming on, blissfully unaware the other bazooka team was close. The STuG moved even closer, filling his sights, and there couldn't be any doubt. They'd designed the warhead to penetrate up to five inches of armor. The frontal armor on the STuG measured three inches. The warhead exploded inside the hull, and the result was spectacular. Shards of steel would've torn through the crew, but a massive secondary explosion told them the missile had found the shells lined up ready to fire. The turret flew off, and the vehicle ground to a stop, with smoke pouring from inside. Nobody got out.

This time, Dan was more careful, and he kept his head down in case there were any more nasty surprises lurking around the corner. They looked every which way, and they found nothing. But it wasn't over. The Tiger was still out there, firing shell after shell, and although the American armor scored plenty of hits, none penetrated the massive frontal armor, five inches thick. The Allied attack had stalled, and they were slugging it out with the most powerful and heavily armored tank in the theater of war. Yet there was nothing they could do. The battlefield was a nightmare of high-explosive and clouds of steel, with shells crisscrossing from both sides, and machine gun fire adding to the inferno.

They retreated into the town and found the Company. They'd taken over a defensive position left by the Germans, and there was no sign of Rooker or the officers. Crockett pointed to a nearby building, which in better times had been a hotel, but the front wall was missing after a direct hit from a shell or a bomb. They were standing at the top, watching the battle raging outside the town. An iron fire escape had survived at the side of the building, and he used it to race up to the top and join them out on the flat roof.

Adams glanced at him and waved him back. "Private, don't come any further. The roof is unstable. What do you need?"

"Reporting in, Lt. We took out two STuGs, so that's two we don't need to worry about. I don't know about the other two."

"Two? All I can see is the Tiger out there, and it's giving our guys a hard time, but there's not a damn thing we can do to help them."

"What about the anti-tank guns?"

He gave him a pitying look. "Listen, Murphy, you don't need to worry about tactics. We'll tell you what to do, all you need is to obey orders."

Rooker interrupted. "Lt, he has a point. As I recall, there were nine PAK-40s. We destroyed five, so where're the other four?"

"Sergeant, Headquarters told us the enemy is falling back on all fronts. I expect they've retreated along with most of their army." He looked at Washington. "I think we've spent enough time up here. This building could come down at any time."

Before he could answer, Rooker went on, "What if they haven't retreated?"

He returned a mirthless smile. "If they haven't retreated, Sergeant, where the hell are they? We can see for miles from up here, and if they were still around, we'd have seen them."

"Not if they were well camouflaged. Don't forget, the Nazi charged with defending Evrecy is a cunning savage. I'm willing to bet he's worked out some surprise, and they'll hit us when we're least expecting it."

"Sergeant, you're wrong. They've gone, no question."

"Sir, I'm not so sure…"

"Keep it yourself, Sergeant Rooker. Captain, it's time we got down from here before the building collapses."

Washington glanced at him, and he had a thoughtful expression on his face. "What if they haven't gone? Where would they be?"

"Captain, they're halfway to Germany by now. Can we get off this roof?"

He nodded slowly. "We're not doing any good up here. We can't see them, so I hope you're right."

Murphy descended the fire escape and they followed. Washington was last, and as he stepped off the final step, the iron staircase moved. The entire building moved, and Rooker shouted, "Run! It's coming down!"

They raced away, keeping ahead of the tons of rubble collapsing around them. They made it just in time, as the entire structure became a heap of masonry where once a hotel had stood. Astonishingly, the iron fire escape hadn't collapsed, and it remained like a black iron finger pointing up at the sky, but with no building to attach it to.

The battle still raged outside the town, and it didn't look good. Washington opined the Shermans had to win out over the Tiger by sheer numbers, and he was probably right. One tank, even the much-vaunted Panzer VI, had to succumb to the overwhelming mass of fire of the surviving Shermans, but it could still do a lot of damage in the meantime. Now they'd left their precarious perch on the roof of the damaged hotel, Adams began to recover his confidence.

"It'll be over soon, that Tiger can't survive much longer. Our guys will enter the town, and we can notify Headquarters the door is open to swing the armies through and get in behind the Germans. They'll have no choice but to surrender, and soon we'll be driving on Paris."

"I hope so, Lieutenant, I truly do." The Captain didn't look so confident, "But I'm still worried about those guns."

"You should be." Loony Lawson appeared, striding from a narrow gap between two ancient, stone, ivy-covered houses, with the elderly Frenchman, Marcel. "We think they've positioned the guns somewhere to the north, and they're waiting in ambush for our tanks to get close before they open fire. The Tiger is pushing them toward the guns, and it's a hammer and anvil. The Tiger is the hammer, and the guns the anvil. When they get the Shermans where they want them, they'll beat the crap out of them. Somehow, we must find a way to stop them. It's not just the artillery, they'd have deployed most of the infantry somewhere out there with the guns, and they're gonna be a hard nut to crack."

Washington looked puzzled. "You mean they abandoned the town? How come, if they know its importance to both sides?"

"You heard about Kursk, that big tank battle last year in Russia?"

"Sure, the biggest in history, they say."

"It was all of that. The Russians pulled back and let the Germans roll toward the defensive positions they'd dug, so when they arrived, they were waiting for them. They call it defense in depth. Giving ground to the enemy, leading them on to your prepared positions."

Adams snorted. "Not on your life, Major. We were on that roof, and we had a clear view of the entire countryside. If those guns and troops are out there, why couldn't we see them? Have you seen them, or is this just a guess?"

A pause. "No, we didn't see them. But we did find several sets of tracks; the kind of tracks trucks towing artillery would leave. They're out there, somewhere."

"With the greatest of respect, Sir, if they'd been there, we would've seen them. Unless they've covered them with a cloak of invisibility?"

Washington interrupted. "Lieutenant, you're out of line. You're talking to a senior officer, and a man with a great deal of military experience. Probably more than you'll ever have in your lifetime. If he believes they're there, he could be right. Major, you must have some idea where they're hiding."

For once, Loony seemed at a loss. "I don't know, and Marcel doesn't know. He knows this area like the back of his hand. He's lived here all his life, and he's been wracking his brains, trying to work it out. It is almost like Lieutenant Adams says; they've covered themselves with a cloak of invisibility."

Adams gloated, but Washington hadn't finished. "If you saw tracks, they must be there somewhere. Could they have used that route to retreat?"

"North-west? I don't think so. It would lead them into a head-on confrontation with the bulk of our army. Our guys would blow away a few Kraut anti-tank guns and fifty or sixty troops like they were swatting flies. We know the guy in charge is a homicidal Nazi, but he's a clever homicidal Nazi. I'm certain they're out there."

Washington believed him, but he wasn't happy. They couldn't fight them if they couldn't find them. Which meant if they'd found some deep concealment, sooner or later they'd show themselves, and the jaws of the trap would snap shut.

"We need a recce. We have to know what's out there. Major, you know the ground, would you do it, and take Marcel along with you?"

The Frenchman nodded eagerly. "Of course I will do it. Anything to beat the Boche and drive them out of France."

"Murphy, Kelly, are you up to going with them? I know you've had it hard, but you men always get the job done, and right now I need to get the job done. If there was somebody else I could send, I would, but…"

"That's okay, Cap'n. No sweat."

"It's appreciated. When this is over, I'll do you a favor and put you both in for promotion."

"Sir, when it's over, do us a favor and don't put us in for promotion."

He looked mystified. "You want to continue as private soldiers?"

Dan Kelly shot a glance toward the Lieutenant. "Promotion ain't all it's cut out to be."

He pretended not to understand the barbed comment. "If you find them, get a message back here fast. We have the men, and we have the machine guns. What we haven't got is somebody to fight."

Lawson led the way out of the town with Marcel, while Murphy and Kelly followed a few paces back, keeping a wary eye out for an enemy that'd proved cunning and resourceful. A half-mile out of town there was still no sign of them. It didn't look good, and they asked the Brit if they could've missed them. He shook his head.

"That's an emphatic no. They're here, and if we keep going, we'll find them."

Murphy wasn't so sure. There was something strange going on, something they couldn't see. Nothing to do with a cloak of invisibility, but what was it? It was Marcel, the Frenchman, who spoke urgently to Lawson; his eyes widened, and he nodded emphatically. "You may have hit it on the head."

He turned to Murphy and Kelly. "He just reminded me about the old French château. They demolished it during the French Revolution, a hundred and fifty years ago, and ever since the locals have removed the stones to build their houses, so there's nothing left of the original structure. But the moat is still there. It's dry. There hasn't been any water for over a hundred years, and it's deep enough to conceal what we're looking for. Artillery, soldiers, and even tanks. They could hide in there and pop out at the last moment to ambush our troops. Marcel will lead us that way, and we'll check it out."

The Frenchman led them, and they approached the site of the old château through a line of trees that got them within four hundred yards, and he called a halt.

"We can't go any further without exposing ourselves to the enemy if they're there."

Lawson nodded. "There must be a way to get closer. What do you suggest?"

He gave a typically Gallic shrug they took to be a no. Murphy stepped up to the plate. "I'll crawl across. There's plenty of long grass to cover me, and I can get close enough to take a look."

Lawson nodded. "As soon as you see anything, get back here. We'll report back to Washington, and if they're there, we'll give them a big surprise."

Murphy started forward, dropping to his hands and knees. When he got out into the open, he crawled on his belly, inching through the long grass. He still couldn't see the old moat, but the Frenchman had pointed him in the right direction. After the first two hundred yards, he became convinced he was on the right track. It was the odors he noticed first, the stench of oil and grease, of expended munitions, and of human waste that often pervaded the temporary camp of a large number of troops. He considered crawling back to pass on what he'd discovered, but he decided he needed more, like the number of guns, troops, and armor.

He crawled on, and the smell became stronger. He estimated he was fifty yards from the moat, and he slowed. Inching forward at an infinitesimal pace to make sure he wasn't discovered, and he worked out he was almost there. Through the grass, he could make out the camouflaged outline of a gun barrel, and another, and another. They were there, and he crawled another yard. There was something bigger, a gun barrel. A gun barrel attached to the camouflaged turret of an armored vehicle. He'd seen enough, and he started to crawl backward. And stopped.

"Wer da?" *Who's there?*

He saw the German helmet coming toward him, saw the KAR-98 rifle angling down toward him. He'd messed up. If he fired a bullet at him to take him down, they'd know he was there. A score of soldiers would emerge, and he'd be dead. If he did nothing, he'd be dead. He had to face it, there was no way out.

CHAPTER ELEVEN

He took the only possible option, and that meant doing nothing. Apart from dragging out his combat knife and holding it at his side, away from the German so it was out of sight. The guy came closer, and when he saw Murphy, his lips formed a smile. He said something in German he didn't understand and worked the bolt on his rifle. Leaned closer and put the steel muzzle against Murphy's chest. He watched the eyes beneath the rim of the steel helmet. It was always in the eyes. Waited until they focused and tightened with a steely expression. The expression he'd seen before a man squeezed the trigger, and he moved.

He swung up with the knife, and the finely-honed blade sliced through the man's finger held over the trigger. The finger fell away in a gush of blood, and the self-satisfied, gloating expression changed. Once again it was in the eyes, and they widened. The mouth opened, and he was about to scream, not a warning, but a scream of agony. It would be loud enough to alert every German soldier in the vicinity. They'd be all over him in seconds. He swung his legs around, scissored them around the German's ankles, and flipped him over. Bringing over the knife at the same time, he plunged it into the gaping maw of his mouth, and instead of a high-pitched, pain-wracked scream, all that emerged was a choking gurgle. He put his hand over the man's mouth to keep him quiet, ignoring the blood pouring from the back of his ruined throat.

He thrashed and struggled, trying to break free, trying to breathe, trying anything. One moment he'd been about to kill an enemy soldier, and now he was dying. He didn't want to die, and in his death throes his strength was almost superhuman. Murphy had to throw himself off his body to hold him down and prevent him from making too much noise. He stayed on top of him, and gradually, the violent movements eased until he lay still. Only then did he relax his grip on his mouth when he was certain the guy was dead.

He left the corpse lying on the ground and continued crawling forward until he was at the edge of what had once been the château moat. Peering through the weeds and grass on the edge, he saw them. Well hidden by camouflage netting, leaves, and broken branches, a Tiger tank, two STuGs, and five artillery pieces, along with fifty or sixty soldiers. The men had relaxed, confident they were safe out of sight of the enemy, and in the middle, close to where he assumed the château would once have stood, he saw the man he'd vowed to kill. Major Gottlieb Kreis chatted to another officer, a captain wearing the black uniform of a tanker. The man acknowledged what Kreis had said, walked across to the Tiger, and climbed onto the hull. He said something to the crew who'd sprawled on the grass. They joined him and climbed inside the armored behemoth.

They were getting ready for battle, and he'd seen enough. He crawled back to where he'd left the body, and began dragging it away from the moat, back toward where the others waited for him. It was a long crawl, pulling the dead weight, but he made it, and it was almost worth it when they goggled at what he'd brought back.

Lawson's eyes narrowed. "If you take a prisoner, Murphy, it's normal to bring him back alive."

"He nearly killed me. Maybe I should've left the body for them to find."

He nodded his understanding. "Point taken, my apologies. We need to get back and tell them what you've seen."

They made it back to Battalion HQ and reported what they'd found. General Shriver was in process of assembling his force, and he looked to be watching while his soldiers counted and checked off from a list a stack of ammo boxes. Washington pointed out the counting could wait. If they moved fast, they could pound the crap out of them while they were still in that moat, blissfully unaware the enemy had spotted them. He refused.

"I'm waiting for more reinforcements. We've lost tanks and men, and I don't intend to make a move until the replacements arrive."

"You could call in an airstrike," Washington pointed out, "Catch them napping, it'll save us all a heap of hassle."

He gave him an irritated glare. "I don't think so, Captain. This is my fight. Our fight, and when we win, it'll be our glory. An airstrike won't give us any medals."

"It'll keep casualties down, General. Save the lives of our men."

"I'll decide how this works, and if you do your job right, we'll keep casualties to the minimum." He forced a smile, "Look, when this is over, you could be a Major. Provided it goes right."

"I'd sooner be a captain in command of a live company, rather than a major in command of a heap of corpses."

The smile faded. "You're out of line, Captain. I intend to follow procedure and attack tomorrow, at dawn. Provided the reinforcements arrived. I'm waiting for two companies of infantry and a squadron of Shermans to replace our losses. That'll give us more than enough punch to chew the enemy into little pieces."

He strutted away, and there was nothing more they could do. Except to wait, the bane of every soldier, and it was worse when those soldiers knew every hour they waited was an hour they were giving the enemy to prepare. Shriver throwing away the advantage of knowing the enemy's position, and when Washington strolled back to where Lawson waited with Marcel and the First platoon, he couldn't help but spell out what the 'military genius' had in mind.

"If everything goes well, Shriver could be right, and we could hit them at dawn tomorrow with enough tanks and troops to tear them apart. What worries me is if he's wrong. The Germans may not wait, and if they decide to come out and attack first, General Shriver is gonna be caught with his pants down."

Lawson agreed. "He's no Patton, that's for sure, but he happens to be the man in charge. There's nothing we can do, except play it his way." He glanced up as a truck arrived, and he smiled, "Except get something to eat. I'll say this about the U.S. Army; you know how to look after yourselves. British Army food is terrible."

"Ours isn't much better," Dan Kelly grunted, "Pig swill."

Nobody argued, but they queued up as the cooks ladled food into their mess tins, and they sat around eating. Murphy finished and was drinking from his canteen to wash down the food he'd just eaten. He failed to identify when a jeep drew up. An MP climbed out. He didn't need to identify the man to know trouble had arrived, trouble in the shape of Sergeant Duane Bishop. He walked toward him, and he wasn't alone. Two more MPs accompanied him, and they were all muscle, like beat cops back home. The kind who believed there were no problems they couldn't fix with the judicious application of a nightstick.

Bishop sneered. "Murphy, I guess you're no angel after all. We know what you did."

"Right. So what did I do, Bishop?"

"Sergeant Bishop to you."

"I'm waiting, so spit it out."

"You murdered two men. Sergeant Abbott and Corporal Pérez. I got them to extract the bullets from their corpses, and you know what they found? Slugs fired from an MP-40, just like the gun you carry around with you. Like the one you're carrying on your shoulder right now."

Lawson interrupted. "Sergeant, there are thousands of MP-40s in this theater, tens of thousands. What makes you think the bullets were fired from Murphy's gun?"

"Because I managed to get hold of a round he fired during the German counterattack. It smacked into a tree, and a soldier got it out for us so we could compare. They're a match."

The Brit looked at Murphy. "Do you have an explanation?"

Murphy was thinking about that MP-40, and unless he'd got it wrong, they'd taken it off him when they captured him. The weapon he carried now was one he'd taken from another dead German. "They got it wrong. Who says the bullet he recovered was fired from my gun?"

He didn't need to ask. He already knew. There was one man who'd do anything to suck up to officers and MPs. PFC Ron Lucas, Lieutenant Adams' driver. A man who'd go to any lengths to keep himself as far away from the action as possible. Probably he'd worked out if he dropped Murphy in the shit, he'd be called to the rear to give evidence as an eyewitness.

"We have a witness," Bishop smiled, "Private Jack Murphy, you're under arrest, pending a court martial on the charge of murder. Men, cuff him, we'll take him back with us."

They stepped forward, and he knew whatever he said wouldn't make a tad of difference. Bishop wanted blood, wanted to make a high-profile arrest for what he had already made up his mind was the murder of his pal, Jeff Abbott. He waited for them to come, considering and discarding the options. There were none, at least, not until they checked his machine pistol and found the bullets weren't a match.

"Hold it!"

Captain Washington appeared and walked up to Bishop. "You can't arrest him, Sergeant. We're about to go into battle, and we need every man."

He shook his head. "It's outside of your say-so, Captain. This is Military Police business, and you have no authority to interfere. Step back."

With no alternative, he let them cuff him. They led him toward their jeep and pushed him into the back, where he sat with a burly MP next to him to stop him from jumping out. Bishop climbed in the front, and the other MP got behind the wheel. They attached a long chain to the cuffs in case he tried to make a run for it. They'd riveted the other end to a steel stanchion fixed to the body of the jeep. The engine roared, and they drove away. Bishop twisted around to regard the prisoner, looking like he was more than pleased with himself.

"Jeff told me about you, said you'd caused him trouble in Whitefish, and he even believed you murdered a girl they found dead in the woods."

The girl Abbott raped and murdered to hide the evidence of his crime.

"What've you got to say now, wise guy? Your ass is mine, and we'll beat the truth out of you when we get back to HQ."

"You got it all wrong, Bishop. Do you want to know why?"

"Why don't you tell me, Angel?"

"Because you're pig shit thick, that's why. You wouldn't know the truth if it fell on top of your stupid head, and even then…"

He should have kept his mouth shut, and he got his reward; a blow on the side of the head, just beneath the rim of his helmet, a blow from an expert. Everything went black like the sky had just fallen in, or maybe it'd exploded, and he almost fell over the side of the jeep. Strong hands grabbed him, and it felt strange as if the ground had moved in an earthquake.

Jesus Christ, that guy sure knew how to hit!

Something strange was happening, and he felt the jeep lurch off the track and shudder to a stop. Somebody shouted,

"Incoming!"

The next moment they dragged him semi-conscious from the jeep, and he was lying on the ground. It was no earthquake. Men were lying flat, holding their helmets tight over their heads, and artillery was exploding all around them.

What the hell!

He was still dazed from the blow, but his mind cleared, and he knew what was happening. General Shriver's plan had failed. The Krauts had got the jump on him.

The MP driving the jeep got back on the track and headed away at high speed, determined to put distance between them and the battle back at Evrecy. They reached Battalion HQ in record time, just behind General Shriver's command car, that'd made even better time away from the action. Shriver was already out, shouting orders, surrounded by confused officers.

"Get the lead out. We're under attack!"

"Where from, General?"

"From the Germans in Evrecy, it looks like they took Washington's unit by surprise. I told the stupid bastard to get there first, but he wouldn't listen. Now we're in the shit."

"What do you want us to do, Sir?"

"Do? Retreat and regroup, of course, just like it says in the manuals. Washington won't be able to hold them, and after they've rolled over his unit, they'll be here in a matter of minutes. We need to get out of here!"

"What about Washington?" a harassed-looking lieutenant asked, "Should we send in troops to give him support?"

"Negative, we're pulling back. Move it!"

Men ran every which way, and a moment later, another shell landed nearby. He doubted they were shooting at them.

They'd just be overshoots from the attack on Washington's company, but they were enough to panic men into even more chaos, with Shriver continuing to issue contradictory orders. Things got even worse when a shell landed next to the MPs' jeep, and it flipped over, spilling men out onto the earth. The MP seated next to Murphy was unlucky. The body of the jeep landed on his belly, crushing him, and when he crawled alongside to see if there was anything he could do for him, there was no sign he was still breathing. More shells landed, and men were still screaming inexplicable orders.

He pitched his voice even louder. "Medic! This man is badly hurt!"

Nobody took any notice, and he tried to put pressure on his chest to resuscitate him, but he was dead. And he had his own problems, like the cuffs securing him to the overturned vehicle. Bishop and the other MP had run, and his priority was to get the cuffs off to join the battle the Germans had so inconveniently decided to start first. He couldn't get the cuffs off, and the enemy was dropping shells all around. He couldn't do anything, except lie on the ground, chained to an upturned jeep, next to the body of a dead MP.

He pulled on the chain, put his boots against the bodywork, and heaved, but he was wasting his time. They'd designed the steel cuffs to restrain a prisoner, and it worked every bit as good as they'd intended. They'd forgotten him in the excitement of pulling out. Jeeps raced away and men charged after them in panicked flight. He was helpless, almost helpless.

"Jack, what are you doing?"

Clemence's voice, and then she was bending down next to him. "Where is the key for the cuffs?"

He glanced at her in astonishment. "What the hell are you doing here?"

"This is Battalion Headquarters, and in case you forgot I work here as an interpreter. At least I did, until now. Jack, never mind what I'm doing here, we need to get you out of here."

"I'm not going anywhere without the key to the cuffs."

She looked at the body trapped half beneath the upturned jeep. "Will he have a key?"

Murphy cursed. He'd forgotten about the MP. It was the obvious place to look, although if he did have a key, it would likely be in his pants pocket or clipped to his belt. Both belt and pocket were beneath the steel bodywork of the jeep.

"I guess so, but there's no way to reach it. You need to get out of here. I'll just have to take my chances."

She returned a look of scorn. "I trust you're joking. Where will I find the key?"

He told her and explained there was no way she'd be able to get to it. "The best thing you can do is get some help, find some guys to lift the jeep, and drag the body out to get to the key."

"There's no time. I can do it."

"Clemence, no!" he shouted as another shell landed fifty yards away.

He revised his opinion. It wasn't an overshoot. The Germans were using an observer to report the fall shot, and now they knew they'd found Battalion HQ, they'd decided to make it a secondary target. Or maybe a primary target, but either way, it was becoming hot. Before he could stop her, Clemence wriggled beneath the jeep, and he could've sworn the gap was no more than four inches, but somehow, she made it and she disappeared completely. He began to worry when she didn't reappear, but after several minutes she hauled herself out, covered in mud and dirt, which didn't prevent her from wearing a triumphant grin.

"I got it!" She held up a hand, and she was holding a small, standard pattern military handcuff key, "I also found this."

She'd recovered his weapons, the MP-40 and his Colt automatic, and she brandished them like trophies. She crawled over to him and unlocked the cuffs. He was free. He grabbed his guns and pulled her behind the jeep as a salvo of shells bracketed the area, throwing up clouds of smoke and flame. He lay over her to protect her until the salvo had ended and dragged her back to her feet.

"I want you to get out of here. This is just the start. They have tanks, and since the military genius pulled back the Shermans, when they arrive there'll be nothing to stop them. Start running toward the rear."

"What about you?"

"Me? My guys are in trouble, so my place is with them. I'm going back."

She hesitated, and he knew he was going to have trouble with her, but he also knew they were out of time. Outnumbered and outgunned, enemy soldiers were about to swamp Washington's entire company. "Get out now! Run!"

He didn't have any more time to waste, and he started jogging back toward the position they were holding outside of Evrecy. He picked up speed and reached them in record time, but time was something that had run out for First Platoon and Bravo Company. The enemy had emerged from the moat, screened by continuous barrages of artillery fire from Kreis' guns. Led by the Tiger and two StuG assault guns, enemy troops streamed toward them. Everywhere was chaos, and Lieutenant Adams was bellowing at his men to grab their gear and run. Sergeant Rooker was doing his best to hold the line.

"Lt, if they run now, they'll be out in the open, easy meat for the tanks. It'd be better to stay and fight them from here. We're overlooking them from the top of this hill, and the men have dug slit trenches, so we can keep our heads down."

The men looked from him to Adams, but the Lieutenant didn't look to be in the mood for discussion. Panicked men rarely are in the mood for anything, except more panic. "We need to run, I tell you. Get out now, while you still can."

"No!" The command came from Captain Washington, who'd ordered the men to take cover in foxholes and trenches. Major Lawson, the Brit officer, was standing beside him, "We have bazookas, we have machine guns, and we can hold them. Lieutenant, control your men. Keep them behind cover, and don't shoot until I give the order. We need to keep the bazookas as a surprise."

"But…" His eyes were rolling, and flecks of spittle came from his lips.

"No buts. Get their heads down!"

He gave the order, and they took cover in their foxholes. It was a scary prospect, infantry facing armor, with shells dropping around them, but they had a job to do. They also knew running would make things worse, a good incentive to stay put. Washington glanced at him. "Murphy, what's the situation at Battalion? Does General Shriver know about this?"

"He knows."

"What's he doing about it? Is he bringing the men

forward?"

"He's quoting the military manual, something about retreat and regroup."

Both officers stared at him aghast. "He's running?"

"He's running."

"Shit. What about the Shermans? If we had the tanks, we might stand a chance of beating them."

He shook his head. "He ordered them all back, men, tanks, everything."

His face fell. "In that case, we're gonna have a problem holding them. Major Lawson, is there another way out of here without exposing ourselves to enemy fire?"

"We can follow the reverse slope of the hill, but when they reached the top, they possibly will see us."

"That's it? There's no other way?"

"None. Not unless we can conjure up a squadron of tanks. Murphy, are you sure those tanks were retreating?"

He was about to answer in the affirmative when a noise in the distance made him look up, and he couldn't believe it. The rumble of tank engines growing louder, and they were there; ten Shermans, racing toward them at full speed, with pennants flying from their radio aerials. When they got closer, he recognized the two figures showing from the turret of the leading tank. The commander, Sergeant Chris Davidson, and somebody had persuaded him to come to their aid, somebody clutching onto the turret as she rode on top. He wasn't sure if he could believe his eyes.

Except this was France, the land where the 'Maid of Orleans' had led the French forces to battle the English invaders when still a teenager. She'd achieved astonishing victories over superior English forces until captured and burned at the stake as a witch.

This was no witch. He was looking at Clemence Delon. Somehow, she'd persuaded Davidson and his fellow tankers to ignore General Shriver's orders and advance toward the enemy.

Somebody was about to get a big surprise. Neither Davidson's Shermans nor the onrushing enemy tanks were aware of the other. Positioned on top of the low hill, Washington's men could see them from both sides. They could also see they were likely to meet on top of the hill, and that was going to be interesting. Theoretically, the Shermans outnumbered the Kraut armor, but the theory goes out the window when the monstrous Tiger tanks were involved. With the heavier armor of the Panzer VI and the low profile of the STuGs, Davidson's crews would be tangling with difficult targets, hard to hit. In the case of the Tiger, when they did hit it, hard to penetrate and destroy.

He worked it out in seconds, and they needed time. Time for the Shermans to crest the hill where they could fire down on the enemy, losing them much of the advantages of low-profile and heavy frontal armor. The 76mm shells crashing down on the top of the hulls would have a better chance of penetrating, and ten Shermans could do a lot the penetration. Provided they reached the crest of the hill first.

He explained what he had in mind to Adams, who was attempting some semblance of command of his platoon, but he shook his head.

"There's no way we can slow them down, Private. That's a Tiger down there. Nothing can stop it."

"Lt, we have bazookas."

He scoffed. "Don't be stupid. A bazooka would scratch the paintwork at best, and anyone who stands up to fire a rocket will get his head shot off. Or had you forgotten the tank's mounted machine guns, designed to take out infantry before they get too close?"

"We need to do something. If they get here first, our guys are toast."

That's their problem," he snarled, "Our problem is staying alive."

Rooker tried to intervene, but he shrugged him off. "Keep your heads down and forget any notions about trying to take on that monster with a bazooka."

Murphy had just about taken enough. Those tanks were rushing to help them, and his girl was riding on top of the lead tank. It gives a man a big incentive when the life of someone you love is endangered, and he snapped back at Adams.

"Fuck you, Lieutenant. They're coming to help us, and when they get here, the Krauts will shoot the shit out of them. I'm going out there with a bazooka."

"I said no!" he snapped, "One more peep out if you, and I'll place you under summary arrest. Sergeant Rooker, if this man disobeys me, you know what to do."

"I know what to do, Lieutenant. Murphy, tell me what you need."

"Two bazookas would be better than one, Sarge."

"You got them. What else?"

"I need every man to open fire, give them something to think about while we get out there."

"No sweat." Adams was red in the face, bellowing he would have every man arrested and charged, locked up, and the keys thrown away. They'd be in disgrace, felons, and once again flecks of spittle sprayed from his mouth, until Rooker had taken enough. He smashed a huge meaty fist into his face, and the flecks of spittle became flecks of blood. He grinned. "I slipped, too bad. Men, we have work to do."

Kelly had already disappeared, and he returned with a bazooka, as well as two more men, a bazooka team. Rooker ran to the nearest machine gun crew, ordered them to grab their BAR and follow him. He glanced at Murphy. "This is your show, what's the plan?"

"Get them to open fire now." He pointed to a shallow defile that ran to the bottom of the hill, "I reckon we can take that route, and with any luck, they won't see us."

He grunted. "Maybe so, but it's gonna be tough. When the Shermans appear, the PAK-40s will open fire, and they'll hit them hard. Then we have the infantry, and there're a lot of 'em. We need to persuade Shriver to get the troops moving forward with the rest of the tanks. Hit them with everything we have, and we can finish this. Open the gap and get our armies moving again. I'll get Captain Washington to send a message back. We need everything he has, and we need it fast. Gimme a minute."

He raced back to Washington, and he agreed they were about to fight the decisive battle. He was on the radio to Shriver when Rooker arrived back. "It's done. Let's go."

"Will he do it? Get those men moving?"

A shrug. "Washington was making it clear as day. Get them off their asses, or he'd spend the rest of his career in command of a storage depot somewhere in Antarctica. He may get the message." His lips twitched in a smile, "They say Shriver hates cold weather. Okay, it's time to get the lead out. Let's move."

They slid down the hillside and reached the bottom without any sign of the enemy seeing them. They crawled forward to find an ambush spot to hunker down and wait for the tanks. They slid into a shallow depression, enough to hide them, and watched the oncoming tide. Three tanks; followed by at least a company of infantry. Behind them, the guns continued to fire HE shells that turned their positions into a hell of explosives and shrapnel.

He looked back, and there was no sign of Davidson's Shermans. The enemy was getting closer, and they'd have to fire the bazooka soon before the mammoth tank rolled over them. Without fire from their own tanks to get their attention, the enemy would be able to take their time and blast the bazooka crews with everything they had. The tanks ground closer, and still, there was no sign of the Shermans. Closer, and when the lead Tiger was within one hundred yards, they got ready to fire. Kelly insisted on taking the shot. Rooker grabbed the BAR from the gunner who didn't look keen to put his head up and do some shooting, and Murphy waited with a spare rocket to reload the bazooka.

The Tiger came closer, and the commander had his head poking out the hatch to get a better view. So close he could make out every feature on his face, and yet still Kelly didn't fire.

He tapped him on the shoulder. "Dan, you're leaving it a bit late."

"If he gets close enough, we can take out the mother."

"How close is close enough?"

"A bit more. I can do this, Murphy."

"Right."

He waited, clutching the spare rocket. Rooker gripped the BAR to deal with the infantry if they got close enough, and still Dan didn't fire. The tank was almost on them, a hundred yards ahead of the STuGs, and he looked at Dan. "He's mighty close."

"Patience. I can do this."

"Yeah, I heard you the first time."

He looked at Rooker, and they shrugged. They were dicing with death. Dan was dicing with all their deaths, but he felt convinced, and maybe he'd do it.

Still, they waited. The monstrous Tiger rumbled past less than twenty yards from where they lay in the shallow depression, and they shrunk into the grass and weeds, trying to make themselves invisible. The earth shook as tons of steel rolled past until the most vulnerable area of the Tiger lay before them.

Dan had gambled the enemy wouldn't see them, and they'd have a chance to put a rocket up their ass. When it had rolled a further twenty yards, he fired. The rocket soared out from the launcher trailing smoke and slammed into the rear compartment. There was an eruption of flame, yet it wasn't enough. The explosive warhead had seriously damaged the engine, and the vehicle ground to a halt. But it wasn't enough.

The commander's head was still poking out from the turret, and he swung round to see where the rocket had launched from. A second later, he spotted them and grabbed the butt of the machine gun mounted on the turret. He swung it around, and they were seconds away from oblivion. Murphy still clutched the spare rocket. He slammed it into the bazooka and tapped Dan on the shoulder.

"You're reloaded, now nail the bastard!"

He swung his MP-40 around, aimed fast, and emptied the

magazine at the Kraut. The burst of 9mm bullets tore into the German, flinging him backward, and a crewman dragged the badly wounded man inside to be protected from further gunfire. It was true, the corpse protected him from further gunfire, but Kelly fired again. Another bazooka rocket hit the rear of the already damaged Tiger. The warhead smashed through the buckled and damaged armor, detonating inside the hull. The result was spectacular. First, a massive explosion that pushed smoke and flames up through the open hatch, followed by secondary explosions as the store of lethal 88mm shells erupted. The once-mighty symbol of Hitler's invincible war machine became nothing more than a useless heap of scrap. A metaphor for the Third Reich, staggering like a punch-drunk boxer under the weight of blows from a superior opponent.

Yet the STuGs were still moving toward them, and they were out of rockets. Their remaining armament consisted of light weapons and a few grenades. It looked like their triumph at the destruction of the Tiger would be short-lived, until everything changed. The Shermans appeared on top of the hill and began firing at the STuGs. The range was short enough for the initial barrage to bracket the nearest assault gun, and a flurry of shells exploded on top of the StuG. The other began to back away, and Kelly jumped up and down, exulting in their victory.

"When the Shermans reach the artillery, they'll turn them into mincemeat. We've nailed the bastards! This time we've got 'em beat!"

Murphy nodded. "That was a smart move, waiting for the tank to drive past, although I nearly had a heart attack. Next time, warn us what you're planning."

Rooker nodded. "I'll second that, but what matters is you

did it. Well done, Private Kelly, you destroyed a Tiger with a bazooka. I reckon that'll rate a mention at Ike's headquarters."

They watched the Shermans roll down the hill, and the second StuG erupted in smoke and flame, hit by several shells. They rolled on toward the artillery, forewarned of their location by Lawson and the Frenchman Marcel. It was all over, bar the final mopping up of the enemy troops, now in full flight and running for their lives.

They got to their feet, grinning and backslapping each other. Davidson's tank rolled past, and he saw Clemence still standing on the hull. He cupped his hands and shouted to her to get into cover. She waved an acknowledgment and leaped lightly to the ground and ran across to them.

"Jack, they told me what you men did. They said you could have been killed."

"They've been trying to kill us since we hit the beach, but we're still here, and they're not."

"Is the battle over? Will the Germans retreat now they have lost most of their tanks and guns?"

"If they have any sense they will. Provided they don't spring any last-minute surprises. They can…"

"Murphy, we got trouble."

He looked at Dan. "What is it this time? Lieutenant Adams mouthing off again?"

"Look to the east."

He looked. And looked again, and again. Couldn't believe it. "What the hell!"

Rooker squinted at the three huge shapes moving out from the smoke and dust of exploding shells. "They told us about these at headquarters. They're Germany's latest weapon."

"Yeah, but what are they?"
"King Tigers."

CHAPTER TWELVE

The tanks began swapping shells, and they ducked back down in the hollow in the ground. Six Shermans had survived the barrage of shells from the battery firing from the moat, and they came on like a cavalry charge from the previous century. Brave, flamboyant, even when up against a superior force. The PAK-40s continued lobbing shells, and now the King Tigers opened up, slamming volleys of 88mm shells into the thinning ranks of the Shermans. It looked like nothing could stop them, and in desperation Davidson's squadron went into reverse, backing away to keep their thicker frontal armor to the enemy. Three made it to the top of the slope and over the other side.

They watched, stony-faced, seeing their victory plucked away at the last moment.

"This fucking town is cursed" Rooker snarled. He glanced at Clemence. "Excuse the language, Ma'am."

Her reply was tart. "It's Mam'selle, Sergeant. Not Ma'am."

"Yes, uh, Mam'selle."

"The question is what're you going to do about this?"

"What do you mean? There ain't a damn thing we can do. Shriver will have to deal with it. It's his problem. Problem is, I don't know if he has the guts. All we can do is hope."

"What about the guns? Isn't there something you can do about them?"

"Uh, no, not without more men and more weapons. There's no way to destroy them, not three men with light weapons."

"There's always a way," she snapped, "Sergeant Rooker, all France has been praying for the success of the Allies, and it looks to me as if all that's holding up that success is a few tanks and a few guns. At least find a way to destroy those guns, perhaps it would give your men a chance against the King Tigers."

He glanced across to the location of the guns, hidden from incoming fire by the dried-up moat where they were able to send screaming salvos of shells with seeming impunity. Looked at Kelly, who shrugged, "Don't look at me. I'm out of bazooka rockets."

"Murphy, any ideas of how we can help our guys and spike those guns? They might just fight off the King Tigers, but the guns are the Krauts' ace in the hole. Our guys have to avoid the anti-tank fire, and the King Tigers will just pick them off, one by one."

"An airstrike would take care of them."

"Except we have no radio, no way of contacting the forward air controllers."

He nodded. "True, but I'd like to see their faces when the bombs fell on their heads."

"Not gonna happen."

"No." He grinned, "I was just thinking about the big surprise the Jerries got when the Brits destroyed those dams with bouncing bombs. They wiped out huge swathes of German war production in a single raid. They called the guys who did it 'The Dambusters.'"

Rooker looked irritated. "That's crazy thinking. We don't have any Dambusters, no bouncing bombs, and no dams to destroy, so forget it."

"I was just thinking, is all." He glanced to the south, seeing two men running toward them. Loony Lawson and Marcel. They took shelter in the hollow and looked over the edge as the guns fired again.

Lawson grimaced. "We were on our way to the town when we saw those King Tigers, so we looked for somewhere to keep our heads down. The guns are bad enough, but those monsters are beyond bad. What're you men doing here?"

"Same as you, keeping our heads down," Rooker replied, "Murphy has been entertaining us with stupid ideas about bouncing bombs."

He raised a quizzical eyebrow. "Bouncing bombs? Not too many of those in Normandy. Not too many dams either."

Murphy had been thinking about dams. Dams held back the water the last time he checked. Didn't moats hold water? He looked at Lawson. "You know this area well, isn't that right?"

"Not as well as Marcel, he's the local expert."

"Ask him where they got the water to fill the moat."

He caught on in a moment and grinned. "That's not bad,

Private Murphy. Right, let's see what he can tell us."

They chatted for a couple of minutes, and the news wasn't good.

"He said they capped off the feed from an underground spring about eighty years ago before he was born. His father told him about it. He said the village was up in arms at the time because the spring also fed the local wells with drinking water. The commotion only died down when they dug new wells. The problem is getting to the cap. It's in the center of the moated area, where the chateau used to stand, and covered with a concrete slab. It'd take a few sticks of dynamite to break it open. And we don't have any dynamite."

"We have grenades."

"Not enough. It'd take a big bang to crack the concrete."

He thought for a few moments. "How about a shell?"

Lawson frowned. "That's an idea, provided you could hit it square on, and those Shermans are tied up enough with the King Tigers. Even then, I doubt they'd hit a small target. It's about a yard square. Forget it, Murphy."

He didn't forget it. He was thinking there was more than one way to deliver a high-explosive shell, like an artillery piece. The Krauts had artillery pieces on site. They also had a heap of soldiers, and they weren't likely to sit back and watch while he took command of one of their precious guns. He popped his head up and looked across toward the cloud of smoke marking the enemy position. For a few seconds, the smoke cleared, and he saw him, Major Gottlieb Kreis. He'd stepped out into the open to survey the battlefield. He had to have something in mind, but so did Murphy, and he felt the anger boil inside him. The fanatic Nazi who'd kept up the pressure to defend the town until the last, the man who'd committed untold numbers of murders. Including his intention to murder him.

He wanted to race over there and fill him full of holes, and the impulse burned inside him. He was still watching the Nazi when he suddenly disappeared inside a dense cloud of smoke. It wasn't smoke from the guns, but more like a grass fire. A grass fire! The incessant fire from the guns had caused smoke and flame to ignite the undergrowth, and they were in trouble. The outgoing gunfire ended, and he pictured the panicked Germans beating at the flames, attempting to put out the fire. Dense smoke and panic, what else did they need?

"Sarge, look at that. They've got trouble."

Rooker joined him with Lawson and Marcel, and Kelly helped Clemence to her feet so they could survey the enemy position. The Sarge smiled. "They sure have trouble. I hope the bastards roast."

"I was thinking of putting out the fire."

"You what?"

He told them what he had in mind. They'd never have a better chance to penetrate the moat, and if the Gods of War were willing, they'd find an unattended gun, point the barrel at the cap over the spring, and hit it with an AP shell.

"It'll never work."

"Forget it, they'll spot us before we can get close."

"It's suicide. No way."

The two French citizens had other ideas. "It could work," Marcel said gravely, "With luck, yes, but we could die in the attempt."

Clemence shot him a look of scorn. "If we do this, we do it for France, to drive out the enemy from our land. It is our holy duty as sons and daughters of France to make the attempt."

Lawson pointed out most of them weren't sons or daughters of France, but she shot him down in a few seconds. "You have come to France to liberate us, and that makes you honorary Frenchmen. General de Gaulle even said so." Nobody argued, even if they'd never heard the prickly General say anything of the kind, "We must do this for the honor of France."

"And to save the lives of our soldiers," Rooker murmured. He looked at Murphy. "What're we waiting for?"

They ran out into the open, keeping inside the thickest smoke blowing toward them by a gentle breeze. There was no problem finding the right direction, which was toward the place where the smoke was thickest. As they got closer to the moat, they heard the shouts of Germans frantically beating at the flames. They reached the edge of the moat, and it was like a scene from Dante's Inferno. Flames and smoke shooting up to the sky, grass that'd dried out after the bad weather was a tinderbox, allowing the flames to spread rapidly.

Their effort focused on the north side of the moat where the flames burned more furiously. They'd abandoned the two artillery pieces on the south side to concentrate on stopping the conflagration from engulfing the area in a pool of fire. There must've been a hundred men attacking the fire with spades, shoveling earth over the burning grass, and some had taken off their coats beat out the flames, but it was a battle they were losing.

Marcel led them unnoticed to the center of the moat, and they had to tie scarves and strips of cloth over their mouths to prevent them choking on the acrid fumes. He pointed to a concrete slab, almost invisible beneath a tangle of brambles.

"In there, it's around two feet thick, and the spring is immediately below. Break open the concrete and the moat will fill with water. It'll stop them firing the guns, but the bad news is it'll also put out the flames." He was looking at Murphy, the man who'd come up with the plan, "When the flames go out, they'll see us."

"We'll worry about that when the time comes. Does anybody know how to use one of these things?" He pointed toward an artillery piece closest to the slab, and Lawson nodded. "I've fired something similar in the past. Marcel, didn't you tell me you were a gunner during the First World War?"

"I took part in the siege of Verdun when we fought the Germans to a standstill. If we'd lost, they'd have taken the whole of France. We didn't lose, and we forced the dogs to retreat."

Nobody pointed out if they'd managed to do the same the second time around, they wouldn't be in this situation. Not to this man, who'd demonstrated his bravery. A true son of France, and with a few more like him, maybe things would have been different. They swarmed over the gun. Lawson checked the breech and found it empty.

"Find the shells. We need to load."

They discovered them in a steel container several feet away, and Murphy carried a 75mm shell to the open breech, inserted it, and slammed the lever closed. Marcel stared down the optical sight while Lawson followed his commands to depress the barrel low enough to hit the low-lying target. They traversed the gun a few inches to make final adjustments, and they were ready. Lawson waved at the Frenchman to take the shot.

"For the honor of France, my friend."

The old man operated the firing lever, and a shell erupted from the barrel, reached the target in a split second, and exploded. Murphy ran forward to check the damage, and it wasn't good news. Although the shell hit the target, it hadn't cracked the concrete.

He ran back to the gun. "Take another shot. The first must've weakened the concrete, but not enough to crack it. Load!"

Kelly picked up another shell, almost a yard long and three inches in diameter. Marcel opened the breech to eject the spent casing. Rooker and Clemence were busy elsewhere. The Germans had heard the gunfire, and half-dozen men were running toward them to investigate. Rooker fired the BAR and knocked several down with a long burst. Clemence used her pistol, aiming and firing in a long, smooth sequence of shots that took down two more. Of the six that ran toward them, only one survived, and he got away to shout a warning. Which meant there'd be others, and soon.

"Fire again!" Rooker shouted, "They'll be here in the next few seconds. Make this one work. We won't get another chance."

Marcel put a hand on the firing lever, and simultaneously, a bullet came out from inside the smoke. He keeled over, his body blocking the lever. Rooker and Lawson grabbed him, dragging him off to access the lever, and more bullets buzzed around them. Several Germans appeared from inside the smoke, firing and reloading their bolt-action rifles. If they'd been using machine pistols at such short-range, they'd have shredded them, but the single shots fired in panic all missed.

They wouldn't miss when they got closer. Rooker and

Lawson finally managed to grapple the body off the firing lever, but the effort caused them to tumble over. A long burst of machine gun fire from further away forced them to keep their heads down. The situation was desperate, and he bounded forward to reach the gun.

"Kelly, cover me."

"We're on it."

They were both firing, Dan and Clemence, who'd reloaded her pistol. Shooting into the smoke, trying to hold back the rush of enemy soldiers, but they couldn't do a damn thing about the machine gun, and he had to play Russian roulette with the bullets. He figuratively spun the wheel of chance. Took a flying leap toward the gun, hand on the firing lever, and he jerked it hard. Praying the barrel had remained pointed at the concrete slab, the shell crashed out of the muzzle. It impacted almost at the same moment, and it was like the earth shuddered as the long, pent-up pressure of water finally found a way out. It didn't emerge in a slow trickle or a fast stream. What appeared was a waterspout, high in the air, falling back to earth, and the ground became wet.

The wet became a puddle of water, and within seconds the area resembled a shallow pond. The water dispersed the smoke, exposing the mass of German soldiers, and they stared at each other, astonished to see them so close. A frozen moment in time, and he knew what Custer had felt like at Little Big Horn. If only the girl hadn't come, but she was here, and he knew she'd die when the shooting started. He looked down, and he was already standing in six inches of water.

"Clemence! Hit the deck."

She gave him a sad glance. "Too late."

* * *

Chris Davidson had done everything he could. Had fired shell after shell at the monstrous King Tigers, without success. Maybe he'd scratched the paintwork, but he wasn't even sure about that.

These fucking things are indestructible!

The problem was the main gun on a Sherman didn't have enough clout to penetrate the heavy frontal armor, not at long-range, and the German commanders were clever enough to keep the fight at long-range.

If they didn't do something soon, they were fucked. One Tiger had stopped, and it looked like it had broken down. But the other two were hammering them, and he'd already lost two Shermans, both destroyed by 88mm shells. He maneuvered his tank behind the cover of the stalled Tiger, and it worked. The other two lost sight of him, a fatal mistake, and he managed to get close enough to make his shots count. One tank came close, within three hundred yards, and it was the opportunity he'd waited for. He aimed the turret, and if he didn't destroy the tank, he'd give the commander a headache big enough to last him until the end of the war.

"Fire!"

The shell left the muzzle of his 76mm gun, traveled the short distance, and it gave the commander more than a lengthy headache. The turret exploded, separating from the tank, and it flew high into the air. He afterward found out some tankers stored ready-use ammunition in the turret to make for faster firing and reloading. Which worked well, until the turret took a direct hit, and he'd just put a major dent in Adolf's armored superiority. Flames belched from inside the hull, and they were down to one tank. One tank, but they were wary after the second loss they'd sustained, and the King Tiger maintained a distance, firing a couple of shells that narrowly missed blasting his Sherman into scrap.

Another Sherman wasn't so lucky, and it took a direct hit on the frontal armor. Two crewmen managed to escape before the ammunition exploded, and he was down to two vehicles.

"Driver, get behind that stalled Tiger before he fires again."

"Sure thing. Say, Chris, how're we gonna get out of this?"

"I don't know. Maybe something will turn up."

"Like a few more of our tanks? Fat chance."

"Just do it."

There aren't going to be any more tanks. Not with a piece of work like Shriver running things. Or rather, running away. Do we stand a chance against this last King Tiger? I don't want to answer that question.

The driver, PFC Orson Rice called back. "Chris, we got company."

Shit!

"Enemy armor?"

"Nope. Allied armor. They're ours, look to the west."

They were racing toward the hill, a full company of Sherman tanks. Their tanks, and in the blink of an eye everything change. For them, it changed for the better. The Germans should have stayed in bed. Before the new vehicles got close enough to open fire, the enemy tank slowed and stopped. Two crewmen clambered out, and they appeared to be attempting to fix a mechanical problem. Without power, the vehicle was defenseless, unable to fight, and the Shermans bore down on it. They surrounded it like hungry wolves, pounded it into scrap at close-range, and when they ceased fire, it was all over.

* * *

The gusher showed no sign of slowing, and the water was already up to their knees. The Germans eyed them uncertainly, trying to make up their minds. Fight, or run. Aware that when the shooting started, they'd wipe out the small force of Allied soldiers, but they'd also lose men. Nobody wanted to die, not when they knew they'd lost the war.

He saw him then, Gottlieb Kreis. Standing on the carriage of a PAK-40, bellowing at his men, waving and gesticulating. He should have saved his breath. Fight or run, and they chose the latter. One man took to his heels, splashing through the water, then another three, and ten more, and they were in full flight. Like some crazy game played out on a vacation beach, racing through the shallows, but this was no game.

They let them go, and Murphy had eyes for just one man. He waded toward him, Kreis saw him coming, and he knew what he planned. He aimed his Walther and fired three shots before the magazine emptied.

Murphy was too close, and he had no time to reload. He hurled the empty gun at him, and it glanced off his helmet. He didn't take any notice, kept paddling toward him, past another PAK-40, rendered useless by water that'd already reached the open breech, and he got to him. The German leaped off into the water and started to wade after his men. He caught him easily, kicked his legs from under him, and he went down into the water. His head went under, and he came up spluttering. The arrogance and the bluster had disappeared, along with the drowning of his guns and the absence of his men.

"I surrender! I am a prisoner of war!"

"You're a piece of shit, Mister, and you're gonna get what you deserve."

"You cannot kill me! The Geneva Convention forbids…"

"Sorry, pal, I can't hear you. Must be all those shells you've been firing, I've gone deaf. You recall those American soldiers you murdered?"

"No!" he shrieked, "I tried them in a properly constituted court. Their sentences were legal. You must not do this!"

"Wrong. I found you guilty, shitface, and you're about to get what you deserve."

The Major struggled and fought back like a wounded leopard, but Murphy had been waiting for this moment. He pushed his head down into the water, holding it down with all his strength. Kreis fought back for a long time, a desperate attempt to survive, but the man holding him wasn't about to allow this man to breathe the clean air of civilized people for a moment longer.

The struggled ceased, and he kept him down for a few minutes more, just to make certain he'd arrived in hell and had time to shake hands with the devil.

The roar of engines made him look up. The Shermans had arrived and halted at the edge of the flooded moat. Kelly was standing next to him, covering him with his gun, and Lawson was there with Rooker, who stood protecting Clemence with his body.

Shriver's command car arrived, and he climbed out and

looked down at the flooded gun position. Something about him had changed. His face had filled with the flush of enthusiasm, his eyes glinted, and he glanced every which way as if he couldn't wait for another chance to hit the enemy.

"Sergeant Rooker?"

"That's me, Sir."

"You did well. Sergeant, I made a mistake pulling the troops back, and I admit I was wrong. That's why I sent in the Shermans and brought up the rest of the men. Where are the Germans?"

"They're gone, General. I guess they knew you were coming."

It was the right thing to say, and Shriver's chest puffed up with pride.

"I took a chance, tore up the manuals, and it paid off." He glanced at his radioman, sitting in the rear of the command car. "Get a message through to HQ. Tell them we've done it. The way is open, you can get the troops moving." He grinned. "Damn! Nothing can stop us now. Major Lawson, what're you doing here?"

"Just observing, General. Private Murphy here did a good job. He deserves recognition."

"Murphy? Don't I know you? Right, that business with the MPs, what were you doing in the water when I arrived?"

"Just drowning a rat, General."

He shuddered. "Good job, I hate rats. I've noted what Major Lawson said, and when I hand out the medals, you'll be first in the queue."

"He doesn't deserve a medal!" The voice was unmistakably that of Duane Bishop, "That man is under arrest.

I'm charging him with murder, escaping custody, and desertion."

Shriver looked puzzled, looking from Bishop to Murphy, back to Bishop, and he looked toward Washington as he arrived. "Captain, this is your man, what do you have to say for him?"

Washington glanced at Bishop, and his gaze dripped with contempt. "Ask him where he was."

"Excuse me?"

"Murphy and the other Rangers took action when the enemy threatened to break through. The last I saw of Bishop and his MPs, they were running. Where were they?"

He tactfully didn't mention the others who'd run. Shriver was on a roll, and he needed to keep him rolling.

Shriver looked at the MP. "Well, Sergeant? Where were you?"

"I, uh, we followed orders and retreated, General. Like the rest of your men."

He exploded. "That's a lie! Are you suggesting I ordered my men to run?"

"Uh, well, Nossir. Of course not."

"Of course not. Sergeant, you seem to hold a personal grudge against this man, and I don't believe a word you say. Neither am I interested. We're fighting a war here, not settling an old score. Do you get me?"

"Yessir."

"You'd better. Here's how it works. You forget this thing with Private Murphy. He's a credit to the Rangers, and I can't afford to lose good men. When we move forward, I want you on point. It seems to me you need a taste of real action. Who knows, you may even win promotion to sergeant."

"Sir, I'm already a sergeant."

"Not anymore, Private Bishop. Now get out of my sight until we're ready to move off. Murphy, you're in the clear."

"Thank you, General."

"I don't like to see innocent men falsely accused."

He glanced up as a jeep arrived, carrying Lieutenant Adams and driven by 'Lucky' Lucas. Shriver, still fired up by the defeat of the Germans, was in no mood to forgive those who'd given anything less than one hundred percent, and he gave the new arrivals a sour glance.

"Lieutenant, you're late. You missed the battle, where were you?"

Adams leaped out and threw the General an immaculate salute. "At headquarters, tidying up important paperwork, Sir."

"Is that right?" He pointed to Bishop, who was slinking away. "You see that man?"

"The MP? That's Sergeant Bishop."

"It's Private Bishop now. He'll be on point when we advance. You can join him."

"General? I don't understand."

"I gave you an order, Lieutenant. Which bit did you not understand? Try a source of action, and you can take that driver of yours along with you. You can leave the jeep here, so make sure you're both carrying rifles. From here on in, I want maximum effort from every man, and that includes you. That's all. Get your asses moving."

Murphy fought hard to hold back a wide smile as the two men charged after Bishop, but the smile soon faded.

"I see you have that girl with you, the French interpreter. I thought I ordered her to stay in the rear."

"She got lost, General."

His eyes twinkled, and his lips twitched. "She looks mighty feisty to me. I doubt that girl has ever been lost in her life. My headquarters has moved up. You'll find it about five miles back, outside a village. Take her there, and if she's to stay on as an interpreter, you'll need to find her somewhere to stay. You have twenty-four hours."

"General?"

"Twenty-four hours to find her somewhere to stay and settle her in. I'll be handing out the medals later, and you might miss it, so if you want to get straight back…"

"I'll take the twenty-four hours, Sir."

"I kinda thought you might. Good work, Murphy, you deserve something for what you did. Anything else I can do for you?"

"That photographer, Sir. Jamie Curtis. He's been pestering us, if you know what I mean."

He frowned. "The photographer? Yeah, I know what you mean. He's a real pain in the ass. Ike's HQ has been requesting volunteers for an airborne operation they're planning over Holland, some kind of a shortcut into Germany. I reckon they'll need a good photographer to go along, get some pictures for the history books."

"I reckon so, General."

"I'll add him to the list. Don't be late tomorrow. We've still got plenty of Germans to kill." He shouted at the MP. "Private Bishop, before you take up your new duties, you can drive them back to HQ, and get straight back here."

"Yessir."

He didn't speak until he stopped inside the village, outside of a small guesthouse. "I won't forget this, Murphy."

They climbed out of the jeep. "Good luck with the Krauts, Bishop. I'll be seeing you."

He snarled a reply. "Count on it."

They watched him drive away, he took her hand, and they entered the guesthouse.

"I want a double room."

The woman behind the reception counter gave him a frosty glare. "This is your wife?"

He was about to lie when he remembered where they were. This was France, and they did things differently. "No, Ma'am. She's my mistress."

She gave him a curt nod of approval. "Enjoy your stay."

Clemence gave her a sweet smile. "Oh, we will. We most certainly will."

As they walked away, Kelly shouted, "Murphy, what was that you always said about generals?"

"Generals are okay, Dan."

"You're sure?"

"Ask me in twenty-four hours."

www.ingramcontent.com/pod-product-compliance
Lightning Source LLC
Chambersburg PA
CBHW020315160726
47992CB00004B/1549